MILLION DOLLAR GIFT

IAN SOMERS

Ian Somers lives in Dublin and works as a graphic designer. This is his first book.

HE HAS THE GIFT, BUT HE'S NOT THE ONLY ONE.

MILLION DOLLAR GIFT

IAN SOMERS

THE O'BRIEN PRESS
DUBLIN

First published 2012 by
The O'Brien Press Ltd,
12 Terenure Road East, Rathgar,
Dublin 6, Ireland. Tel: +353 1 4923333; Fax: +353 1 4922777
E-mail: books@obrien.ie.
Website: www.obrien.ie.

ISBN: 978-1-84717-307-2

British Library Cataloguing-in-Publication Data
A catalogue record for this title is available from the British Library

1 2 3 4 5 6 7 8
12 13 14 15 16

Printed and bound by CPI Group (UK) Ltd, Croydon, CR0 4YY
The paper used in this book is produced using pulp from managed forests.

The O'Brien Press receives assistance from

I dedicate this book to my family – Lucy, Kevin, Alan, Paula &
Luke – who always believed in me.
And to Edyta for her support through some difficult times.

contents

CHAPTER ONE –

The Impossible Stunt

Night was fast approaching and I was running out of time. The back door of the abandoned factory was hanging off its hinges as I squeezed through the gap to find the light inside already fading; I raced up the rickety staircase to the first floor; the rays of the evening sun were pouring through the tall windows, but the light wouldn't last much longer; I had to get to work immediately.

I pulled the back-pack from my shoulders, placed it on the dusty floor and began pulling out the tools I needed. There weren't many, just my smart-phone, a measuring tape, a face mask and the two pieces of a wooden ramp that I'd been building in my spare time. I had everything worked out in my mind and it wouldn't take long to get the stunt set up.

First I extended the tape from the wall and marked out two points: one five metres from the wall and another eight metres from it. I constructed the ramp and put it at the five metre point, sloping up towards the wall, then carefully placed the phone at the eight metre point and set its video camera to record. I took one last item from the back-pack: my skate-board.

I pulled my facemask on and dropped my foot onto the board. With one deep breath I pushed myself forward and gathered as much speed as possible before I was launched off the floor by the ramp. I shot about four metres into the air then did a 360 in mid-flight. I angled my body so that the wheels struck the flaking paintwork of the wall cleanly; I then defied gravity by slowly rolling down the wall, backwards, and somersaulting to the ground. The board flipped through the air and I caught it with my right hand. I raised a V sign to the camera with my left and cried, 'Victory!'

I'd just performed an impossible stunt, one that no one else on the planet could pull off. I'm not the kind to brag though, hence the facemask; I'm quite a modest person actually.

My hometown was called Maybrook, the furthest suburb from the city and a place so boring that I renamed it 'Dull-brook'. The people of the suburb knew me simply as 'Ross Bentley' or 'Ross Bentley the loner' or 'Ross Bentley the weirdo', but millions around the world knew me by my online alias, 'Gotcha365'. They knew me because videos of my impossible stunts were all over the internet.

I performed and recorded the skateboard stunt twice more, and would have tried it a third time, but the sun was in a hurry to get away from Dullbrook that evening and my time had run out. I packed up my stuff and sneaked out the back door then hopped on my board and headed for home. The exciting part of my life was over for another few hours. The real, and very boring, side of my life had returned.

I put in my earphones and maxed the volume on my phone as I rolled along the Dullbrook road towards the housing estate. I'd downloaded three albums the day before and was buzzing to the best and liveliest of them. I was always listening to music, without it my life in suburbia would've been unbearable.

I hated Dullbrook and everything about it. The older generation were a crew of old fashioned gossipers and their offspring were a collection of hideous morons; most of them were mindless fools that only moved around in large groups. Both generations were as bad each other.

When I got home I pushed the hall door open and found the house as it always was in the evenings; the lights were off and everything was quiet, except for the sitting room. As I let my earphones dangle around my chest I heard the low murmur of the TV and saw its blue light strobe through the doorway.

As I took to the stair the familiar voice from the sitting room said, 'That you?'

'No,' I replied as I climbed the creaking steps.

Of course it was me! Who the hell else would it be? We hadn't had a single visitor for about three years, since my former head teacher came to have a *chat* with us about my attitude in class.

I always gave Dad a smart answer when he asked a stupid question. It seemed like the appropriate thing to do. Sometimes I'd spice it up and say,

'No, this is a holographic representation of Ross Bentley sent to put your mind at ease. The real Ross is out spending all the money he earns from his crappy job at the supermarket.'

Dad always laughed at my answers. Maybe that's why he asked stupid questions. Who knows? We didn't talk much other than that; there'd been a rift between us for years.

I kicked off my runners when I got to my room and slid my board under the bed. After I emptied my back-pack and put it in the wardrobe I jumped on the bed and powered up my laptop. It was time to delve into my secret life and excitement was tickling me all over; I was about to do something that would stun the world… or at least a few thousand people who regularly used Youtube. That was my way of living a secret life; I'd record myself doing amazing tricks and stunts and upload them onto the internet. It was my only way to escape the tedium of living as Ross Bentley in the sleepy suburb of Dullbrook.

I connected my phone to the laptop and transferred the three video files, then watched them on the larger screen. I decided to keep one and threw the others in the recycle bin. I named the remaining clip 'The Impossible Stunt'.

I thought it was a good name and it seemed to be an accurate description of the video. I logged on to my Youtube channel, which had over twenty similar videos available on it, and uploaded the one-minute clip.

The Impossible Stunt was the most ambitious and revealing clip I'd ever made and nerves zapped my stomach as I watched it going live to the world, or anyone who happened to be looking. The nerves were mostly because my previous recordings had got a mixed response; a lot of people thought they were clever fakes. That really annoyed me. One thing I hate being called is a *fake*.

Why would that bother me so much? Because I've always been *real*. So real that I didn't even have any friends, because I didn't try to be someone I wasn't, I didn't pretend to like people I hated and I didn't act like I disliked people I was fond of. I got lonely from time to time, but that's the price you pay for keeping it real. My skateboarding and free-running videos were as real as I was; there was absolutely no trickery involved.

It always took a while before the comments flowed in so I aimlessly surfed the web. Nothing grabbed my interest and I found myself staring at my Facebook page. It was like watching a mousetrap; it was hard to take my eyes away from it just in case something happened, but it always took a long time for anything to happen. I only had seven friends, and six of them were people I hardly knew, so it usually took a very long time for anything to happen.

The fact that I'd only seven Facebook friends didn't bother

me in the slightest. I actually got a lot of friend requests, mostly from local girls who were a year or so younger than me. I never added them, although sometimes it was tempting.

The only reason I stared at Facebook each night was one of the older girls from Dullbrook, Gemma Wright. We'd been mates for ages and used to share some classes in school. I once had a serious crush on her, but to her credit she never once mentioned my constant gawking and drooling. That all changed when I actually got to know her. We became instant friends and any attraction that there'd been quickly fizzled away. Gemma was the only person in the world that I felt I could talk to and she always gave me good advice.

Some nights she'd appear online and we'd talk about every-day stuff and work (we'd been working at the same supermar-ket since finishing our final year of school) but I sometimes wanted to talk about more serious stuff, especially about how to mend my relationship with Dad. Falling out with him had really hurt me and I wanted to tell someone about it. I was sick of feeling so isolated.

But I'd sound like a total dumbass if I did that, and so we talked about everyday stuff and bitched about our co-workers. There was something else I wanted to tell her about, but I figured I'd never be able to tell her – or anyone else. How do you tell someone your deepest, darkest secret? I don't know. I couldn't afford for my secret to get out – it would spread like wildfire and my life would end up being even more unbearable. I often got pointed at by some of the other teenagers. They'd say, 'There's the loner!' or some crap like that, but if my secret got out they'd shout, 'There's that freak! Keep away from him, he's dangerous.' I didn't need that type of hassle in my life.

It didn't look like Gemma was going to appear so I put the laptop into hibernation and looked for something to do. I sat at my desk and gathered the sheets that covered it. These were my conceptual drawings; before I made my 'impossible' videos I'd plan them out in meticulous detail. These were not rough sketches, they resembled architectural drawings with precise angles and exact measurements and calculations of the effects of lift and drag. I guess I was never your average teenager – that was obvious from the objects that made up the clutter in my room.

I had, of course, the usual items that everyone my age possessed: a Playstation 3, an iPod docking station, an old pair of football boots, *Harry Potter* and *Maximum Ride* books, collections of DVDs and video games, but there were also odd contraptions everywhere. These were my special puzzles. I invented them to keep me occupied and I felt they were unlike any others; I truly believed that no one else on the planet could play them.

The puzzle I'd spent most time on, and the only one I was yet to conquer, was *Marble Star*. Basically, there was a piece of thick card with a hole at its centre. On the card were a number of small marbles arranged in the shape of a five pointed star. Just outside the star was a larger marble. The object of this game was to roll the larger marble towards the centre, scattering the others, and to land it in the hole at the middle of the card. It might sound easy but the hard part of this game was to have the marbles back in a star shape before the large one reached the hole. But of course nobody had the speed of hand to complete this puzzle.

One-Minute Ping-Pong was the first I'd ever invented. It consisted of a business card and a ping-pong ball. You lay the card on the floor and bounce the ball on top of it. You could only touch the ball once, but it had to bounce for at least one minute and it had to bounce on the card every single time.

Horizontal Card was one of the most difficult. You had to stand a playing card on its edge. It was as simple and as impractical as that.

There were normal games too, but I had adapted them to my own specific talents. There was a dart board hanging on the door, but I liked to play Three Shot Blind Bullseye. I'd sit with my back to the door and fire the darts over my shoulder, without looking. I always hit the bullseye within three shots. I could have been the most successful darts player in the world if I wanted, but I never played in public. I'd learned my lesson about playing sports in public when I was younger.

I'd once been a very special soccer player and averaged six goals a game, from all sorts of improbable angles and crazy distances. I even had big football clubs from the premier league in England chasing my signature. But I turned them all down, even Manchester United, because they kept asking how I could score such incredible goals. I couldn't give them an honest answer; my secret had to remain with me and I hung up my boots at the age of fourteen.

This had created the rift with my father who was a football fanatic. He couldn't understand why I turned my back on such a promising career and I couldn't give him an honest answer either. Three years had passed and we still weren't on good terms with each other. He lost his job a year after my 'early retirement' and we were always short of money, which seemed to exaggerate the problems between us; I could have earned a lot of money from soccer and our lives wouldn't be so miserable. I kept refusing to give him a straight answer, though, and he eventually stopped asking the question.

I simply couldn't play sports in public and that's what led to me recording my free-running and skateboarding stunts as a masked man by the name of Gotcha365. My only audience was strangers from other countries who spent too much time surfing Youtube.

The mask was a necessity. A part of my life. You see, all my puzzles, games, sporting exploits and stunts were totally impossible. Only a person who could move things with their mind could do them. That's my secret – I can move things with my mind.

I stared at the Youtube and Facebook mousetraps for a couple of hours more, but no one went for the cheese so I powered off the laptop and got into bed. When I was ready for sleep I simply thought about darkness and the light switch flipped down, plunging the room into blackness.

By the way, I was the only one in the world who could do that.

CHAPTER TWO -

'No Mere Prankster'

The alarm clock woke me at 8am. I pointed at it and hissed, 'shut up,' and it suddenly went quiet. I'd perfected a way of using my power to press down on the 'silence' button. I rolled out of bed and took my laptop to the desk; I was dying to know what sort of remarks had been made about The Impossible Stunt.

I logged onto my Youtube channel; over two hundred people had commented on the clip. I got the most comments from American viewers so they were usually posted while I was asleep. A lot were one-liners like: 'Wow, that's incredible!' or 'How does he do it?', but I just flicked past most of those and focused on the longer posts. Some were a little negative, others were in foreign languages, but one really caught my attention.

'This is the most amazing video I've ever seen. He's not a skateboarder, he's a wizard!'

Now that was a good way to start the day! It took a nose dive two minutes later when I read some of the latter comments.

These were the usual rubbish:

'This vid is a fake. There's nobody on earth that can do this', 'He must be on strings or something', 'I think this was created with computer-generated effects', 'I'm sick of doctored videos. It spoils it for all the real skateboarders out there', 'Fake, fake, fake!'

Others tried to protect me and argued there was no point in producing a fake video because there was nothing to be gained from Gotcha365's channel, I had no adverts and wasn't selling anything or revealing my identity. The word *fake* kept cropping up though and I hate that word. I was detecting a bad mood coming on until I read one of the most recent posts.

'I've watched all of Gotcha365's clips and can't find a single flaw in any of them. He defies gravity and logic, but I believe he's genuine. This guy is no mere prankster. I just hope that I get to meet him some day.'

The comment had come from Mark Jones, a renowned free runner from England. That one post made all the planning and preparing and sneaking around worthwhile. I wasn't looking for fame or fortune; I just wanted some recognition for my skills because I *wasn't* cheating. I was just using my natural abilities like everyone else. Okay, my abilities were rare, even unique, but I wasn't cheating. I've never been a fake.

As The Impossible Stunt gained popularity, the hits, as well as the comments, appeared every minute or two. I could have stayed there all day reading them, but I had to leave for work; another day at the dreaded supermarket was looming.

It was twenty minutes to Delaney's Supermarket by car, but I could make it there in fifteen on my skateboard. I could generate incredible speed, but I had to be careful not to do anything too extravagant in public so I usually travelled through the maze of alleys that dissected the housing estates.

Before I left the house my Dad shouted from his room, 'You heading to work?'

'No, I'm rolling there,' I shouted back before slamming the door shut.

I set off along the avenue at a modest pace, not fast enough for the elderly to report me for speeding, but once I got to the entrance of the nearest alley I instantly picked up speed. Unlike everyone else, I didn't have to use one foot to propel the board, all I had to do was think about the board moving fast and it simply happened. I had also perfected the technique of pulling the board towards my body, some sort of anti-gravity I guess, so it stayed glued to my feet and I never fell off.

I increased speed as I moved through Dullbrook Close and Dullbrook Place. My hood fell back and my hair was whipped by the breeze. I raced out of one lane, across a narrow road and into another. Junk was sent flying as I rolled along and a sleeping dog leapt into the air with fright. It was the fastest I'd ever managed, but I wanted to find out just how fast I could push the board – I wanted to push the boundaries of my power.

There was a wider alley up ahead and when I entered it I put all my energy into moving the wheels beneath me. I was amazed at the speed I'd reached, and I wasn't easily amazed. It was so liberating to do something that no one else had ever done and to do it right under the noses of Dullbrookian horde. I just couldn't contain myself and I laughed and cheered as I darted between the narrow walls.

Suddenly, a little orange cat appeared and crouched down directly in my path, hissing as if a thousand stray dogs were bearing down on it. I couldn't swerve around the little pest, but at the last instant I managed to force energy downward which propelled the board into the air. I vaulted over the cat and five feet into the air.

When I came back to earth I looked back at the little feline without slowing down.

'Sorry 'bout that, Kitty! Didn't mean to scare you.'

My blood ran cold when I turned around. I'd taken that route every day for over a month and should have made a mental note that there was a concrete pillar standing in the centre of the alley's exit, it had been placed there to stop trouble makers on motorbikes from driving through the alleys. I was hurtling towards it at a phenomenal speed and I knew I couldn't leap it or swerve around it. There was no avoiding it! I'd reacted too late and was about to crash into a hefty block of concrete at a hundred miles per hour! Panic electrified my brain and a sudden surge of energy and heat radiated from my chest. Just before the impact I instinctively raised my right hand and I felt the heat and energy flow from my chest and through my arm and fingers. I was subconsciously focusing my power at the pillar.

It blasted into a million pieces and I skated straight through the cloud of debris and into the street beyond. I slid to a halt, my heart pounding like a hammer in my chest. I was covered, head to toe, in dust but I'd come through it without a single scratch or bruise. Not to mention the broken bones I should have had.

How had I done it?

I lifted my hand in front of my face and stared at it for a long moment. Could I smash concrete? A grin grew on my face and the hairs on the back of my neck stood up. I had just discovered a new side to my power. No longer was I confined to simple tricks and stunts. I could also smash concrete!

I gazed at the cloud of dust that was sweeping out into the road. The cat emerged from it shaking its head furiously and licking its paws. I erupted into an uncontrollable fit of laughter.

'Hey, Kitty. I can smash concrete!' I roared, thumping my chest. 'No mere prankster am I.'

The cat shook itself, as if in disapproval, and darted off down the street. My excitement faded when a car turned the corner. The driver stared through the windscreen at the dust cloud then at me. I simply shrugged my shoulders and smiled cheekily. I took to my board and quickly left the street, but not quite as quickly as before, I'd had enough of breaking records for one day.

I dismounted before entering the car park in front of the supermarket because, apparently, it gave a bad impression of Delaney's. This was according to my boss, but what did he know? According to him my hairstyle gave a bad impression of the place too, and the way I wore my uniform. Oh, my shelf arrangements weren't helping either.

I clocked in just on time and went to the changing room and put on my uniform: a bright red shirt, brown slacks and a red and white tie. Seriously, a blind person must have come up with the colour scheme. I walked onto the supermarket floor and proceeded to look for something to pretend to do.

I skulked around the aisles, trying to avoid the watchful eye, and eventually found myself moving boxes of cereal around in no obvious order. I'd perfected the art of looking busy since I started working in Delaney's. I could spend entire days looking busy without actually doing anything productive, which I considered a skill in itself.

Amazingly, I got away with my dossing for almost an hour and was trying so hard to look busy that I didn't notice the early morning shoppers staring and frowning as they wheeled their trolleys down the aisle. An old woman even stopped to gawk at me, but I tried to ignore her, thinking she'd only ask me to fetch something she couldn't find for herself. That was one of the things that really bugged me about working in the supermarket; people never left me alone for very long. They always wanted me to clean, move or rearrange something. My most common task was to find items for customers.

I had a defence mechanism though. I had humour. Sometimes if they asked where the toilet rolls were, I'd answer, 'There's a half roll in the cubicle out back,' or if they asked where the pasta was I'd say, 'It's boiling at the moment and I should have it ready for you in approximately three minutes.'

My defence mechanism often landed me in trouble though. Apparently smart talk to the customers gave a bad impression of Delaney's. And the uniforms didn't?

My boss, Mr Reynolds, loved the uniforms, but that was probably because he was the only one working in the place who didn't have to wear one. Reynolds was my worst enemy, although he claimed *I* was my own worst enemy.

There was a lot of coughing and chuckling being done by the shoppers and it grabbed my attention. It was only then that I noticed the curious looks I was getting from them. Even the girls at the deli counter were snorting in my direction.

'Bentley!'

It was Reynolds. His voice was very nasal and sounded like the horn of a vintage car.

I slowly turned around to see his tight, thin face coming close to my own. I knew he was going to give out about something but I tried to act cool, just in case he wasn't.

'How's it going, sir?' I asked with a smile.

'Oh, my day is already turning out to be an eventful one, like every other day since I hired you.'

'Why's that, Mr Reynolds?'

'Have you a dandruff problem, Bentley?'

It was only then I noticed my hair and shoulders were coated in the dust of the exploding pillar. The first rule at Delaney's was to look presentable at all times while on the floor, which meant I was giving a bad impression of the place – yet again.

'It's quite a serious dandruff problem by the looks of it,' Reynolds continued. 'Any explanation of how you developed such a problem since I saw you yesterday?'

'It's not actually dandruff.'

'Really,' Reynolds said sarcastically. He folded his arms and feigned interest. 'What is it?'

'It's actually dust. I was er … cleaning out the … attic … this morning and it was dusty up there. It's been years, decades even, since it's gotten a good tidying.'

'Cleaning out the attic, eh. Sounds like a very *sane* activity to engage in first thing in the morning.'

'I would say it's *therapeutic*. I suggest you try it some time.'

'I have a suggestion of my own: you should go and dust yourself off immediately,' Reynolds lowered his face and narrowed his eyes at me, 'and make sure you don't take too much time doing it.'

I knew how to take an order so I saluted him and turned

stiffly on one heel then made my way towards the store room. I was leaving a faint trail of dust in my wake, but nobody was too concerned because I was the one who swept the floors. It was turning out to be a bad day and just when I thought it couldn't get any worse, Gemma barged through the swing doors from the store room. She stopped dead in her tracks and looked at me like I had five heads. She gazed at my dusty hair for a while before speaking.

'What happened to you this time?' she asked, her face amused.

'You don't want to know and you wouldn't believe me if I told you.'

I spent the rest of the morning sweeping floors and helping to deal with the big weekly delivery. I tried my best to stay out of trouble and even fought off the desire to use my gift at one point; I'd spotted Reynolds leaning over a refrigerator unit and was tempted to give him a little nudge that would have sent him face first into a stack of frozen peas. I often felt the urge to be mischievous when Reynolds was around, but I hardly ever indulged in that kind of skullduggery. Something deep down inside told me that the gift was never to be used to hurt others. It was as though my powers were only intended for the good of mankind … but this could have been from watching too many superhero movies.

I got some respite at 12.30 when my half-hour lunch break arrived and I went to sit in the rear yard to enjoy a bottle of juice in the fine weather. I couldn't stop thinking about how I'd destroyed the pillar that morning.

How did I do it? Could I summon such power at will or did I have to be angry or afraid? I was almost eighteen years old and I had noticed that the gift had been growing in strength for the seven years since I discovered it. I wondered just how powerful I could become. Could I become so powerful that I would be a danger to others?

There were so many unanswered questions about my powers, every day there seemed to be a new one to ponder. The most difficult question to answer was: how to use the gift? I knew I couldn't waste the power on pulling pranks and making anonymous videos. There had to be a higher calling. There had to be a way to put the gift to good use.

'Hey, Dusty.'

I looked up to see Gemma standing there, smiling from ear to ear. She had her hands on her hips and a teasing look in her big brown eyes.

'Please don't call me that,' I moaned.

'Too late. All the staff have agreed to call you that from now on.' She sat down next to me and swept her silky brown hair over her shoulder. 'Don't worry, you'll always be "Ross" to me.'

'Thanks,' I said. 'You seem very chirpy this morning. What's behind that big smile of yours?'

'Well, I am feeling quite happy with myself. My two friends

and I found an apartment in the city that we're going to rent when we start college in September!'

'How interesting,' I said rather glumly. I hated when she mentioned college; her leaving Dullbrook meant I would have to endure the place on my own. 'You must be really looking forward to it.'

'I am.' There was a brief flash of concern in her eyes. 'You still haven't any plans for after the summer?'

'No plans past this week. I won't get good enough results for college, so it's either stay here at Delaney's or find some other bottom-feeding job.'

'It's your own fault that you didn't do well in school, Ross.'

'Oh?' It wasn't like Gemma to be so forward. 'How'd you figure that out?'

'I could give you a thousand examples.'

'Give me two.'

'Okay. When Mr O'Donnell asked what the difference between Stratus and Cirrocumulus clouds was, you said, "One is made of candy floss and other is simply a figment of your imagination, sir."'

'Oh yeah,' I chuckled. I'd tormented Mr O'Donnell for the five years he taught us geography.

'And then,' Gemma continued, 'when he said, "What sort of idiot are you, Bentley?" you answered, "What sorts are there, sir?"'

'At least I called him *sir*.'

'It's not *funny!*' Gemma snapped, she'd always been the model student and hated my reckless attitude. 'You made school impossible for yourself and now you're seeing the result. You're gonna be stuck here while everyone else is moving on.'

'No need to rub it in.'

'I'm not *trying* to rub it in. I just can't figure you out, Ross Bentley! You're the strangest person I've ever known. You were one of the smartest guys in St Francis', but you failed all your exams. You were the best at sport, but you gave it up. We all wanted to know you better, but you barely talked to anyone and lots of girls in Maybrook fancy you, but you've never had a girlfriend.'

'I'm not like other guys.'

'Tell me something I don't know.'

'I *could* tell you something that no one knows.'

Gemma turned to me sharply and placed her hand on my shoulder. 'Ross, I'm your friend. You can tell me anything.'

'Gemma, I'm—'

'Bentley!' a voice barked from behind. 'Doesn't your lunch break finish at one o'clock?'

I turned to see Reynolds standing behind me, tapping the face of his wristwatch. 'It's now three minutes past! I'm not paying you to *shoot the breeze.*'

'How does one shoot the breeze?' I wondered aloud.

'How many times have I warned you about that smart mouth of yours, Bentley? It gives a terrible impression of

Delaney's.'

I ambled off the ground and headed back inside for four hours of excruciating boredom. What made it worse was that I had opened the door to Gemma; she now knew something strange was going on in my life. She would hound me until I told her what was really going on. And if I didn't come clean she'd see it as me pushing her away. Did I really want to let my secretiveness ruin our friendship? Would telling her about my gift make her afraid of me or think I was crazy?

Perhaps it didn't matter; I was slowly losing her as a friend anyway. In a couple of months she would relocate and find lots of new friends at college and I'd become a virtual stranger to her, someone she occasionally spoke to on Facebook. That made me truly alone in the world.

There had to be more to life! There had to be people out there who I could be myself with. There had to be others out there like me. People who wouldn't think I was weird because I had a special gift. People I could learn from.

Where were they though and how could I find them?

CHAPTER THREE

The Million Dollar Gift

I was in a very dark mood as I boarded home. I was in such bad sorts that I even dared to use my gift in public. There was a gang of no-brainers a couple of years older than me hanging out on a street corner on my route home. They'd been shouting abuse at me every night since I started at Delaney's. I usually ignored them, but that night I wasn't in a passive frame of mind.

'Here's the sweetheart with the skateboard,' one shouted. He was a stocky twerp with a flat nose and a shaved head. 'You're about the best-looking girl in Maybrook!'

They all laughed and another threw a stone over my head. I turned and blew a kiss to the one with the shaved head. He instantly gave chase, but no matter how fast he ran I was always just out of reach. Then inexplicably, he lost his footing and fell hard on the pavement. It looked like he simply fell but I knew better. I'd sent a little burst of power at his feet that knocked him off his stride.

I treated myself to a sly grin when I heard the thump.

It made me feel strong, not weak like I always felt when I was at work or when people called me names. I felt powerful and wicked, but these feelings were quickly replaced by guilt; I *hated* using the gift to cause harm to others, it wasn't fair. What was worrying was that the crappier my life got the angrier I became. The angrier I was, the more I was tempted to harm people. It was a vicious cycle that had to be severed before I got myself into serious trouble.

I put on my earphones and listened to music as I rolled on towards Dullbrook Avenue. I made sure to avoid angry or depressing tunes, opting instead for more mellow songs. Music always calmed me down and I was feeling something akin to normal as I entered the avenue.

When I got home I slammed the hall door shut and made the lights in the hallway come on. When I plucked the earphones from my ears I heard the low murmur of the 6 o'clock news coming from the sitting room. Life at my house was terribly predictable.

As I took to the staircase Dad called out, 'That you?'

I didn't give my usual answer. 'Yes, it is I, the famous shelf-stacker of Dullbrook. Also known as the biggest loser in the world.'

'What did you say?'

'Nothing,' I shouted back as I reached my room. 'Nothing important.'

The lights in the room came on and I flung my skateboard

into the corner then angrily kicked off my runners. Frustration had been building inside me for a long time and I was really struggling to keep it in check. I tried to clear my mind of all the difficulties that dogged me. I banished Reynolds, the local gang, my job and the failures of school from my thoughts.

I searched for a positive thought to focus on and remembered what I'd done to the concrete pillar. All the bad thoughts evaporated and I became excited again, just like I was when I rolled out of the dust cloud. I wondered if I could do it again, but without putting my life at risk. Could I destroy or move something bigger than a block of stone? But what could I use as a test?

Walking over to the window, I lifted the net curtains over my head and I looked along the avenue. There was nobody around. My gaze hopped from one garden to the next, but nothing caught my attention; there were only potted plants or garden ornaments. I needed something more substantial. I needed a *real* test!

I turned my attention to the road beyond my garden and grinned mischievously. I was staring at a Volvo that belonged to Mr Kirwan, the grumpy old man who lived in the house opposite ours. I tapped into the frustration that I was feeling and channelled it towards the vehicle … nothing happened.

I needed to concentrate harder. I needed to put everything I had into this attempt. I focused on all the things that made me angry, then pressed the palm of my right hand against the window. I pushed every ounce of anxiety, energy and frustration from my chest and imagined my hand as a conductor. My legs suddenly stiffened then shivered violently. Condensation began to spread on the glass.

Then it happened. The car began to move, only slightly, from side to side. As I focused harder the vehicle actually began to bounce on its suspension, as if an invisible rhino was scratching its backside off it. I clamped my eyes shut and pressed forward against the window that was now covered in tiny moisture droplets. The car moved off the ground, only by a couple of centimetres and only for a split second, but it moved. As it touched back onto the ground the car's alarm screamed and broke my concentration. The link was shattered.

I fell back onto my bed, out of breath. My heart was pounding hard and my head was spinning. I felt physically drained – almost ready to pass out – but emotionally I was in rapture; I'd always been able to move small objects using my will alone, but now I was able to lift objects as big as cars! I felt like the most powerful person on the planet. The possibilities were endless … if I was willing to use the gift more openly. That would be a big step forward though; I didn't want to be seen as some sort of sideshow freak.

I climbed off the bed and moved to the window. Mr Kirwan was standing by the road in his leather slippers looking awfully annoyed. He had his hands on his hips and was vigorously shaking his balding head. I'd never liked him and couldn't contain my amusement. I ducked away from the window and laughed until I got a pain in my gut. When I finally stopped laughing I started to wonder if I needed to be frustrated or angry to be more powerful.

And moving the car was nothing compared to what I did to the pillar. Maybe panic fuelled the gift even more. Panic was difficult to recreate though.

I was tempted to move the car again, but as I peeked through the net curtains I saw that Kirwan was still outside, looking up and down the street and he'd been joined by more Dullbrookians who had been attracted by the siren of his car alarm. I decided not to risk another stunt and went downstairs to heat up my dinner.

I was still grinning to myself while I waited for my meal, but the blandness of the kitchen soon wiped the smile off my face. It was like everything else in Dullbrook, grey and old-fashioned. What use was a superpower in such a place – I couldn't let people know about it, and I couldn't escape Dullbrook *and* my job because I'd messed up my exams. I really was an idiot.

The negative thoughts returned as I sat at the kitchen table and my mood turned black once more. I realised that I could entertain myself by using the gift, but that my problems remained; if I really wanted to be content I would have to change the way I was living. That was easier said than done, though. An interesting job in the city would turn things around for me, but jobs were hard to come by. I tried to think of ways of escaping Dullbrook as I picked at my dinner. There was a world of opportunities out there, but more often than not you needed money to start a new life; something I had little of. It's what some people call 'the poverty trap'. I was caught in it and there was no obvious way out.

I was cleaning off my plate when Dad came in. I felt pretty uncomfortable; we rarely occupied the same room for more than a few seconds and this situation could have easily led to a conversation, which was a dreadful proposition. It would be the first in months. The last conversation we had ended up in a blazing row and I wasn't in the mood for one of those.

'There you are,' Dad remarked, more politely than was necessary.

'Yes, here I am,' I replied without turning.

'Always the comedian,' he said as he moved to the counter and made himself a cup of coffee. 'How's work going?'

'It's riveting,' I answered, never taking my gaze from the sink. 'When I was finished sweeping the floors today I got the opportunity to study the differences between four types of nappy. Fascinating job, isn't it?'

'There's no need to be so smart all the time, Ross.

'Yes, that's just it; there is no need to be so smart to live my life. In fact, only the basic brain functions are necessary.'

'It's a job, it keeps money in your pocket and you should be happy to have it.'

'Maybe you should do it if you think it's so great.'

'I'd be happy to have a job.'

'Why don't you get one then? Maybe if we both had jobs we wouldn't be living on a shoestring all the time!'

I could see by his expression that my words had cut deep and I regretted them as soon as they left my mouth. I didn't have the courage to apologise, though. I returned my gaze to the sink and scrubbed my plate harder.

'Do I not spend my days looking for work?' he raised his voice. 'I hope you never know what it's like to face rejection on a daily basis.'

'I don't intend to.'

'I never *intended* to end up in the dole queue, but it happened anyway.'

'You'll never catch me in the dole queue.'

'I know you're embarrassed by me, Ross,' he said. 'I'm embarrassed by myself. It hurts that my only son sees me as a failure. I'm just glad your mother isn't—'

'You *had* to mention her, didn't you? I can't wait to get out of this place.' I slammed the plate against the counter. 'I want out of this situation!'

He was about to reply, but I cut him off, 'I know you're gonna say: if I hadn't turned down the contract with Manchester United then we wouldn't be in this situation.'

He took his cup and moved to the door, 'I was actually

going to say that you won't be in this situation forever because you're too talented to end up like me.'

I wanted to say something as I watched him making his way back to the sitting room, but no words came. For the first time in years I saw my father as a human being and not just another piece of furniture. He was a real person with feelings, not just a fixture of this house that wasn't a home. He'd also had to endure the loneliness that had been haunting 57 Dullbrook Avenue for seven long years, since Mam died, and he also had to deal with the shame of unemployment. He'd been an out-standing carpenter in his day and now he walked the streets looking for jobs that no one else was willing to do. My life was utopian compared to his.

Now I felt guilty as well as frustrated. It hadn't been a good day at all and I wanted to put it behind me. I made a cup of tea and headed back to my lair, even though I knew I should have gone to the sitting room and apologised. I walked past the sitting room door and saw him staring out the window. There was nothing out there but lines of little grey houses. Hardly inspiring. I just walked on by and went to my room.

I turned on my laptop and checked out The Impossible Stunt. There were hundreds more comments now and I read through every single one. Unfortunately reading them didn't cheer me up at all, almost all of them were calling the video a fake or daring me to reveal my identity.

I read the latest comment: 'I have to agree with previous

posts. This is so obviously a fake that it's laughable. No wonder 365 won't take off his mask. Don't give up your day job, mate!'

I caved in at that point and deleted the video I'd worked so hard on from my Youtube channel. I doubted that I would ever record another like it. I gathered up my conceptual drawings from the desk and dumped them in the bin.

I actually considered making one last video without the mask, but quickly decided against it; they'd still call me a fake, and they'd know my identity and would pester me even more. I'd never be left alone. There'd be no escape from the cyber vultures.

Making the videos was the only thing that kept me sane, but it seemed my favourite past-time was over. I would have to find something new to do. I couldn't think of anything though so I logged onto Facebook to pass the time. There was no activity. None of my seven friends were online.

I updated my status by typing, 'Worst day ever!' then went to log out. But before I did, a chat box opened.

'Why was it the worst day ever?'

I squinted at the screen and saw that it was Gemma; she'd just logged on. Part of me was happy that she'd decided to contact me, another part of me didn't really want to talk to her at all; I was sure I would face difficult questions.

'It just was,' I typed.

'It's my fault, isn't it? I was way out of line this afternoon.'

'It wasn't that. Everything just seemed to go wrong for me today.'

'We all have days like those, Dusty.'

'Hey!' I typed. 'I thought you said you wouldn't call me that!'

'Ha, ha. I'm sorry, Ross.' She followed that up with a difficult question. 'Why were you covered in dust this morning?'

This really caught me off guard. The *cleaning-the-attic-in-the-morning* excuse wouldn't wash with Gemma, not that it had with Reynolds. I couldn't tell her the truth though because that was even more implausible.

I placed my fingertips on the keyboard and gave her the only explanation that she would believe. 'I fell off my skateboard on my way into work.'

She took a while to send a reply and I knew she was probably crying with laughter.

'Were you hurt?'

'No.'

'OK, then I don't feel bad saying, HA, HA, HA!'

'At least nobody saw me falling. That's the most important thing!'

There was a long silence and I felt the urge to direct the conversation back to where it had been that afternoon. I surprised myself when I managed to say, 'You were right today. You know, I'm not like other guys.'

'Duh! That's pretty obvious.'

'I'm not joking, Gemma. I really am different.'

'In what way?'

'It's hard to explain.'

'You can tell me, Ross! We're best friends.'

'I've never told anyone about it before.'

'Are you gay?'

'No! Christ!'

'Well, what then?'

'It's so difficult to explain.'

'Try.'

'I can't.'

'Typical man. Maybe you should sign up to The Million Dollar Gift if you're so different!'

'Oh, don't get your knickers in a twist!'

'Listen, my Mam is telling me to turn off the computer. I better go.'

'Fine.'

'I'll see you in work on Friday.'

She went offline and left me to curse myself for being so open with her. Twice in one day I'd tried to let her inside and it turned out disastrously on both occasions. I didn't even bother to log off or to shut down the laptop properly. I pressed my thumb on the power button and the screen went black, which I never did. I put the laptop on the floor and wrapped the duvet around myself. The lights in the bedroom went out.

What a day! I'd argued with Gemma and Dad, Reynolds was on my back the whole day, I got hassled by the Dullbrook gang and I was nearly killed by a rogue pillar.

It had been an exhausting day for so many different reasons and my eyelids were growing heavy. I couldn't remember being so tired in all my life and within a few minutes I was drifting off into sleep. Finally I was calm.

'Hold on…' I said as I sat up. 'What the hell is The Million Dollar Gift?'

CHAPTER FOUR

A Day to Forget

The alarm clock buzzed at 8am, but I was already awake. In fact, I'd barely slept at all. I clicked my fingers and the alarm was silenced, then I returned my attention to the laptop. I was on Youtube, but wasn't checking out my alias' channel; I had been watching an unusual clip over and over since late the previous night – The Million Dollar Gift.

This video sent my imagination into overdrive; it began with a gold symbol, an atlas globe contained in the letter 'G', rotating on a black background and the words 'Golding Scientific International' scrolling along the bottom of the frame. A moment later the video faded to a TV studio. The camera first focused on an attractive woman, who was apparently a famous presenter on American TV, but I'd never heard of her before (I didn't watch a lot of TV). Sitting opposite her were two men, both in their fifties. One was smartly dressed, tanned and had neat, greying hair. The other was painfully thin, had a short white beard and wore thick spectacles.

The presenter began a few seconds into the clip. 'Hi, I'm

Melinda Johnson and today I'll be talking to two very different men who have come together in a joint venture that sees one million dollars up for grabs. It's a very unusual competition and it's aptly titled The Million Dollar Gift. Here to talk to me about it are the men behind the idea: Professor Mark Foster and, billionaire businessman, Paul Golding.'

The camera then focused on the guests and the well-dressed man began to chuckle. He crossed one leg over the other and leaned back confidently in his chair. 'Billionaire businessman isn't my official title, but I guess it could be worse!'

All three laughed, but the one who found it most amusing was Golding who continued laughing long after the others had stopped.

Johnson then took control of the interview by directing her words to Professor Foster, 'Now, Professor, a lot of people out there may be familiar with you, but unfortunately not for your actual work in theoretical physics.'

'Yes,' Foster said with a smile. 'I have made my way into the public eye in recent months, unintentionally of course.'

'Of course,' Johnson said with a smile. 'A lot of people will know you because of your very public spat with Johan Van Goor, the famous, or now infamous, psychic medium.'

'Yes, I commented during an interview with a newspaper journalist that I thought Van Goor was a charlatan and that he was robbing vulnerable people, who were mostly in the grieving process, of their money.'

Johnson interrupted the professor and talked directly to the camera, 'For anyone who is unfamiliar with Johan Van Goor, he had a TV show where he claimed to speak to the dead relatives of his studio audience. The show had been mired in controversy because of the high cost of getting a seat in the audience.'

Professor Foster butted in, 'One thousand dollars per seat if I remember correctly. Van Goor didn't react well to my criticism and launched quite an aggressive verbal assault against me. And so I challenged him to put his talents under scientific scrutiny. Needless to say, he lost the challenge.'

'And has that *challenge*, as you call it, led directly to this venture with Paul Golding?'

'I guess you could say that. I was swamped, after the televised contest with Van Goor, by people claiming to have special gifts. I said if I had a million dollars I would offer it up to anyone who could prove me wrong. Obviously I don't have a million dollars to throw around and I thought that was the end of it.'

Johnson turned to her other guest. 'And that's where you come in, Mr Golding?'

'Yes, I had worked on a number of projects with the professor in the past and I heard about his offer and thought it would be interesting if I put up the cash.'

'You don't have any vested interest?'

'None whatsoever, apart from getting some publicity for

my latest hotel.'

'Which we'll come back to in a moment. But you're not looking for potential employees? I'm sure a psychic would come in handy for someone like you. It would sure give you an edge during your business meetings.'

Golding laughed loudly and shook his head. 'I can read people well enough so I don't need a psychic to do my work for me. I guess ever since I read my first *Superman* comic I've been fascinated by the idea that there may be someone out there who actually has a *superhuman power*.'

'So, you're not just looking for someone who can speak to the dead?'

'Not at all,' Foster interjected. 'We are looking for anyone who has any type of extraordinary gift. Be it the power to read minds, to speak with the dead, to make things disappear or reappear, to communicate with animals or even move objects without touching them.'

Johnson then continued by asking Foster, 'It sounds a bit like *X-Factor* or *American Idol*. Will you be the Simon Cowell of this contest, Professor?'

Professor Foster seemed quite insulted by the comparison and straightened himself in his chair.

'Certainly not,' he scoffed. 'This will not be a televised contest.'

'But surely there will be hordes of fame-hungry people entering the contest?'

'That may be the case, but they will be turned away quite quickly if that's their only reason for entering. This is not about fame.'

'But—'

Golding interrupted the presenter saying,

'We'll only announce the identity of a winner if that is their wish. If they prefer to remain anonymous, I can assure you that the public will never know their name.'

The presenter seemed a little flustered, but composed herself and asked, 'When does this competition take place?'

'It starts on 1 June,' Golding answered. 'It'll take place in London, England, at the Golding Plaza Hotel, which I own. Interviews and tests will be conducted in the conference centre by qualified personnel who will be hand-picked by the Professor.'

'And I understand it will run for one month?'

'Yes, for a month only. We'll be officially opening the hotel in late July so we've decided the last day for interviews will be 1 July.'

Johnson turned back to the camera and smiled. 'That is sure going to be one intriguing month. If you wish to enter The Million Dollar Gift you can go to the official website for more details.'

The clip ended and my mind was buzzing with possibilities. I'd already checked the currency exchange rates online and it worked out at well over three quarters of a million euro. It was a lot of money, enough to change my life forever, but it was already late June and there was only one week left before the contest closed.

Not only that, it was in another country and Dad wasn't the type of parent to let his seventeen-year-old son wander off to London for a few days. What excuse could I give? I'd thought about it all morning and no convincing reason to go to London on my own came to mind. If I was to go, I'd have to keep my reasons to myself, which would mean big trouble. It would also mean giving up my job, not that that sounded too bad, but if I was unsuccessful I would return to a gloomier life than the one I left behind.

The thoughts of a new beginning excited me, though. With that type of money I could do anything! I could move to California, get a cool tattoo, loads of designer clothes, a new board … actually I could get a hundred new boards and a slick pad by the coast. I smiled as I pictured a much cooler version of myself rolling along Venice Beach. Could I really do it though or was I just daydreaming? I'd regret it forever if I didn't enter the contest, that much was for sure.

My train of thought was broken when my Dad tapped on the bedroom door. Talking to him was the last thing I wanted, especially after the argument from the night before, but I had to respond, I needed things between us to be better if I was going to convince to let me travel to London.

'Come in,' I said.

'I'm going out for a few hours,' he said as he entered cautiously. 'I thought I'd look around for some work again. Guess I've gotten into a rut these last few weeks.'

'Dad, I didn't mean most of what I said last night. I know you try your best to get work.'

'Haven't been trying very hard lately though.'

'Can't say I blame you; how many times have you been told "Your application has been unsuccessful"?'

'I've lost count.'

As he moved closer I clicked the backspace button on the laptop, I didn't want him seeing the Million Dollar Gift video. My internet explorer immediately jumped back a page and a free runner video started playing.

'So, this is how you spend your time,' he said, 'looking at these crazy clips.'

'They're not so crazy.'

'Looks insane to me. People jumping off walls.'

'It's called free running. It's a very popular sport.'

'Good wages in a sport like that?'

'I don't want to get into that conversation again.'

'Neither do I. It does look dangerous, Ross. You could break your neck doing stunts like that.'

'*I* won't.'

'Oh, so you're special in some way?'

'You have no idea ...'

'Everyone thinks they're special until they realise how vulnerable they really are.'

I was about to reply with a smart remark, but then thought about our conversation the night before and how that had ended up. I simply shrugged my shoulders and remained silent.

'Well, I'd best get a move on,' Dad said as he examined the clock by the window. 'Are you in work today?'

I glanced at the clock on the window sill. It was already 9.05 and I was running late. 'I am, I'll be leaving in a few minutes.'

'Right. Have a good day,' he said as he left the room.

'You too,' I hollered after him, 'and good luck.'

It had been the most civilised conversation we'd had in years. I figured we were both beginning to regret the long silence that had sucked the life out of the house. Maybe things were starting to change. Maybe the tough times were at an end. If only I'd explained to him why I turned down Manchester United … things could have been so different. If only Mam had been around, she would have smoothed things over. She always did that. Maybe I wouldn't be hiding my powers if she were still alive; I don't think I would've been able to hide it from her, or have wanted to hide it from her.

I turned off the laptop. I'd return to the Million Dollar Gift when I finished my shift at Delaney's.

CHAPTER FIVE -

Living The Dream

I left the supermarket at 7pm and rolled home at a snail's pace. The job often left me drained and it just seemed to get worse each day. As I neared Dullbrook Place, the local gang started shouting at me from across the street, but I didn't react this time. I hadn't the energy to use my gift like I had the night before. I thumbed my earphones into my ears and listened to some upbeat tunes. I thought it might liven me up, but I remained zombie-like as I made my way home.

When I got inside the house I staggering up the staircase, dragging my backpack and skateboard behind me. My eyes were almost shut and my feet felt like lead.

'That you?'

'What's left of me.'

'Tough day?'

'You could say that.'

'You want me to make you some food?'

'No, I couldn't handle being poisoned right now!'

I heard him laughing as I pushed open my bedroom door;

at least I'd brought a bit of cheer to someone's day.

I fell face first onto my bed and shouted, 'I need a holiday!' into the pillow. 'A very long holiday in a place where there aren't any supermarkets! The Sahara, Greenland, even outer Mongolia will do.'

Exhaustion soon got the better of me and I nodded off into a deep, dead sleep that lasted over four hours. When I woke I knew I'd be up half the night with nothing to do but think about the contest. This would be a dangerous time. It always was when I got to thinking, because my thinking usually turned into scheming and my schemes usually led to trouble.

I left the room and traipsed downstairs to make some food. Dad had already gone to bed and the house was unbearably quiet. I imagined how quiet the place would be if I left for London, how empty and haunted it would seem. How alone and isolated would Dad be when I eventually left the nest? I felt sorry for him in many ways, he never really got over Mam's death and I guess he was the only thing keeping me from leaving Dullbrook and entering The Million Dollar Gift. I couldn't blame him for not being the same person after she passed away. They were very close and my mother was a really special person. My life would have been so different if she'd still been around. She always knew what to say, no matter how hard things got, she would throw her arm around my shoulder and say something inspiring. I missed her so much. I remember Dad saying at the funeral that only two things outweighed his grief: the love he still felt for her and the sense of luck that he'd gotten to spend twenty years of his life with her. At least he had memories. I sometimes wondered if I would have similar luck; to meet a really special girl who loved me no matter what.

Dad was the only obstacle. What could I tell him, though? How could I make him understand?

A crafty plan entered my mind, but it was risky. I surprised myself by even considering it. Could I really go through with it? I contemplated going upstairs and waking him, but thought it would be best left until morning. I'd put my plan into action if I still had the guts when I woke up.

I took a hot cup of tea to my room and went online to do some research on the contest. There were very few facts, most of what was going on was being kept under wraps but there were some photographs of a queue stretching from the Golding Plaza Hotel's front entrance to the corner, which was about a kilometre away.

There was one confirmed detail on the official website: *We have yet to find a winner*. I still had a chance at that million dollars, but if I wanted to take that chance I'd have to make a decision soon; there were only a few days left and I had a lot to organise if I was going to leave. I'd need money, but I didn't get paid until the end of the month, which would be too late.

I reached under the bed and pulled an out old shoebox. Inside were my meagre savings: two hundred euro in small notes. I went online and checked for flights to London, but I'd left it too late; every flight was booked solid. I would just have to make the journey by boat and bus, which wasn't a very exciting prospect.

I looked at the pitiful bundle of notes. What was I doing? It was ridiculous! I was actually considering it? I'd be a laughing stock if anyone found out I was entering the biggest freak show in the world! I got enough flak as it was.

I stuffed the money back into the shoebox and kicked it under the bed. I needed to get my head out of the clouds. I was only giving myself false hope.

As I took my uniform out of the wardrobe for the next day, I glanced at a poster pinned to the inside of the door. It was an old poster of a Tony Hawks video game. It used to be my favourite game.

If I won that contest they might make a Ross Bentley video game. I smiled and thought about a digital version of me skating and leaping from the rooftops of one building to another. Kids asking for my autograph. Girls asking for my autograph … My smile grew wider. Within seconds I'd retrieved the shoebox and was counting through the loose notes once more.

I'd finally made up my mind. I was going to take the chance and enter the contest.

I awoke with a start to the sound of my alarm clock. I instinctively swiped my hand at the clock and it flew off the windowsill and hit the wall on the opposite side of the room.

'I need to be more careful with this thing,' I said, staring at my hand.

Most mornings I just thought about the alarm turning off and it did. Sometimes I clicked my fingers at it, but now I was realising that swiping my hand to channel energy made the gift much more effective, if a little unpredictable.

I had woken up in a determined mood. This was the day that I was going to start living the dream, and so I leaped out of bed and got dressed then headed for the kitchen where Dad spent each morning. I'd waited a long time to do this and I wasn't going to wait any longer.

'You're up bright and early,' Dad said as I strode confidently into the kitchen. 'What has you so sprightly?'

'You fancy a kick-about in the back garden before you leave?'

He almost choked on his Weetabix. 'You want to play football with me? In the back garden? Now?'

'Yeah.' I ducked out of the room and returned a moment later with a leather ball under my arm. 'Come on.'

'Aren't you a bit old for a kick-about with your Dad?'

'Can you ever be too old?'

'I guess not.'

'Just for five minutes.'

'I don't think so, Ross.'

He slowly rose from the kitchen table, took his bowl and cup to the sink then headed for the hallway. I felt totally deflated and dropped the ball on the kitchen tiles. My plan was already falling apart.

He paused in the doorway and looked back at me. For a long moment we watched each other before he cracked a smile and said, 'Go on. Five minutes.'

I laughed then picked the ball up and moved to the back garden with Dad in tow, chuckling to himself and continually shaking his head at how absurd the situation seemed. I paced to the back of the garden and he stayed near the house.

I started the game by kicking a simple pass and Dad flipped the ball up and volleyed it back (he'd been quite a player in his younger years). We passed it back and forth for a few minutes without sharing a word. We were simply enjoying a game that we'd played so many times in the past.

Dad eventually broke the silence. 'I haven't seen you kick a football in years, lad. I used to love watching you play. You were such a good footballer.'

'Did you ever think I was *too* good?'

'I thought you were the best I'd ever seen. I couldn't understand how you could give it up so easily.'

'It wasn't easy.'

'Why did you quit? It's been gnawing at me for such a long time. I know you think I was just concerned about money, but I was more worried because you'd lost your ambition. You'd always been a bit of a loner and I didn't want to see you become more isolated. I just want to know your reason for quitting. I'm not going to judge you. And for once in our lives let's not make this about money.'

I took my time answering. It was the most difficult question I'd ever been asked. It was so hard to explain, and so much pressure had been built on me turning my back on soccer.

'I can't really tell you,' I eventually said, 'but I can *show* you.'

I kicked the ball, gently, and it rolled along the lawn. It began to spin and before it reached Dad's toe it changed direction and came back to me. I stood on the ball once more.

My dad couldn't quite grasp what he'd just seen. 'How did you…?'

'It wasn't a fluke,' I told him. 'I'll show you again.'

I kicked the ball a little harder this time. It rolled quickly over the lawn then bounced up over his head, smacked the patio doors then moved at incredible speed though his feet and eventually settled under my heel.

He was dumbfounded. 'How…?'

'I couldn't play anymore, Dad. It wasn't fair on the other players.'

'But—'

'Do you understand? It's not just with a football.'

I pointed towards the house and a hanging basket began to spin faster and faster until its chain snapped and it crashed to the ground. 'Do you understand now?'

'I don't believe it…'

'Believe it, Dad. It's real.'

I pointed at another hanging basket and performed the same trick then made the washing line loop round and round like a skipping rope.

'I can move things without touching them. I just have to think of an object moving and it does.'

'Why didn't you tell me?' Dad asked when he caught his breath, and when everything in the garden stopped moving around.

I crossed the garden and stood in front of him.

'I didn't tell you because I knew it had been your dream to play for Manchester United when you were young. But you put the hopes of achieving that dream on my shoulders when I started playing football. I didn't want to let you down, but I couldn't go through with it either. I'm not a cheat. I'm *real*!'

'When did you discover this talent?'

'It appeared in me just after Mam died. I was alone in my room after the funeral and I got real angry. Objects started breaking apart and others simply floated around me. At first I didn't want to say anything because I wasn't sure what to think about it. You weren't really acting very normal, and you weren't really listening to me either, so I kept it to myself and over time it became my secret. It was something no one could know about.

'Then I discovered I could use this gift when I was playing soccer and that excited me at first, but over time I became ashamed of what I was doing. The look in the other players' eyes when I scored always made me feel guilty. I couldn't pretend to be just another normal player who happened to score fantastic goals all the time. I couldn't live a lie and I'm sick of hiding all this from everyone. I'm not a child anymore and I have to face up to it and use this gift for something more than putting a ball into a net or making a skateboard move at a hundred miles an hour.'

'You move your skateboard at a hundred miles per hour? Do you realise how dangerous that is?'

'Not while I'm on it…' I lied. 'I'd have to be nuts to do that…'

He reached out and hugged me for the first time in many years.

'I'm sorry, Dad.'

'Don't apologise, lad. I'm the one who was in the wrong.' He squeezed my shoulders then leaned back and looked me in the eye. 'Why are you telling me this all of a sudden? Has something changed?'

I took a deep breath. 'Well, here's the thing… There's a video I want you to see.'

I felt like a different person when I arrived at work that day. The old Ross was gone. The new Ross had arrived. I was going to live the dream.

The morning seemed to pass quickly and before I knew it, I was on my lunch break.

I spent it sitting at the back of the building with the sun on my face. I hadn't been so at ease in years; I felt confident, calm, excited and powerful all at the same time. I felt so complete that I could have moved a mountain with a hand gesture.

Eventually Gemma appeared from the storeroom and sat on the wall next to me. She was about to say something, but the words never left her mouth. She was staring into the yard in disbelief.

'What the hell is going on?' she breathed.

In the corner of the yard there were two large metal recycling bins. It was my job to empty rubbish into them each day, but I always left a lot of paper and cardboard cartons strewn across the yard. Gemma and I sat there watching the loose rubbish slowly swirling off the ground and into the air as if each piece had a life of its own. The rubbish formed a skeletal column twenty feet tall that rotated very slowly.

'How is this happening?' Gemma gasped. 'There's no wind, not even a breeze.'

The column began to waver and then collapsed, leaving the loose rubbish to float around the yard.

'That was so weird,' Gemma said as she watched the paper falling to the ground.

'The world is a weird place,' I replied. 'Hey, if you had a chance to live your dream, would you take the chance no matter how much risk was involved?'

'Honestly, I don't think my dreams require me take any major risks.'

61

'Let me put it this way: if you had a dream and there was only one chance at achieving it, would you take it, even if it meant there was a lot of risk involved?'

'Theoretically—'

'Come on, Gemma!'

'Yes. I would go for it and I wouldn't let anything get in my way. But what are we talking about here? Really?'

'It's hard to explain.'

'Being secretive again, are we?' Gemma rolled her eyes and turned away. 'You're always so secretive, Ross. *Too* secretive!'

'I'm not being secretive. In fact, I'm being open and honest for once in my life. I'm gonna live the dream, Gemma.'

'What are you on about?'

'Do you think people should live life without regret?'

'Of course.'

I was going to live my life without regret; I was going to do all the things I wanted to do.

'I'm not going to regret doing this,' I said before I stood and paced purposely towards the supermarket. 'I'm *definitely* not going to regret this.'

I passed through the store room and unloaded my locker then strode onto the supermarket floor. I pulled the tie from my collar and held it tightly in my hand.

When I reached to the tills I saw Reynolds glowering at me. 'Bentley! What have I told you about wearing your tie while on the floor?'

I threw the tie at him, 'You wear it because I've had enough of listening to you and I've certainly had enough of this god-damn job, it's almost as bad as your moustache!'

The entire staff and all the customers sniggered as I walked paced through the doors. Reynolds just stood there as if he'd seen a ghost. His face was white and he put his hand over his moustache. He spun round to the girls at the tills and hissed at them, 'Get back to work!'

But everyone continued laughing, even the little kids who were standing with their parents pointed at his fuzzy upper lip and giggled.

I dropped my skateboard in front of me and rolled through the car park towards the street. With a sweep of my hand I sent hundreds of trolleys spreading out across the car park in different directions. It was one last parting shot at Reynolds for being so mean to me; it would take him over an hour to round up so many trolleys.

I put my earphones on, played some music and pumped my fist in the air as I skated along the middle of the street. People on the pavements watched in amazement as I rolled down the street faster than most cars can travel and roaring, 'Living the dream!'

All afternoon my voice echoed through the streets of Dull-brook.

'Living the dream! Living the dream!'

CHAPTER SIX -

The Journey

It was late in the evening and the adrenalin rush of the day had faded from my body. I'd spent much of the evening on the net checking bus timetables, both British and Irish, and departure times for the ferries. There was a boat leaving Dublin port the next day at noon, which meant I'd have to be on my way early the next morning. The ferry would take me to Wales where I could catch a coach that would bring me into the heart of London. I had it all planned to perfection. I'd even cleared it with Dad. Amazingly.

When Dad had gotten home from his job hunting he called me downstairs to the sitting room. I sat beside him on the couch and he talked about the video I'd shown him that morning. He understood why I wanted to enter The Million Dollar Gift, after all, the prize money was immense, but he was also worried, mostly because I had insisted on travelling alone.

'I just don't feel right about it all, Ross. You're only seventeen years old!'

'But I told you, it's only gonna be for a couple of days.

What's the harm in that? I'll be back before you know it.'

'I still think you're too young and inexperienced to go alone. London is very different to Maybrook. There are a lot of dangerous people in big cities like that who are on the lookout for a kid travelling without an adult.'

'You remember what I told you about the pillar?'

'Yes.'

'Did you drive past it on the way home today?'

'I did.'

'And?'

'It looked like a missile had hit it.'

'Exactly,' I said, 'I can look after myself. Anyone who looks for trouble from me will wish they were never born by the time I'm finished with them.'

'That frightens me just as much! I don't want you losing your temper on some mugger. They'll be picking up pieces of him for weeks and you'll be languishing in a prison cell!'

'That's not going to happen. I'll be going straight to that B&B I found online when I get off the bus. The next day I'll be rolling to the Royal Gold Hotel. Once I'm there, I'll win that contest and I'll be on my way home, I swear I will.'

'I'm still worried.'

'There's no need to be. I'll have my phone and I'll call you every day. I promise.'

'You better. Or else they'll be picking up pieces of *you* for weeks.'

He left the couch and took an envelope from coffee table on the opposite side of the room.

'I've been putting some money away for the last few months, enough to pay the bills through the winter.' He dropped it onto my lap and smiled. 'It's not much but just enough for you to catch a flight back if there's an emergency.'

'I can't take this, Dad. How are you going to pay the bills without it?'

'My son is going to win The Million Dollar Gift.'

I reached out and we shook hands. I don't know why I did it; it just seemed like the thing to do. I don't think we'd ever shook hands before, except when I was really young and we shook hands in church … I don't think that counts though.

'Don't go buying a new skateboard with that,' he warned me. 'I'm out of touch but I'd recognise your board anywhere because of that strange cartoon character you have printed on it (There was an image of Jack Skellington from *The Nightmare Before Christmas* on the underside of the board) and I'll know if you've bought a new one.'

'I'm not going there to buy a new board, Dad. I'm going there to prove something to myself… and to win a million dollars.'

'Don't get too obsessed with money, lad. It's not a healthy way to be.'

'I won't. I wouldn't even know what to do with a million quid.'

'I'm pretty sure you'd come up with a few crazy ideas on how to spend it.'

'Just a few,' I grinned. 'I better start getting ready.'

After our chat I busied myself with picking some appropriate clothes for the trip. 'Looking good is always half the battle,' my mother once told me, and I did like to wear quality stuff. I ironed everything I'd be bringing, then ironed them again (I hadn't quite mastered the art of ironing). When I'd banished enough creases I filled my back-pack with everything I needed.

More important than clothes was music. I'd go nuts on the way over if I hadn't got enough good tunes to listen to so I connected my phone to the laptop and transferred a heap of albums to it.

I'd barely finished uploading all the music when a text message made my phone buzz across the keyboard of the laptop. It was Gemma.

'What came over you today? I went in after lunch to find the supermarket full of people laughing at Reynolds!'

I hadn't any credit to text her back and made a note to buy some before I got on the boat the next day. I logged onto to Facebook hoping she'd be online. She was, and none too pleased with me.

'There you are! What happened today?'

'I'd just had enough of not doing what I wanted to do.'

'Not doing what you wanted to do … Lord, you're cryptic

at times.'

'I was sick of being someone I'm not! I wanted to walk out of Delaney's since the day I started, but was afraid to. I'm not afraid anymore.'

'What's changed?'

'Everything. I'm leaving the country tomorrow.'

'What? You're having a really weird week, aren't you?'

'I am and it's all your fault.'

'How did you come to that conclusion?'

'You told me about The Million Dollar Gift.'

'The X-factor for freaks?'

'That's the one.'

'But why would you be entering that?'

Suddenly my phone started to ring. It was Gemma and I took my time to answer, she seemed in a really bad mood.

'Hello,' I said, 'how's things?'

'Things are starting to make sense, Ross.'

'They are?'

'I couldn't quite understand how the rubbish in the yard was moving like that today, but now it makes sense. It was you, wasn't it? You made it happen?'

'It was me.'

'How did you do it?'

'I just did. I don't know how or why. I can just move things around without touching them. I've had this ability for years but I've always kept it to myself.'

'And now you're going to reveal it to the world?'

'No! The winner's identity won't be announced.'

'Don't be so naïve, Ross. Every newspaper in the western world has a reporter following the contest.'

'But nothing is being announced. They even had to blur the faces of the contestants in the photos they've published.'

'It'll be different if someone wins it.'

'I don't care, Gemma. I've made up my mind.'

'When are you going?'

'First thing in the morning.'

'So soon…'

'I can't wait. There's only a couple of days left to enter.'

'And if you win… will you be coming back?'

'I don't want to live in Maybrook anymore, Gemma.'

'You're full of surprises this week. I never knew you had actual feelings, you usually act like a caveman.'

'I'm more than a caveman.'

'I know, Ross. I wouldn't be friends with a caveman.'

'I'll take that as a compliment.'

'You really are crazy, Ross Bentley. You make sure you stay safe over there and keep in touch!'

'I will. See you soon.'

'Good luck, Ross.'

The line went dead. Nothing more needed to be said though. I locked the phone, powered off the laptop and climbed into bed. There was a big day ahead of me and I'd need a good night's sleep. I winked at the light and the room plunged into darkness.

The alarm clock buzzed at 8am and I pulled off the duvet and jumped from bed. The big day had arrived and my entire body was tingling with anticipation. I pointed a finger at the clock and it went silent. Then I dragged my bag into the middle of the floor and checked that I had everything I'd need for the journey. The phone was fully charged, my best clothes were all packed and there was a roll of twenties in my pocket. I was almost ready; all that I needed was breakfast and a hot cup of tea.

I heard Dad in the kitchen and the familiar clank of the tea spoon.

'Pour me a cup!' I shouted down the stairs. I went to the bathroom and dragged a glob of Brylcreem through my hair then slid down the banister into the hall.

'Before it goes cold,' Dad called to me as he pulled a chair from under the kitchen table and sat.

I took a large gulp of the freshly poured tea and Dad grimaced at me.

'How can you drink tea like that? You'll burn your tongue and have a mouthful of blisters for the trip.'

'I drink the way live,' I joked. I put on a funny voice, '*fast and without fear.*'

Dad rolled his eyes and snorted into his cup. 'A little too fast for my liking.'

I splashed some milk onto a bowl of cornflakes and started crunching, all the while I kept looking at the clock above the kitchen doorway.

'Don't worry, you won't miss the bus. I'll drive you to the stop.'

'No need. My board can go faster than that old banger you drive.'

'That might be true, but I want to drive you anyway.'

'If you insist,' I sighed. 'But you're only contributing to climate change. My board is pure green energy, 100 per cent environmentally-friendly.'

'I didn't know you cared so much about the environment.'

I raised a V-sign. 'Respect Mother Nature, dude.'

'Maybe you'll keep that in mind in the evenings when you've got your phone charging, and your laptop, TV, Playstation and lord knows what else on. Bloody electricity bill was bigger than my bank balance last month.'

'Soon you won't have to worry about the bills, Dad.'

'You're very confident.' He took his cup to the sink and washed it out. 'I guess you have good reason to be, but have you considered that you might not be the only one who can prove they have a superhuman gift?'

I hadn't contemplated this scenario; it hadn't once entered my mind. 'I don't mind sharing. Five hundred thousand dollars will still be enough.'

The thought lingered in my mind. What if there were others

like me at the contest? Maybe if I could find them I would get the answers I'd sought for so long.

'Ross?' my father said, clicking his fingers. 'What's on your mind?'

'Nothing,' I replied with a smile, 'nothing to worry about.'

Twenty minutes later I was getting out of the car at the bus stop and saying farewell to Dad.

'I'll keep in touch,' I assured him. 'Promise I will.'

'See that you do … and be careful!'

'Will do. Now get out of here, you're cramping my style. I'll never hear the end of it if anyone sees me near this car.'

Dad laughed and saluted me before slowly driving off. I suddenly had an ominous sensation for the second time that morning. It was as if something was telling me that I'd never see Dad again. It was disturbing and doubts about what I was doing plagued my mind.

'Nonsense,' I whispered to myself. 'I'll be back before I know it.'

I leaned against the bus stop with my bag over my shoulder and my board under foot. My real journey had just begun, a journey that I would undertake alone. There were one or two butterflies fluttering in my stomach, but all in all I was still excited and bursting with confidence.

It only took a few minutes for the bus to arrive and I flipped up my board and climbed up the step. I moved to the back of the bus and gazed out the window as the quiet streets of

Dullbrook faded into the distance. I was finally doing it. I was leaving home. A surge of enthusiasm coursed through me and I smiled and took a deep breath of freedom. I was finally doing it!

I took one last look out the back window and that strange sensation took me again. For some reason I believed this was the last time I'd lay eyes on Dullbrook. I shrugged and made myself comfortable. My eyes would be better off without having to look at Dullbrook.

It was a clear morning in Dublin city centre and the streets were bustling with people trying to get to work on time. I smiled at them as they streamed past me on the pavements; I'd usually be hurrying to reach Delaney's at that time of the morning. Boy, was I glad that I'd made the decision to leave. It didn't take very long to reach Dublin port and I soon boarded the ferry and found a seat in the corner of the bar. I sat there for a while, but boredom got the better of me so I went strolling around. There wasn't much to see or do and I quickly ended up on the outer deck.

It was beautiful and calm, the waters glittered in the strong sunlight and there wasn't a single cloud in the sky. I felt so good as I rested my elbows on the side rail and sucked the salty air into my nostrils.

'The scent of freedom!' I said with a smile.

I spent the most of the journey on deck watching for signs of land. It first appeared as a faint grey shape on the eastern horizon before it grew into a dark coastline. My sense of freedom was suddenly tinged with fear. There was something ominous looking about the Welsh coast and for the first time I felt anxiety about the journey, and the contest. I couldn't quite explain my feelings, but I didn't have long to dwell on them; I was soon queuing to disembark.

Holyhead was a nice place, but rain was starting to drift from the darkening sky so I couldn't hang around and sought out the bus shelter. I couldn't wait to reach the bright lights of the big city; it was something I'd been dreaming about for years. I spent an hour on the bench before the coach to London squealed to a halt in front of me.

I climbed the steps and nodded to the driver and paid him a few pounds.

The journey was an uneventful one. The landscape was monotonous and the sky had dimmed an hour after we left Holyhead. The only thing that kept me entertained were the signposts. I was fascinated by the Welsh place names such as *Caergeiliog*. *Trewalchmai*. But the one he was most amazed by was *Llanfairyneubwll*. I couldn't quite comprehend how anyone could pronounce such a word. It was kinda like I'd entered Middle Earth or something.

After the second hour I was dozing off, but was snapped out of it by a text that made my pocket vibrate. It was from Gemma.

'Good luck, Ross. I'll have all my fingers and toes crossed

for you!'

I'd gotten some credit in Dublin that morning and replied, 'Thanks! Just the fingers will do. You'll probably get a bad cramp if you keep your toes crossed for too long.'

She replied with a smiley face.

I slipped the phone back into my pocket but a few minutes later another text came through. This one was from Dad, which amazed me because I didn't know my old man could operate a mobile phone.

'I know I said I was worried about you going to London, but I'm also very proud of you. I always have been. Your mother would be too if she were still with us.'

It took a lot of effort not to cry. Dad and I had finally built a bridge, and we were talking about Mam. I missed her so much. I wished she was still alive to see me win the contest. The world was a greyer place without her.

I plucked my wallet from my pocket and opened it. There was a photograph of her inside; it had been taken ten years before. She was smiling and her long red hair was slightly disturbed by a friendly breeze. I rubbed my thumb over the picture then rested my head against the window. I put the wallet away. I knew if I dwelled on thoughts of her that I'd burst out crying; it happened from time to time.

I wiped away a single tear that had crept down my cheek and took some deep breaths to free the weight that was gathering at the bottom of my throat.

Tiredness soon overcame me.

'Hey, you!'

I opened my eyes and found an old man with massive nose and beady eyes only an inch from my face. I jerked back and almost whacked the stranger.

'Get off,' I hissed, 'I've nothing for you.'

'Nothin' for me? Wha' you on about?'

'You're trying to mug me!'

'No, I'm not. The driver asked me to wake you up. We're in London.'

I looked out the window and we were moving slowly through the big city.

'So we are,' I muttered.

The old man stood up and moved back to his seat. 'Weird kid,' he whispered.

It took about thirty minutes for the coach to reach Lewisham where I thanked the driver and reluctantly nodded to the old man who grunted at me.

I stood on the side of the road and tried to get my bearings. I'd studied the area on Google Maps the night before and figured I ought to be moving west.

I travelled up and down the street for a while before finally spotting the small B&B, The King's Rest. It was a rundown building and I figured there wouldn't be many kings wanting to rest in such a hovel.

It was a three-storey Georgian place that had probably been a grand home for some wealthy family in the distant past, but now it was only home to people like me who couldn't afford a decent hotel.

I leaped up the tall stone steps and lifted the brass knocker on the front door. I hadn't let it fall when the door swung inward to reveal a small old woman with a harsh face and purple hair. This was Mrs Pilkington, who I'd spoken to on the phone the previous evening. She leaned through the doorway and squinted at me.

'You must be Bentley.'

'That's me.'

'I imagined you'd be older … and earlier; don't usually have people arriving this late.'

'I'm afraid I lost my bearings when I got off the bus.'

'Lucky you didn't get lost. The big city can be a cruel place for a young man on his own. Come on inside, your room is ready.'

She shut the door behind me and handed me two keys, one for my room and one for the main door.

'Up the stairs,' she said, 'yours is the room at the end of the hall. Do you need me to wake you in the morning?'

'No, I'll be up at the crack of dawn. I've got a big day ahead of me.'

I locked the door as soon as I was in the room. It was bland

and outdated like something from an old horror movie. The air was stale and there was a lot of dust on the furniture. I dropped my backpack on the floor and instinctively checked under the bed. There was nothing but dust under it and I had disturbed it, which started me coughing.

I crossed the room to the window; the place seriously needed fresh air. I unbolted the catches, but struggled to open it. I pushed with all my strength, but it still wouldn't budge so I decided to use my gift.

I focused on the window then channelled my energy into my right arm. I threw my hand into the stale air and the window rattled then opened with a loud bang. I realised I was gaining more control over the gift. I was learning to use it in a more precise way than before.

Now wasn't the time to ponder the gift though, I needed to preserve my strength for the contest. I climbed into bed and before long I was out cold. The long day had finally caught up with me.

CHAPTER SEVEN

Running Out of Time

All tests conducted during The Million Dollar Gift contest are documented by Golding Scientific Security Division under the direction of Derek Shaw. The following test took place on the morning of 1 July. 8.00am - 8.27am and was remotely monitored by staff member William Adams.

TRANSCRIPT No. 181,217:

(Interview, phase 2)

Contestant: 27,710

Name: Felix Cross

Stated power: Animal Communication

Control conditions: Animals unknown to contestant supplied by local animal shelter

Test Location: Golding Plaza Hotel. Room 102.

Test supervised by Dr Mark Jones.

Jones: Morning, Felix.

Cross: Good morning. May I ask a question before we start?

Jones: Certainly.

Cross: Where are my pets? They were taken from me by your colleagues an hour ago. I can't possibly pass this test of yours without them.

Jones: I can assure you they are very safe. You see, we cannot conduct a proper analysis of your talent unless the animals are independent. We have to rule out tricks.

Cross: Tricks?

Jones: Tricks, Felix. Every pet owner can teach their pets tricks. You know: roll over, give the paw, play dead. We're going to test you with some animals supplied to us by the local shelter. I think it's time we began, don't you?

Cross: Oh … yes of course.

Jones: Could you bring in the first subject.

Staff Member Maria Collins enters the room with a bull mastiff on a leash. She sits the dog down next to the contestant.

Jones: I would like you communicate with Bruiser here. Would you be so kind as to tell him to stand up and walk in a circle?

Cross: I shall try, but to him I'm a stranger and he may not take orders from me.

Jones: I see.

Long pause. Contestant massages his temples.

Cross: I have established a connection with Bruiser. I will now relay your orders to him. Bruiser, you shall stand and then walk in a circle. I command thee.

Long pause. Contestant moves his chair closer to the dog.

Cross: I command you, Bruiser!

Dog becomes very aggressive towards contestant. Maria Collins removes the animal from the room.

Cross: That was not fair. That animal is insane. I cannot communicate with animals who have mental disorders.

Jones: That's why we brought a second subject for you.

Cross: What is it this time? A wolverine?

Jones: No, he's much smaller than that. How about you ask this little fellow what age he is.

Dr Jones takes a mouse from a box on his desktop.

Cross: I don't know his name. It helps to be polite.

Jones: I don't think he has a name. But let's call him Mr Mouse for the sake of politeness, shall we?

Cross: Very well. What is your age, Mr Mouse?

Long pause.

Cross: Ah, he has spoken to me. He is almost a year old.

Jones: Is that so?

Cross: It is so.

Jones: Well, this little guy belongs to my son and we bought him at the local pet shop a month ago, when he was a newborn. So, either Mr Mouse is lying to you or you're a fake.

Contestant takes his coat and leaves the room.

Results of test: Fail. The contestant does not possess any of the known gifts

All tests conducted during The Million Dollar Gift contest are documented by Golding Scientific Security Division under the direction of Derek Shaw. The following test took place on the morning of 1 July. 8.05am - 8.17am and was remotely monitored by staff member Clive Monroe.

TRANSCRIPT No. 181,218:

(Interview, phase 2)

Contestant: 27,742
Name: Jane Smith
Stated power: Clairvoyance
Control conditions: Contestant required to contact the dead relatives of staff member, Dr Peter Ferguson
Test Location: Golding Plaza Hotel. Room 105.

Test supervised by Dr Peter Ferguson.

Ferguson: Is there a spirit in the room at the moment?

Smith: There is ... it is your grandmother. She has returned from beyond to speak with you one last time.

Ferguson: That's strange. My grandmother lives in Glasgow and should be down at the local newsagent collecting the morning paper right about now.

Smith: Obviously it is your other grandmother.

Ferguson: She lives in Edinburgh.

Smith: Perhaps she has died.

Ferguson: No, she was on the phone not more than an hour ago, wanting to know if I had any other funny stories about the loonies I was interviewing.

Contestant leaves the room.

Results of test: Fail. The contestant does not possess any of the known gifts

All online and telephone conversations involving Golding Scientific staff are recorded and documented by Golding Scientific Security Division under the direction of Derek Shaw. The following discussion took place on the morning of 1 July. 9.08am - 9.12am and was remotely monitored by staff member Sandra Weir.

TRANSCRIPT No. 181,229 (Red Flag)
Note to security director: I have flagged this instant messaging conversation under the Golding Scientific Security Division Act of 2004, Section 49, reference B-018, "Any employee of Golding Scientific who openly questions or contradicts Paul Golding is subject to investigation by Golding Scientific Security Division".
(Flagged for investigation: Professor Mark Foster)

TRANSCRIPT No. 181,229:

Golding: How have the latest hopefuls fared?

Foster: It would appear they are no more than charlatans.

Golding: 28,000 contestants and not one has made it to the third round of tests. I thought you would have come up with something better than these by now.

Foster: It's hardly my fault! My job is to identify the gifted, not produce them. I thought the latest five showed some promise, but there is no trace of what you are looking for.

Golding: Promise! Don't make me laugh. They were probably as bad as the supposed pyrokinetic who nearly burned down the hotel last week. And let's not forget the girl who could control electricity, who just happened to have eighty-seven batteries and half a mile of copper wire under her clothes. How she didn't electrocute herself is a mystery.

Foster: I had hoped for better, but no contestant has showed any sign of one of the **true** gifts.

Golding: And not one with the particular gift that I'm searching for.

Foster: There has been nobody with that gift, nor even a trace of it. It seems our hopes of finding a powerful psychokinetic are all but gone. I truly believed we might have found one in time.

Golding: This is the last day of testing.

Foster: We could extend the contest for a week or two. We make our own rules.

Golding: No. I can't change my plans for the hotel's opening. Today is the end of this freak show. I had hoped we would have found a replacement for **her** by now.

Foster: Perhaps we can renegotiate with her. She must have some weakness you can exploit.

Golding: Weakness? Have you met this woman?

Foster: Unfortunately I have. She has always given in when you offered her more money though.

Golding: That's the point of this, Foster. Her wage demands are too high. She'll bankrupt me if I continue to employ her.

Foster: There must be a way to keep her content.

Golding: I have already exhausted all possible avenues. There's only one way to sort her out: to get rid of her and replace her with someone new, but that looks unlikely. Unless someone very special shows up in the next few hours.

CHAPTER EIGHT -

No. 29,108

I'd always wanted to sight-see in London, but I wasn't paying much attention to my surroundings as I skated along the pavements in the direction of the Golding Plaza Hotel. I had a few close calls when meandering through the traffic and scuffed up a few wing-mirrors.

'Watch it you little brat!' one driver shouted. 'I'll stick that board up your—'

'Chill!' I roared back. 'You'll give yourself a coronary!'

'I'll give *you* a coronary!'

It wasn't the only high-speed argument I had that morning, but it was the least foul-mouthed! The London cabbies had a colourful lexicon when they lost their tempers; I could match most though when it came to swearing.

Eventually the Golding Plaza Hotel came into view; it was a twenty-storey tower that looked like it was made entirely of glass. Every inch of it was covered in dark, tinted panes, apart from the name that spanned the top floor in gold lettering and a symbol above the tall front doors. It was the Golding

Scientific symbol, the same one I'd seen on the internet; the gold atlas globe contained in the letter 'G'.

As I neared the building I wished I'd taken my time; there was a long queue coming from the entrance at the front. I figured there were at least five hundred people lined up outside. I despondently took my position at the end of the line and put my earphones on. I'd need music to get me through this because I hated waiting in line for anything and it looked like I wasn't going to reach the top of this one any time soon.

After a while there were people gathering behind me and I'd moved about ten feet closer to the entrance. The other hopefuls were a very colourful bunch and I'd avoided getting into conversation with any of them until I got poked in the shoulder by a scrawny-looking guy with *The Million Dollar Gift* printed on his t-shirt, a walkie-talkie hooked to his waist belt and a name tag reading *Damien*. He was carrying a clipboard and a bundle of small cards and was now staring at me and nodding impatiently. I reluctantly removed my earphones.

'What's your name?' Damien asked.

'What you wanna know for?'

'You have to be registered if you want to enter the competition, or are you just standing in the queue for the good of your health?'

'Yeah, this is what I like to do. I travel around the world looking for queues that I can stand in. Haven't you heard of me before? They call me Dr Q!'

'Are you going to tell me your name or not?'

'Ross Bentley.'

Damien wrote my name down then handed me a card. It was plain except for the number *29,108* printed in black ink on one side.

'Is this how many people have entered so far?' I asked.

'Unfortunately, yes.'

'What's unfortunate about it?'

'Because every last one of them has been a waste of space,' Damien snapped as he moved his pen to the clipboard. 'So … what's your *gift*?'

'Dunno. Not sure there's a name for it.'

'Doesn't matter, you won't win anyway.'

'You're so sure?'

'Listen, Ron—'

'My name's Ross!'

'Whatever. Nobody's gotten to the third round so odds are you'll be chucked out five minutes after you get through the door … that's if you even get in. It's the last day and believe me, everyone wants to get out of this circus early today.'

Damien moved away and started to antagonise the next in line, a grotesque man with enormous lips who was wearing a yellow leather outfit.

I wasn't put off by his negative attitude at all. On the contrary, I was filled with confidence because now I was sure the prize money would be all mine.

By 4pm the people in the line began to disperse, most had only come along for something to do or to attract attention and had got fed up with waiting. I was starting to worry that if I didn't make it inside before closing it would make for a disastrous journey and I would probably regret it for the rest of my life.

At 4.55pm the girl in front of me, who was about six feet tall and built like a rugby player, was allowed inside.

At 4.58pm Damien came to the entrance, grinned at me through the glass doors and bolted them.

'Hey, it's not five yet!' I shouted as I pounded on the glass. 'Come on, give me a chance at least.'

Damien walked away into the crowd of people inside and a burly security man came to the door and waved me away. 'Don't hit that glass again!' he said.

'I've been waiting out here all day! Just let me in! Look, I've got a number!' I pressed the card against the glass, but the security guard turned his back on me.

My temper was growing and I slammed my board against the door.

'I'm not going to tell you again!' the guard shouted. 'Get out of here!'

A surge of energy was rising from my chest and I could feel my arm tingling with power. I wanted to force the energy out of my body and at the glass doors; I retracted my arm before the temptation grew too great. I didn't know how powerful the surge could be, but knew I could kill the guard if I unleashed all the frustrated power that was flowing through my body.

I turned my back, bashed my board on the ground and walked away. It seemed it had all been for nothing. I'd made a mess of it all because I didn't get out of bed early enough.

I was going to look like a right tool when I got home. Dad would say he told me so, Gemma would think I was a moron and I'd have no job!

I felt terribly alone in that moment, as if my whole world had come crashing down around me. I felt lost in a city full of strangers and wanted to click my fingers and disappear off the face of the earth. And on top of all that I'd just broken my beloved board in half. It seemed my luck was out.

'Ron!'

I turned round to see Damien sticking his head out of the entrance. 'Come on, there's room for one more!'

I raced back to the entrance, glancing at my skateboard that was lying on the pavement in two pieces.

'Why'd you change your mind?' I asked him when I reached the door.

'Cos you're cute,' he said, and something akin to a smile brightened up his skinny face. 'Now get inside before I change my mind.'

The immense foyer of the hotel was bustling with staff trying to organise the last of the contestants and others were hastily removing posters and equipment. Workmen were taking down scaffolding that had been holding up large banners and a giant, plastic Golding Scientific logo was being carried past by five burly men.

I had made it in by the skin of my teeth and would probably be the last person to be interviewed. That didn't bother me though, I'd gotten over the first hurdle.

There were still about twenty contestants waiting to be brought into the hall for testing. Anyone with a funny costume was ushered into one line and anyone who looked relatively normal was ushered into another. This was the most nerve-racking moment for me, when I was within minutes of putting my mysterious powers to the test for the first time. Having time to think about it was the worst part and I was afraid I might get stage fright at the crucial moment.

'I don't know what you're going to do now that you've broken your skateboard.'

I looked over my shoulder to see Damien smirking at me. He'd seen me doing a few stunts to entertainment myself a couple of hours before and probably thought that was my only skill.

'I've still got a few tricks up my sleeve,' I told him. 'And I can buy a new board with a million dollars in my pocket.'

'That's the spirit.' He gave a soft jab in the arm. 'Knock him dead, kiddo!'

I didn't have a chance to reply. A tall man pulled back a curtain and called, 'Bentley, Ross. Number twenty nine thousand—'

'That's me.'

I stepped forward and the man led me through the curtains and into a small cubicle closed in on all sides with Perspex; he told me to sit at a small square table and wait. I sat on a very uncomfortable plastic chair and took off my hoody. After a few moments a man wearing a name badge that read 'Dr Jones', who looked like he'd a very long and exasperating day, sat down at the other side of the table and yawned.

He placed his notepad and a cup of tea on the table and stared at me with red-rimmed eyes.

'Okay,' he looked at a sheet of paper that had been left on the table, 'Bentley, let's make this as quick and painless as possible, eh.'

'Sounds like you're gonna give me a tetanus shot.'

'There were quite a few I would have liked to shoot today.' He wrote a couple of lines into the notebook then asked, 'So, what's your gift?'

'Not sure how to describe it really.'

'It doesn't have a name?'

'I'm not completely sure. I don't think anyone else has it, so how could it have a name?'

'Teenagers,' Jones muttered under his breath. He rubbed his forehead and scribbled into his notebook again then checked his wristwatch.

'How about I just show you?'

'Oh, you'll get a chance to do that once we've ascertained

the possibility that you actually have a gift. You see, we can't waste lab time on everyone who comes through the door.'

'I don't need a laboratory to show you.'

'You've got a card trick, is that it?'

'Not quite.'

Jones was about to pick up his cup when it began to slide across the table. It didn't glide, it made a heavy scraping sound, as if it was being forced down onto the table top and dragged towards me at the same time. The tea inside began to swirl rapidly and tiny bubbles popped on the surface.

When it had crossed the table I picked it up and took a sip. I grimaced and spat it out on the floor.

'Yuk! What sort of tea is that?'

Jones just sat there staring at me as if he was in a daze.

'It's ... mint ... Hold on, how did you do that?' He pushed his chair back and examined the underside of the table top. There were no strings or magnets. He looked at me again then pulled the cup across the table. 'Do it again?'

Once more the cup slid slowly across the table until it reached my hand. I picked up then placed it back down.

'Ta-dah!' I chuckled. 'Bit better than a card trick, eh?'

Jones reached over and grabbed hold of the cup, spilled its contents on the floor and inspected the inside and outside. It was a normal cup. There was no trickery involved, he was sure of it.

'Give me a moment. Don't go anywhere,' he said as he got

to his feet. 'In fact, don't even move.'

He disappeared out of the cubicle, but returned a few moments later with a mobile phone. I could see he was texting someone. He stood by the table and looked down at me and smiled politely. 'Would you like something to drink or eat, Mr Bentley?'

'Mr Bentley? You can call me Ross if you like.'

'Okay, Ross, would like me to get you something while you're waiting?'

'I'd love some apple juice, but I don't want to put you out.'

Jones clicked his fingers and Damien came in through the curtain.

'Would you get Mr Ben– Ross, a nice, cool glass of apple juice, please?'

Damien looked at me then smiled cheekily and gave me a thumbs-up.

Jones sat back down and asked me to move the cup again, which I did. He got very excited and his fingers drummed the table. He didn't say much, though, and I got the feeling he was waiting for someone more important to arrive.

I had barely taken the first sip of the apple juice Damien had brought in when two more people appeared. I recognised one of them immediately; it was Professor Mark Foster from the video I'd seen on Youtube. His presence meant they were taking me seriously and my heart began beating a little faster; I knew I was getting closer to the prize money. Foster was accompanied by a bland-looking woman with short blonde hair and round spectacles, who introduced herself as Professor Mary Blackmore. Seconds later, two of the hotel staff entered and replaced the table in the cubicle. I figured this was to make sure I hadn't somehow rigged the previous table.

'Can you move the cup again, Ross?' Jones asked as he made way for the newcomers.

I didn't bother replying. I focused my energy once more and the cup moved back and forward for a moment. Jones, Foster and Blackmore all crouched down together and looked under the table. Foster rubbed his hand on the underside of the table then lifted it off the ground before placing in back on the floor and examining it again.

'What do you think?' Jones asked Foster.

He didn't answer the question.

He spoke directly to me, 'Place your hands behind your back and,' he took a pen from his jacket pocket and placed it on the table, 'move this ... if you can.'

I clasped my fingers behind my head, leaned back casually in the seat and a few seconds later the pen began to twitch. My audience moved closer and stared at the pen as it started to rotate. I started giggling, couldn't help it, and the pen spun rapidly across the table and fell onto the floor.

Jones and Blackmore gasped, but Foster remained calm. He stooped to pick up the pen, took a close look at it and returned it to the table.

'Keep your hands were they are,' he said, 'and lift the pen.'

This was a pretty easy test for me; I'd been expecting something much more difficult. Again I focused on the pen and it was lifted into thin air by an inch or so, then I made it float as if in zero gravity.

'Dear God, he's a telekinetic,' Blackmore breathed. 'A *true* telekinetic!'

'A tele-what?' I asked.

'The proper term is psychokinetic,' Foster pointed out.

'That sounds better,' I laughed. 'Makes me sound like a bad-ass.'

Foster gave me a cold stare as he took the pen from the table. 'Oh, you don't want to be one of *them*.'

'One of *them*?'

'Never mind. There will be more tests tomorrow morning.'

'What time shall I come back?'

'Come back ... Where are you from?'

'Ireland.'

'And you travelled here to enter this contest?'

'Yeah.'

'Where are you staying and who are you with?'

'I'm on my own, have a flea-bitten room in an old B&B.'

'I'll organise a driver to take you there, collect your things and bring you back here. I'll make sure one of the rooms on the third floor is prepared for an overnight stay.'

'I don't think I can afford a room in a place like this, mate.'

'It's free of charge. I would also like you to remain inside this building until the tests are complete.'

'Well, I'm—'

'And I'd prefer if you didn't talk to strangers.'

'You sound like my Dad.

'It's for your own safety. I will get one of the drivers to look after you.' He left the cubicle leaving me with Jones and Blackmore who were both gawking at me like I had two heads.

I should have been over the moon with the way the first round of tests had gone, but instead I felt a sense of foreboding. Foster had said he wanted me to stay in the hotel for my own safety. Did he mean I wasn't safe? That someone might harm me because of the gift I had?

I didn't like the sound of it at all. In fact, the short conversation with Foster had left me feeling very uncomfortable and more than a little suspicious about the contest.

Foster had also said 'one of them'. What could he have meant? I couldn't quite figure it out but I was getting the feeling that The Million Dollar Gift was more than just a talent show.

SECURITY ALERT
1 July

Note to security director: I have forwarded this alert to you under the Golding Scientific Security Division Act of 2004, Section 02, reference A-005, 'Security Director of Golding Scientific Security Division must be notified immediately if a member of the public is identified as possessing a true gift'.
(Flagged for review: Ross Bentley)

(Interview, phase 1)

Contestant: 29,108
Name: Ross Bentley
Stated power: Psychokinesis
Control conditions: Contestant has displayed the ability to move objects without any physical connection
Test Location: Golding Plaza Hotel. Lobby.
Results of test: Success. The contestant appears to possess one of the known true gifts.

Test was supervised by Dr Mark Jones.

CHAPTER NINE -

Put To The Test

I was escorted to the underground car park of the hotel by a tall, stocky man wearing a grey suit. He had an ear-piece and I had also glimpsed the tan leather of gun holster under his jacket. He didn't introduce himself or say a single word as we made our way through the hotel and down into the cavernous car park, where a black BMW M5 was waiting. He opened the back door for me then climbed into the front passenger seat.

'The King's Rest', he said to the driver, a young Asian man with an aggressive face and long black hair slicked back over his shoulders.

It all seemed a bit surreal and I was growing more and more uncomfortable with the situation. Nothing about it seemed normal. These people were starting to scare the crap out of me. Why did I need an armed escort? What possible danger could I be in?

Everything about The Million Dollar Gift was obscure. Foster had spoken in riddles and the security guys refused to talk to me, even when I asked them a direct question. I'd expected the contest to be very different to this and, even though I was used to being on my own, I was starting to feel terribly isolated.

'Come on, guys!' I moaned as they drove through the city. 'What's with the silent treatment?'

There was no response from either the driver or the armed man in the front.

'I'll just keep talking until you answer me!'

And I did. I yapped aimlessly for ten minutes until the armed man turned to me.

'Don't you ever shut up? On and on and on you go about music I've never heard of and bloody skateboarding! I hate skateboarders!'

'Gotcha to talk, didn't I?'

'What do you want?'

'Just wanted to know what the big fuss is with the limo and your gun.'

The man sighed then nodded. 'This probably seems really strange for a kid like you, but we're both under orders not to speak to you and especially not to tell you anything about the contest. Our job is to look after you.'

'Why?'

'I don't know. I don't get paid to answer questions; I get paid to follow orders. There's no point asking me anymore questions because I can't and won't answer them.'

'All right,' I said, shrugging my shoulders. 'Suit yourself.'

I shifted over to the window and watched the city and the busy Londoners passing on the pavements from behind the tinted glass of the BMW. It was a fascinating place and I would much rather have been travelling on foot and taking everything in properly. I'd always liked the idea of being driven around in a limo, but now that I was in one, it felt alien and wasn't how I'd imagined it.

I thought about my board, how I'd had it for so long, how I'd maintained it over the years and how it was now lying on a pavement in pieces. I'd have to be more careful with my temper in future. Lord only knows what could happen if I used my gift while I was in a rage!

We didn't stay long at the B&B, just enough time for me to grab my belongings, and we didn't make any stops on the way back to the Golding Plaza where my new best friend showed me to an extravagant room on the third floor. I was left alone as the evening drew in, or so I thought. After spending an hour admiring the room, trying out all the gadgets and watching the giant TV, I decided to leave and take a stroll around the hotel, but there were two more, sterner, security men outside in the hallway. They towered over me as I stepped outside, then a small woman dressed in a pin-striped suit approached me. I didn't like the look of her at all; women weren't meant to be that muscular and she had a face like she was sucking on a lemon.

'I can't let you leave the room,' she barked.

'What?'

'You're confined to the room for now.'

'I'm a prisoner here?'

'Of course you're not. Professor Foster said it would be good for you to conserve your strength for tomorrow's tests.'

'I don't give a damn what Foster said. I want to go for a walk and get some fresh air.'

'If you want fresh air I suggest you open your window.'

'I'm outta here! You hear me? Outta here!'

'You're free to leave at any time, Mr Bentley. But doing so may jeopardise your chances of winning the prize money…'

I went grudgingly back to the room without saying another word and sat watching the widescreen TV opposite the bed. There were about a thousand channels to choose from, but I soon got bored and when I had my phone charged I sent texts to Dad and Gemma telling them I'd passed the first round and was staying in a swanky room at the Golding Plaza.

Dad complained that I hadn't called that morning, but congratulated me on my success so far. Gemma was still cautious about the whole thing, she warned me to be careful and to leave if anything felt wrong.

I thought about what she said; actually, it *all* felt wrong, but I wasn't going to leave. I wanted to see this through and win. Not just because of the money involved, but also because I'd never completed anything in my life; I gave up soccer at a young age and had shied away from skate-boarding professionally. I was determined to see this through to the end, no matter what was thrown at me.

Night rolled in and I stood by the window and admired how beautiful the immense city was at night. I figured after I won the money I'd probably buy an apartment in London, it was my type of place. There was so much activity out there but it also appeared peaceful from the fourth storey of the Golding Plaza Hotel, apart from the occasional siren screaming in the distance.

Something caught my eye before I pulled away from the window. There was a dark figure leaning against a lamp-post on the opposite side of the street below. It was a tall man, wearing a long black coat, and he appeared to be looking back at me. I couldn't make out his face, but he had pale skin and wild hair. I thought it was just some weirdo; London was probably full of them. I was sure that there were thousands of people out there with nothing better to do with their time than to stand around looking in windows.

The stranger unsettled me, though, and I turned from the window and decided to avail of the opulent surroundings. I went to the bathroom and got into the luxurious bath tub.

The bath certainly helped me to relax and I was in there until the water grew cold and my fingers pruned. I dried myself off, pulled the plug then wrapped a towel around my waist. I returned to the main room and switched on VH1 then proceeded to dance around the room wearing just the towel.

I didn't want anyone seeing my dreadful dance moves so I went to the window to draw the curtains. The man was still leaning against the lamp-post. I was almost certain he was looking at me, and if I needed confirmation, I soon got it. The man pointed at me and shook his head slowly. I felt very cold all of a sudden and snapped shut the curtains.

'What a freak!' I sighed.

He'd really given me the creeps, but I wasn't going to hide. There was no way I was putting up with this stalker! It was my first day of freedom and I wasn't going to let that oddball ruin it for me. I was going to teach that man a lesson!

I parted the curtains and the man was still there, now waving at me. I pressed my hand against the glass and focused on an overflowing bin that was on the pavement close to him. I concentrated on the rubbish, intending to dump it all on the stalker's head.

The glass frosted and my body shook. I watched a few bits of rubbish float into the air. Then …

Nothing happened. The rubbish stayed put and the few pieces I'd managed to lift floated harmlessly down the street. I was beginning to weaken and drew my hand from the glass. My heart was pounding and my head felt light. The last thing I saw before losing consciousness was the man shaking his head again then walking away.

I was woken the next morning by a loud knock on the door.

I was still lying on the floor by the window and it took more than a minute to muster enough strength to get to my feet. Whoever it was kept knocking, but I ignored until I'd gotten dressed and checked my phone. It was 6.10am. Why would anyone be knocking on my door this early? The knocking grew louder and louder.

'Yeah, Yeah! Give me a minute!' I shouted crankily as I made my across the room.

I was stunned when I opened the door to find five members of the testing team standing outside accompanied by two security guards.

'Morning, Mr Bentley,' one of the men in white coats said, a little too loudly for that hour of the morning. 'We're here to bring you to the laboratory.'

'That's nice,' I mumbled, as my eyes adjusted to the bright hallway, 'but could you come back in a few hours?'

'I'm afraid not. Professor Foster was very particular about you being in the lab by 6.30.'

'I bet he was. I'm starting to seriously dislike that man.'

I couldn't believe my eyes when I saw the multi-roomed laboratory in the hotel's conference centre; one of the white-coated men told me that it had been built especially for The Million Dollar Gift and had been intended for the third stage of testing, but they were making an exception for me, the last remaining contestant. I was escorted there by Foster's team, along with security, and once inside was shown to a cubicle and told to put on a set of white pyjamas that were hanging up. After a moment I stuck my head outside and asked, 'You don't have any stripy ones, do you? Or maybe pale blue with clouds...?'

Nobody humoured me and I soon emerged from the cubicle barefoot and wearing the white pyjamas that were one size too small.

'This is a bloody joke! Who's the comedian who came up with the idea of making me wear this jackass outfit?'

'It was my idea.' Professor Foster said as he entered the lab. 'Don't worry, no one's going to laugh at you.'

'They'll be sorry if they do.'

'Follow me.'

He led me into a brightly-lit room with a chair at the centre of the white tiled floor. There were thermometers, microphones and lots of strange laboratory instruments in the room; it looked like these were hooked up to five computers on a long table; the five laboratory assistants sat at the table and I guessed they were monitoring the instruments' results. There were also a number of video cameras and I figured these were remotely-connected to a PC that a young woman with red hair was sitting in front of. Most curious of all was a long mirror on the opposite wall that I immediately suspected was two-way. I couldn't explain it, but I felt the presence of someone on the other side. There was definitely someone watching me.

The professor sat at a small desk at one end of the room, I didn't need to be told that mine was the lonely seat in the centre of the room. I sat and looked directly at Foster.

'What now?' I asked.

'Now you face some *real* tests.'

I didn't like Foster's tone. Actually, I didn't like one single thing about the man; he gave off a bad aura.

'Bring it on,' I said confidently.

I wasn't so positive on the inside though, I couldn't get what had happened the night before out of my mind. My gift had failed. What if it failed again? And who was the stranger watching me? I had a suspicion that the strange man had something to do with my gift failing, which was inspiring all sorts of questions in my mind.

Another assistant entered, an elegant Japanese woman with alert eyes and short black hair. She flicked a switch on the wall and a myriad of conflicting red lasers surrounded me on all sides.

'Now I know what it feels like to be the Mona Lisa,' I joked.

Nobody laughed.

'It's just so we can be one hundred per cent certain that there are no strings, wires or devices of any kind being used during the experiments, Ross. These lasers cannot hurt you in any way.'

'So I can touch them?' I waved my arms about, breaking the lasers, which set off a loud alarm in the room.

'Yes, you can touch them, but I'd rather you didn't,' Foster said, when the alarm had been silenced

'Righty-oh.'

'There will be four tests, Ross,' Professor Foster told me. 'We'll begin with something relatively simple, just to get you warmed up, but they will get more difficult as the day goes on. If at any time you need a break, just say so.'

'I need a break.'

Foster blew out his cheeks.

'Okay, okay, no more jokes. So, what's first?'

'You'll see soon enough.' Foster turned to his Japanese assistant. 'Mizuki, could you place the items in front of Mr Bentley.'

She first brought a very simple table, made completely of glass, into the middle of the room, about two metres in front of me. She then placed an A4 sheet of white paper on it before returning to her seat beside the camera girl.

'Let me explain how we will do this,' Foster said. 'We will place a number of items on this table for you to manipulate in certain ways. Think of it like a game-show; you will have three chances to be successful with each item. Fail to be successful and you fail to win the prize money.'

'I got it,' I nodded. 'So what's the deal with the piece of paper?'

'Simple. Stand it on edge and straighten the sheet. *Perfectly* straight.'

It was very similar to Standing Card, the game I had played so many times in my room. I closed my eyes and took a few deep breaths before beginning.

The page fluttered a couple of times before it rose into the air. It then fell very slowly until one edge touched the glass counter. It was standing in portrait-orientation on the table, but curling to one side. I saw it was very light paper, purposely thin to make the test more difficult. I also realised this was not like Standing Card at all, that game only had one objective, this test had two: stand the paper on its edge *and* keep it straight, which was the hard part.

I was successful after four minutes of manipulating the page. I'd imagined it being wet and fixed onto a piece of glass and it worked a treat.

'Excellent,' Foster declared, 'you may release your hold on the piece of paper.'

The page fell over and see-sawed to the floor. The assistant took it away and returned with a glass box that had one side covered in a black cloth. She placed it on the table and I noticed a kitten inside.

'Can you see the cat?'

'Actually, it's a kitten.'

'OK ... Can you see the *kitten* then?'

'Yes.'

The assistant abruptly rotated the box on the table so that black side was facing me and I could no longer see inside.

'I want you to lift that kitten off the bottom of the box.'

It sounded easy at first, but I realised I had never before moved an object that I couldn't see. I thought long and hard before I began, but couldn't figure out how I was going to do it. So, being me, I decided to take a short cut.

I channelled my energy out of my body until it had surrounded the large box. After a moment of concentration I jolted the box up into the air and back down with a loud thump. The kitten had been propelled off the bottom of the box when it had fallen. Technically I'd passed the test.

'That wasn't what I meant,' Foster barked as he crossed his arms. 'You were supposed to—'

'Did the kitty go airborne?'

'Your ingenuity is to be applauded. You outsmarted me on that one.'

'I outsmarted a professor. Wait till I tell my Dad.'

After the few moments the box was removed and an old-fashioned egg-timer was put in its place. It was small and the bottom half was full of fine white sand.

'You know how this device usually works, Ross?'

'I do.'

'I want you to reverse the sand's normal course. Can you make the sand leave the bottom and fill the top?'

'You bet I can.'

This was as new to me as the previous test and was just as perplexing. I was very good at moving objects, but multiple objects were difficult, even Marble Star had evaded me for months. There were thousands of grains that would have to be moved at the same time and then needed to be held in place. This would be difficult to say the least.

A single grain flew into the top half of the egg timer. Then another and another after that. Before long there were a hundred grains at the top of the jar but I was struggling to lift any more while keeping those already in the top from falling. I spied the professor grinning and I allowed the sand to fall.

'That is strike one,' Foster announced with a smirk on his wizened face.

I tried again, but couldn't lift anymore than twenty grains or so.

'Strike two.'

'Do you want me to fail?' I shouted. My patience was running thin and the lasers around me flickered as my temper rose. 'This isn't a game of baseball!'

The professor apologised. 'I didn't realise I was being offensive, Ross. Please try again.'

Didn't realise my eye! Foster was purposely trying to get me agitated so that I would fail. I was determined to pass the test though. I would not fail!

I focused on the egg timer. How would I do it though? It was impossible to move so many objects at once and I couldn't focus on single grains, they were too small. There had to be a way though…

Then I had a moment of inspiration. I couldn't lift each grain so I'd have something else do it for me.

I focused on the air within the top half of the egg-timer. Nobody could see it, but the atmosphere inside was beginning to move in a clockwise motion. After a moment the air began to swirl faster and grains of sand were being sucked up one by one. I used all of my power to twist the air as quickly as I could, creating a vacuum inside which sucked up more and more of the sand.

Foster stood up from his chair and took a closer look. The sand was spinning in the top half of the egg-timer and not a single grain was left at the bottom.

'You can stop now,' he said. 'Do you want to take a break? That must have been incredibly draining.'

'You wish.'

There was little respite; the final test was upon me. Mizuki walked to the table with a length of rope that had a large and complicated looking knot in it. I guessed what the objective was before professor Foster told me.

'I would like you to untie the—'

'Yeah, I get it,' I said. This would be next to impossible; not only would I have to control the entire length of rope, I would also have to figure out a way of untying it at the same time. I tried twice, but failed miserably; I'd barely loosened the knot. Sweat was pouring from my face and my body was growing weak. I doubted I would have the strength to complete this last test.

I couldn't fail at the last hurdle though. There had to be a way. The knot was the hard part but I couldn't figure out how to untie it, it was far too intricate.

I stared at the rope and began channelling energy out of my body until it surrounded the table. I took full control of the rope then thought about how they had tied it ... if only I knew how they had tied it.

Suddenly my mind tuned out and I almost fell out of the chair. Then a flash of white light came into my mind and I stiffened up. I was having a vision of some kind – it was Foster and Mizuki tying the knot in the rope, the vision was playing out in reverse and I saw *exactly* how to remove the knot.

Foster watched in awe as the rope hovered over the table and began to untangle itself until it was levitating and completely straight. The alarm screamed when I collapsed out of the chair and onto the floor, breaking the lasers around me.

When I eventually came to I found myself looking directly into Professor Foster's eyes.

'Are you all right?' he asked.

'I think so,' I muttered. 'Feel a bit sick.'

'I'm not surprised. That last test was meant to be virtually unsolvable. I don't know how you did it, but I must congratulate you. Your skills are *extraordinary*.'

I felt myself blacking out again. I heard a phone ringing just before I lost consciousness and saw Foster walking away to answer it.

CHAPTER TEN

The Third Round

All online and telephone conversations involving Golding Scientific staff are recorded and documented by Golding Scientific Security Division under the direction of Derek Shaw. The following discussion took place on the morning of 2 July. 11.42am - 11.47am and was remotely monitored by staff member Alan Dowd.

TRANSCRIPT No. 181,315 (Red Flag)
Note to security director: I have flagged this phone conversation under the Golding Scientific Security Division Act of 2004, Section 49, reference B-018, 'Any employee of Golding Scientific who openly questions or contradicts Paul Golding is subject to investigation by Golding Scientific Security Division' and reference B-023, 'Any employee who questions, or shows contempt for, the authority of security director, Derek Shaw'.
(Flagged for continued investigation: Professor Mark Foster)

TRANSCRIPT No. 181,315:

Golding: He appears to have the gift we're looking for, wouldn't you agree?

Foster: I would. It's in a raw form, but he certainly has significant power.

Golding: Can he pass the next round of tests?

Foster: Possibly, but do you think we should put him through such an ordeal? He's already at breaking point.

Golding: Yes, I want him to fail at least one test so I won't have to give the little brat a million dollars.

Foster: I'll rig one of the tests.

Golding: Good. How powerful is he?'

Foster: I'm not sure yet. I didn't expect him to pass the egg-timer test. If he can control air then he may just have the purest form of the gift.

Golding: Has he shown any signs of the other **true** gifts?

Foster: I can't say for sure at such an early stage. I still haven't figured out how he untied the rope. It may be the case that he can see into the future and past, that he's a time-scanner. It's the only way he could pass that test, and he blacked out after it, which usually happens when someone transports their mind through time.

Golding: Could he be precognitive too?

Foster: It's a possibility, but precogs are very different to time-scanners.

Golding: Maybe he has three of the true gifts.

Foster: Let's not get carried away.

Golding: The third round will tell us more. When will you conduct the stress test?

Foster: I think we should leave it for a few days. He's running on empty now and I don't want to push him too hard.

Golding: I'd prefer if the stress testing begins tomorrow. I also want you to investigate his precognitive skills.

Foster: We can't push him too hard, Golding.

Golding: We can do whatever we want with him, Foster.

Foster: Have you forgotten how dangerous these people are when they are put under stressful conditions? Have you forgotten what happened when we tested ... **her**? One glance at the face of your pit-bull, Derek Shaw, should remind you of what you are dealing with.

Golding: I'm sure Shaw will be happy to hear that you openly talk about his unfortunate disfigurement.

Foster: It was simply an example of how dangerous the gifted can be in certain circumstances.

Golding: Begin the third round of tests tomorrow morning.

Foster: I don't—

Golding: Remember who pays your wages. Don't make me repeat myself again or I will have you deal directly with Shaw.

Foster: We will conduct the stress test first thing in the morning.

I watched the professor enter the modest canteen of the conference centre where his team was attending to me. Even though I was very groggy I noticed his face was greyer than it had been before and his brow was furrowed deeply.

'How are you feeling, Bentley?' he asked.

'I've never been drunk, but I'd say this is what it feels like to have a hangover. I'm wasted.'

'Can't say I'm surprised, but your strength will return soon enough. It will have to.'

'What do you mean?'

'I wanted to wait a few days before putting you into the third round of tests, but I've been instructed to start them first thing tomorrow morning.'

'Another day of *this*?'

'Yes, I'm afraid so. Tomorrow will be different though; there will only be two tests, but they will extremely difficult.'

'You think today was a walk in the park?'

'No, I know it wasn't.' Foster sat next to me and looked me in the eye. 'I need to ask you something.'

'Shoot.'

'How did you pass that last test?'

I didn't want to tell the professor about the vision I'd had, primarily because I couldn't quite get my head around it, but also because my instinct was also telling me to keep my mouth shut and not to tell these people any more than was necessary.

'I … I guess I got lucky with that one.'

'I don't believe that for one second.'

'You don't believe in luck, professor?'

'As much as I believe in the Tooth Fairy.'

Foster pestered me about the rope test for a while, but I wasn't opening up. After an hour or so, when I felt well enough to stand, they brought me back to the hotel where I got a good meal in the restaurant. When I'd eaten my fill I told them I wanted to sleep and they allowed me to go to my room.

Once there, I got undressed and stood under the shower for what seemed like hours and pondered the day's events. I'd thought the contest would be a piece of cake, that I'd move an object or two and stroll out with a suitcase of cash, but it was turning into a nightmare. I had never been so exhausted in all my life and, according to Foster, I was heading into an even more difficult day.

But that wasn't what was bothering me the most. I was making new discoveries about my powers and I couldn't quite figure out what had happened with the rope. I'd actually seen into the past, like I was rewinding a video of something I'd recorded with my phone. How the hell did that happen? Was this another part of the gift? Then I wondered if I could see into the past ... maybe I could also see into the future ...

When I left the shower I went to the main room and sat on the bed. I'd intended to watch some TV, but kept thinking about the incident the night before when my gift had failed as I tried to use it on the stranger ...

I looked at the window. Something was urging me to go to it. To look outside. I knew it was unwise to go near that window. If he was out there, I'd probably only encourage him. I couldn't resist though so I crept off the bed and crossed the room. I parted the curtains and looked at the lamp-post across the street. There was no one there.

'You're losing it, Ross,' I said to myself. 'You're going nuts. Just some oddball trying to...'

As I began to pull the curtains together I spied a figure leaning against the window of the department store across the street. The lights in the building were off, but I could make out the silhouette of a man. I knew it was the stranger from the night before, and I could feel the man's gaze on me.

I told myself I had a good mind to go down there and bounce him off that window if I could only leave the room. I wouldn't have admitted it, but deep down I was scared stiff of the shadowy character.

I took a step back and gathered my thoughts. I tried to bring forward some anger, knowing that it made me stronger.

When I felt a surge of power inside, I stepped forward and placed my hand against the glass. I concentrated on moving a large potted plant that was in the centre island of the street. I intended to hurl it at the man. The glass around my hand started to frost, but the pot didn't move.

I looked at the stranger and to my amazement the glass the man was leaning against became misty.

I pulled my hand away. I couldn't believe it! He *was* stopping my powers because he had the same power. He made the glass steam up just like I did when I used the gift. He had the gift too! I had to talk to him. I needed answers. But why was he watching me?

Maybe he's not friendly…

Suddenly the man left the shadows of the department store and walked into the glare of a streetlamp. He took a notebook from inside his coat and plucked a small pencil from the behind of his ear. He started writing.

I considered calling the security guards into the room, but curiosity got the better of me and I stood there watching him.

The man slid the pencil over his ear and tore a page from the notebook then threw it into air. It was as if a mighty gust caught hold of the sheet of paper and sent it upward and across the street. I watched very carefully as it floated up and up until it was right outside the window. I looked back down at the stranger and saw that he was smiling and gesturing at the page.

'What's he trying to do? Is he telling me something...? Ah, I get it! It's a game!'

I focused on the page. It sapped my strength at first, but eventually I gained total control over it and pulled it towards me. The page pressed against the glass and I could see the writing clearly.

GET OUT! GET OUT NOW!
YOU ARE IN GREAT DANGER!

I opened the window and took the piece of paper in hand then raced across the room and got a pen from the bedside locker. I wrote: *Who are you? Why do you think I'm in danger?*

I walked back to the window and was about to throw the paper out, but paused. The man had raised his hands and began to move his fingers rapidly. The sheet of paper began to fold itself over and over until it became a perfectly symmetrical paper plane. It shot out of my hands then glided across the street at great speed. The stranger held out his hand and caught it, then read my words.

He rolled it into a ball and threw it over his shoulder, then it whizzed away and found its way into a nearby bin. He wrote in his notepad once more then ripped out another page and held it in his hands. He nodded at me.

This was like some magical version of texting, but a lot more complicated!

'What does he want now? Oh, I get it. He wants me to make it into a plane.'

I stared at the page and made the edges fold over themselves until I had made it into a rudimentary plane. The stranger fired the small white plane into the air and it flew directly into my hands.

I CANNOT TELL YOU WHO I AM.
YOU WILL HAVE TO TRUST ME!

SOMEONE WILL TRY TO KILL YOU
IF YOU DO NOT LEAVE SOON!

I looked across the street and the man nodded at me. I

placed the paper on the window sill and wrote: *I can't leave yet!* then sent the paper back. The man shook his head angrily when he read it. The situation was starting to freak me out! I was doubting everyone around me; I didn't know who to trust.

He started writing again then tore another page from the notepad and sent it flying towards the window.

THE MONEY IS NOT WORTH IT!

YOU ARE ENTERING A WORLD YOU KNOW NOTHING ABOUT. IT IS A DANGEROUS WORLD.

DO NOT THROW YOUR LIFE AWAY!

I shut the window and drew the curtains. I waited a few minutes then peeked out to see the stranger still standing there staring back at me. I paced away from the window; he could wait there all night if he wanted to. I wasn't going anywhere with some weirdo I didn't know, and I certainly wasn't going anywhere without my prize money. This was getting way too weird! Who would want to kill me? And why? I gazed at the untidy handwriting and focused on the word *dangerous*. I had been sensing that all was not as it seemed with the contest, and that there was something else behind it all. It now seemed there was something dangerous, possibly life threatening, behind it. But I couldn't walk away before the end. Why would I trust the words of a stranger? He could have been a total psycho! The money *was* worth it.

Either way, the situation was becoming disturbing and I wanted to get out of London as soon as I completed the tests.

Before I went to bed I decided to do my duty and ring Dad, who answered after the second ring.

'Hey, Dad. How's it going?'

'Finally! You said you were going to ring twice a day, Ross! I tried calling about twenty times and couldn't get through.'

'I know. I had to turn my phone off because we were doing tests. It's part of the rules.'

'And?'

'And what?'

'And how are these tests going? Is it finished?'

'Almost. I've got two more tomorrow. If I pass them, I get the money.'

'Is everything all right? You seem a bit down.'

'I'm tired, Dad. It's been a real long day and quite a weird one too.'

'Weird?'

'I'll tell you all about it when I get home.'

'And when will that be?'

'Not sure. Maybe the day after tomorrow. I'll let you know when they tell me. I just want to get some sleep now, I'm wrecked.'

'I think I should come over there. I don't like you being on your own like this.'

'No. The tests are hard enough without you hanging around and making a show of me.'

'Why do you always think I'm going to make a show of you?'

'Er … because you always do! Listen, everything is fine. There's no need for you to be here. Remember we talked about my gift and how dangerous I could be if someone messed me around?'

'I remember.'

'I'm perfectly safe.'

'Right. You'll call tomorrow?'

'Yep.'

'See you then.'

I hung up then decided I'd give Gemma a call. I needed to hear a friendly voice for a change. She didn't answer the first time, but when I called again she picked up.

'Ross?'

'The one and only.'

'How did the competition go? Did you win?'

'It's still going on. I was doing tests all day and I've a few tomorrow before they make the decision.'

'You sound tired.'

'This isn't as easy as I thought it would be, Gemma.'

'When will you be coming back?'

'Hopefully I'll get out of here the day after tomorrow. I'd like to spend some time in London after that, but I kinda promised my old man that I'd come home when the tests are done.'

'You haven't spent much time sight-seeing then?'

'None at all.'

'What have you been doing with your time?'

'They haven't let me leave the hotel without a … an escort.'

'That doesn't sound like fun.'

'I'm sure it'll change after tomorrow. It's probably all to do with making sure I'm not cheating.'

'It still doesn't sound good, Ross. Did you tell your dad that they haven't let you leave?'

'No. He'd only want to come over.'

'That might not be such a bad thing.'

'I don't want him involved. Listen, don't worry, I can look after myself.'

'You can call me whenever you want, you do know that, right?'

'I know, Gemma.'

We chatted aimlessly about the tests and the hotel, then Gemma told me all the scandal from Delaney's and how Reynolds had shaved off his moustache and how he notified all staff never to allow me on the premises ever again. I was barred for life which made me laugh.

I was about to tell her that a strange person was watching me, but I got cut off. I'd run out of credit again! And there was no landline in my room. How could they have a luxury hotel suite without a phone? I made my mind up that I would demand that Foster let me leave and get phone credit the next day. And he'd be paying!

The morning began in an irritatingly familiar fashion; there was a loud thump on the door and someone was calling my name. I took my time getting out of bed and putting clothes on. I knew they'd wait. Again there was a team of people outside waiting for me and they brought me to the conference centre, but not to the laboratory. I was taken to a bland hall, which was intended to be a gym when the hotel officially opened. It was set up in a similar way to the lab with instruments of all kinds and cameras everywhere.

I was shown to a seat in the centre of the hall and a large mechanical contraption was wheeled up behind me. Two technicians worked on it for a moment then switched it on. I was suddenly surrounded by sensor lasers that shot from the top of the machine.

'You must be getting used to this by now,' Professor Foster said as he inspected the paths of the lasers.

'I'll never get used to this.'

'It won't take long. We'll get the test set up as quickly as we can.'

'Take your time.'

I watched the team setting up the equipment around me, when all was in place five men rolled in a huge trolley with a very large block of silver material on it to the middle of the hall, about fifteen metres in front of me.

After that, Mizuki and another Japanese woman taped electrodes to my arms, legs, stomach and one to the back of my neck.

'What the hell are these?'

'It's part of the test,' Mizuki answered.

'I guessed that, but what are they for?'

She refused to answer. Foster came to me as they were connecting the wires to a black box with a number of red switches on it. 'No need to panic, these are just to make sure you can maintain the right type of concentration during the test.'

'Hold on … you're going to electrocute me?'

'A slight pinch, you'll barely feel it.'

'What has this got to do with the ability to move things with my mind? Haven't I already proved to you that I have the million dollar gift?'

'We had a list of possible gifts, psychokinesis being one, and we had a number of tests designed to prove the gift was genuine. This is one of the tests and you cannot be successful without passing it.'

'Let's get the show on the road, professor. I don't feel very comfortable with this all of a sudden.'

'The test is a simple one. Do you see the silver block on top of the trolley?'

'It'd be hard not to. It's about the size of a car.'

'It is a new type of material, manufactured by Golding Scientific, it's called Metaliglass.'

'Glass?' At first I had thought it was just a simple block of metal, but as I focused on it I saw it shimmered unusually under the strong lights in the hall. There was a rainbow effect radiating from it and I'd never seen a metal so highly polished. 'Doesn't look much like glass to me.'

'It's not the type used for windows, Ross. It's a metallic glass consisting of many layers and mixed with platinum then blended together at extreme temperatures. It is one of the strongest materials ever created. Stronger than any type of metal or rock.'

'And I'm supposed to break it.'

'Not exactly. We don't expect you to be able to destroy it, that would be totally impossible, we are hoping you could possibly dent it or even put a slight fracture in it. Shall we begin?'

'I guess so.'

When everyone had taken to their seats and had their instruments set up, Foster gave the nod to begin.

I focused my gaze on the huge plate of Metaliglass, started

to suck the energy from my body and gather it in my mind. Just as I was about to release it there was a buzzing sound and I jumped in my seat. It was one of the minor shocks that Foster had mentioned. He had told the truth; it wasn't painful at all but it had broken my concentration and the link.

I sat and tried to compose myself with deep breaths. When I'd gotten over the shock I mustered my power once more and began to send it towards the metallic glass, but again I was buzzed, twice this time.

I was starting to get seriously irritated. 'Right, ignore the shocks. Focus everything on the glass,' I whispered to myself. 'Remember, they *want* you to fail.'

Again I prepared myself and began to force the energy out of my body – I got zapped; I was being shocked on both arms then on both feet. I ignored it as best I could, but as I was about to force all my strength at the block there was another shock, this time on my neck. I stood up and broke the lasers and the alarm rang.

'Goddamn it!' I roared over the wailing siren. 'How am I meant to do this with you shocking me?'

'It's part of the test. You can quit at any time.'

'I'm not a quitter, Foster.'

'Then please proceed.'

The shocks started before I had time to focus. My temper was boiling over and I clenched my fists and gritted my teeth. The shocks were constant and I growled as my rage grew out of control. I was angry enough to stand and fire the chair at the professor, but I remained focused on the block. One last shock was sent into the back of my neck and I let out a roar.

The centre of the block of Metaliglass bloated and melted for a split second. When I sent all my rage towards it there was a deafening blast. The entire block cracked then blew into a thousand pieces that were fired outward and spun around the floor of the hall.

A stunned silence filled the room. The professor stood still and raised his hand to his face. He was left utterly speechless by what I had done. I had destroyed a thick block of the hardest material on earth.

'Incredible,' he said under his breath. 'They never cease to amaze me.'

'They?' I asked him.

The professor didn't respond to me. His mobile phone rang and he excused himself and quickly left the hall.

I expected to be drained but I wasn't, I was actually full of energy. I thought back to when I blew up the stone pillar in Dullbrook. I didn't feel drained after doing that, not as much as I was when I played Marble Star. Maybe when I was angry I used some other source of energy and when I was calm I used my own. So much about the gift remained a mystery to me.

Mizuki disconnected the electrodes, turned off the lasers and took away the machine. A group of men in boiler suits entered and started to clean up the pieces of the metallic glass and I took a walk around to cleanse myself of the anger that was still lurking inside.

All online and telephone conversations involving Golding Scientific staff are recorded and documented by Golding Scientific Security Division under the direction of Derek Shaw. The following discussion took place on the morning of 3 July. 10.28am - 10.34am and was remotely monitored by staff member Alan Dowd.

TRANSCRIPT No. 181,387 (Red Flag)
Note to security director: I have flagged this phone conversation under the Golding Scientific Security Division Act of 2004, Section 49, reference B-018, 'Any employee of Golding Scientific who openly questions or contradicts Paul Golding is subject to further investigation by Golding Scientific Security Division' and reference B-023, 'Any employee who questions, or shows contempt for, the authority of security director, Derek Shaw'.
(Flagged for continued investigation: Professor Mark Foster)

TRANSCRIPT No. 181,387:

Foster: That was exceptional! He broke the Metali-glass as if it were polystyrene! I've never seen anything quite like it.

Golding: Exceptional indeed. Is he as powerful as her?

Foster: He could be. Although he doesn't control his gift as well as she does.

Golding: That could be because of his lack of years.

Foster: Possibly. But remember she has three gifts. She's a Psychokinetic, but she is also an Emotomagnet and a Metallisir.

Golding: He may have three gifts of his own, Foster. He did show signs of being a Time-Scanner yesterday, and he could also be a Precog.

Foster: We will need further tests to prove that.

Golding: Give him one more test, a Precog test. Tell him he must complete it to win the money. If he's successful I will give him the million, I think it's time to get young Bentley on our side.

Foster: Which test shall I give him?

Golding: Foosball. I want him to play against Paolo.

Foster: Paolo is in London?

Golding: He arrived late last night. I wanted him to

face Bentley.

Foster: But Paolo's a fully-fledged Precog. Bentley won't stand a chance against him at foosball.

Golding: He will if he's a Psychokinetic **and** a Precog. If he has both gifts, he will beat Paolo. I'm sure of it.

Foster: I think this is unwise. We shouldn't put him into a duel so soon after the stress test. He will still have residual power in his body from drawing up negative energy, if he were to lose his temper during the game ... Paolo would be ...

Golding: We'll be scraping Paolo off the ceiling, I know.

Foster: But you still want to do this?

Golding: Paolo isn't very important in the grand scheme of things. Bentley, however, could change everything.

Foster: Remember that I warned you against this, Golding.

Shaw: You don't warn Mr Golding. He calls the shots around here and you follow orders. Now get moving, Foster!

Foster: Shaw? You weren't supposed to be involved in this.

Shaw: I am now.

I turned to see the professor entering the hall, he was accompanied by a skinny, sallow-skinned guy in his twenties with lots of tattoos on his arms. Behind them, two men in boiler suits were pushing a foosball table. This was just getting stranger by the minute. Was this supposed to be light relief?

The table was rolled into the middle of the hall and the professor stood beside it and asked me to stand at one end.

'Have you played before?'

'Of course I have,' I snorted. 'I'm pretty good at it too.'

'You will be playing against Paolo,' he nodded at the sallow skinned guy who was standing opposite me. 'Best of five.'

I looked down at the table and frowned when I saw that I was missing a very important player. 'Hang on, I don't have a goalkeeper, and he does. That's not fair.'

'You're psychokinetic, Ross. You won't need a goalkeeper.'

'Be nice if I had one though…'

The professor took a small white ball in hand and dropped it onto the table. Before I focused on it, the ball was sent flying into my goal.

I arched my eyebrows and looked at my opponent. 'Christ, you're fast!'

'I have never been beaten.'

'There's a first time for everything.'

Paolo sniggered at me and told the professor to restart the game. The ball rattled around and got kicked a few times before it dropped kindly for Paolo. He spun a handle and sent it whizzing towards my goal.

I deflected the ball out of its path with my mind. I felt quite proud of myself, but Paolo reacted faster than me by sending the loose ball rattling into my goal.

'If Paolo scores one more he will be declared winner.'

'I can count,' I grunted. 'Start the game!'

Again the ball was dropped onto the table and the duel continued. I knew I could control the ball with my mind, the problem was the speed at which it was travelling. I had to try and predict its path. It was the only way to stop Paolo scoring again.

Paolo banged the ball with all his strength – I knocked it away before it crossed the goal-line. Again and again and again he tried, but I found that I could almost see where the ball would end up. After a minute or so the game seemed simple to me. I eventually struck the ball and sent it into my opponent's goal.

'Two goals to one,' the professor announced. He dropped the ball again and the battle raged on.

'Two goals all,' he said when I had again gotten the better of Paolo. 'The player who scores next will be deemed the victor.'

'Let's go,' I said, staring across the table. I smiled at Paolo who was absolutely fuming. 'This is getting boring.'

The ball dropped and we gave it everything we had. I blocked his every attempt to score; I could see where the ball would land before it was hit. But Paolo could too; I knew he had some sort of special gift. The rally lasted for over four minutes, which in foosball terms is like four years. I could tell Foster was getting a headache from trying to follow the ball, it was moving around so fast that the human eye could not trace it properly. On it went until there was a loud *bang*. Paolo had tired and I'd finally defeated him.

'No!' Paolo screamed. 'How could he beat me? No one could ever beat me!'

I raised my arms and sang, '*Champiole, champiole, olé, olé, olé.*'

'Take a break, Bentley,' Foster said. 'You deserve it and congratulations, you're the world's latest millionaire.'

'Oh, I like the sound of that!'

'I thought you would. I'll be back in a few moments. Paolo, you may leave us.'

'Whatever!' Paolo moaned, and he kicked the table. 'Another time, Bentley!'

'Ciao, Paolo.' I gave him a little wave before he left.

'So, this is the end?' I asked the professor.

'It would seem that way. You must excuse me, Ross, I have a phone call to make. I'll be back soon.'

All online and telephone conversations involving Golding Scientific staff are recorded and documented by Golding Scientific Security Division under the direction of Derek Shaw. The following discussion took place on the morning of 3 July. 11.16am - 11.22am and was remotely monitored by staff member Alan Dowd.

TRANSCRIPT No. 181,399 (Black Flag)
Note to security director: I have flagged this phone conversation under the Golding Scientific Security Division Act of 2004, Section 52, reference A-001, 'Any employee of Golding Scientific who openly threatens Paul Golding or endangers the corporation is subject for removal by Golding Scientific Security Division'.
(Investigation closed: Professor Mark Foster)

TRANSCRIPT No. 181,399:

Golding: I would say that was proof that he is a Precog, wouldn't you, Foster?

Foster: I would say so, but his psychokinesis is his most powerful asset.

Golding: Indeed. Is he as tired as he was yesterday?

Foster: No, he's showing no sign of fatigue.

Golding: Good. He's got quite the temper, hasn't he?

Foster: It's terrifying.

Golding: 'Terrific' is the more appropriate word. I think we should give him a day or two to relax and to think about how he'll spend his fortune before we introduce him to the violence test.

Foster: The **violence** test?

Golding: Yes. It's designed to damage the subject psychologically. Permanently so.

Foster: And how would you do that?

Golding: It's quite simple actually and there are two purposes of the test: first, to remove any inhibitions about using the gift on other people. Second, to make the subject naturally violent and able to instantly tap into negative energy.

Foster: Explain the test, Golding.

Golding: We find someone who Bentley is attached to ... a family member or perhaps a girlfriend, if he has one. Then we a send one of our special teams to ... make them disappear. We wait a few weeks, allow the subject's anger to rise then we present him with a patsy. We tell the subject that a particular person is responsible for murdering his loved one and allow nature to take its course. Basically, we let Bentley kill an innocent man and after that he'll be a right nasty piece of work. And we tell him that we're the only ones who can protect him from the law, so he does what we tell him.

Foster: That is the most disgusting and immoral thing I've ever heard. How could you even consider something like this?

Golding: Immoral, but effective. It does work.

Foster: You've done this before?

Golding: Yes, Shaw devised the test and carried it out.

Foster: On who?

Golding: On Marianne of course ... how else do you think we made her so violent?

Foster: I'll not be a part of this! You people need to be stopped. Leave the boy be! If you follow through with this, I'll go to the press.

Golding: I open the door for you, Foster, and you slam it in my face. I expected more from you. I'm removing you ... from the testing process. Shaw is waiting for you outside the hall. He wants to have a word with you face to face.

I'd waited in the hall for over an hour and was getting bored. I was just about to ask if I could leave when the main door opened. I'd been expecting Foster, but it was someone I hadn't seen before. He had a shaved head and was wearing a grey suit; he strode across the hall in a very confident manner. As he got closer I saw there was a horrific scar running from his chin, through his lips and across his right cheek to above his ear.

'My name is Shaw,' he said as he shook my hand and smiled. He noticed me staring at the scars on his face and head, but he didn't get offended by my curiosity. 'Don't let these fool you, I'm actually a nice guy.'

'How did it happen?' I asked, examining the most horrendous of the cuts on his face.

'I was a … gamekeeper of sorts in a previous life. One of the animals went crazy one night and did this.' He ran his hand over face. 'Ghastly, isn't it?'

'What sort of animal could do that?'

'A really nasty one. But let's forget that for the moment.' He revealed an envelope and offered it to me. 'I have here some documents containing the details of your new bank account.'

'Bank account?'

'I set it up for you, and the balance will blow your mind, I'm sure.'

'The testing is over then?'

'It is. But you know, Ross, there's a lot more money where this came from. You should set yourself up here in London and I could probably sort you out with a part-time role in one of our companies. A handy job with a very handsome wage.'

'Sounds interesting.'

'It will be really interesting, believe me. But let's not talk business right now! You need a few days off to enjoy yourself.'

'I was thinking the exact same thing. I wish I'd been dealing with you the whole time instead of Foster.'

'You won't have to deal with him again, I promise.'

I reached out and took the envelope. I opened it and took two pages from it. One was the usual bank details, with a debit card attached, and the other was printed balance with *£629,000.00* written at the bottom. The sterling equivalent of a million dollars! I looked back at Shaw and smiled. 'Thank you. I was starting to think you people were all monsters.'

'Not at all!' Shaw laughed and clapped me on the shoulder. 'We're the good guys.'

'I can see that. Where is Foster anyway?'

'Oh … he's tied up somewhere.'

'Hope you don't mean literally.'

'Of course not.'

CHAPTER ELEVEN -

Danger Everywhere

I used a land-line in the reception area to ring Dad before returning to my room. The old man congratulated me, but seemed more concerned with getting me home safely. I assured him that I'd be back within a couple of days and told him not to be worrying so much. It seemed to put his mind at ease – I suppose he imagined me relaxing in a four-star hotel and being waited on hand and foot. I spent the rest of the afternoon near the window in my room, watching for any sign of the stranger, but he didn't show up. I thought long and hard about the warning I was given and about who could possibly be a threat to me.

Why would anyone want to harm me? After all, I didn't pose any danger to anybody that I could think of. My time at the Golding Plaza was growing tedious, and a little disturbing. If the prize money hadn't been so substantial I would have already bailed out of there.

My thoughts were interrupted by a tap on the door. I opened it to find Shaw standing in the hallway, smiling pleasantly. Well, as pleasantly as he could considering the scar on his face, which made him look rather sinister.

'Hey, Kiddo. Has your new financial status sunk in yet?'

'Not quite. It might once I get to spend a little of it.'

'You should go out shopping,' Shaw suggested as he entered the room. 'Victor and Tsuyoshi are waiting at your car in the underground. They're all yours for as long as you want them. They will bring you anywhere you want.'

'Victor and Tsuyoshi?'

'Tsuyoshi is your driver, Japanese fellow with long hair. Victor is your bodyguard, the grumpy guy who's been following you around for the last few days.'

'So that's his name.'

'He was under orders not to talk to you. He's a good man and he'll take you wherever you want to go.' Shaw grabbed one of my hoodies from the back of a chair and passed it to me. 'Come on,' he said, 'you need to get some fresh air; you've been cooped up in this room too long.'

'You're right. There are a few things I need to get anyway.'

'Take this.' Shaw offered a huge wad of cash. 'A little spending money for you.'

'I can't take it, Mr Shaw. You've already given me a million dollars today.'

'Mr Golding gave you the million; this is from me, personally. You've had a few rough days and I feel bad about it. Come on, take it, humour me.'

'If you insist.' I reached out took the roll of notes. 'But you really shouldn't.'

'Ross, this is only pocket change in the world that you've just stepped into. You've got some powerful friends now and money will never be an issue for you again. Come on, I'll walk you down.'

The black BMW was running as we entered the underground car park, Victor and Tsuyoshi were sitting in the front and the rear door was hanging open, as if they were expecting me. I paused before I got in; the competition was over and I didn't want to start my new life like this, I wanted to be the free spirit that I'd always aspired to be.

'Listen, Mr Shaw, don't take this the wrong way, but I'd rather go out without the car and the guards. It's just not my style, you know.'

Shaw didn't seem offended, but he was determined at the same time. 'I'd prefer if you used the car for the next day or so. There's still people from the press hanging around and I don't want them talking to you. *And* you've had a busy morning and it might catch up with you. I'd like Victor to be there if it does. Do it for me, Ross. I worry.'

'You don't seem like the worrying type, but I probably wouldn't be able to find a skateboard shop on my own anyway!'

'Is that the only place you're going?'

'No, I wanna get some credit for my phone and I'd like to buy a laptop too.'

'Okay. Hey, give me your number, just so I contact you if I have to.'

I gave him my phone number then climbed into the back of the car. Before I shut the door Shaw leaned in and said, 'I'll be in the restaurant having dinner at about seven, would you like to join me?'

'Sounds good to me.'

'Great, we'll get us a couple of steaks. My shout.'

'Thanks again.'

'My pleasure. Okay, Tsuyoshi, take Mr Bentley wherever he wants to go.'

It took over an hour to find a place to buy a quality board, and it took even longer for me to choose which one I wanted. I eventually emerged from the store with two that I liked. I was tempted to use one to escape Victor and Tsuyoshi, but I didn't want to let Shaw down, and the warnings from the stranger were still preying on my mind. We went from there to a nearby electrical store were I bought a modest laptop. Then we made our way back to the Golding Plaza, but stopped along the way at a convenience store so I could get some phone credit. Victor accompanied me inside despite my protests.

'I don't need a babysitter, you know,' I said when we got inside. 'I'm not a—'

An overhead light fell from the ceiling without warning and

bounced off Victor's head. I wheeled around to see my body-guard falling face-first to the floor. He was out cold and people rushed to him to loosen his collar, to inspect his injured head or just to gawk.

When everyone's attention was focused on the unconscious man, I felt a hand grasping me and pulling me away from the crowd. It was the stranger from the hotel and he was a lot taller and crazier-looking than I'd first thought. He towered above everyone in the store and had to stoop to look me in the eye. 'You did not heed my warning.'

'What are you doing?' I snapped. 'You're a crazy bast—'

'Shut it!' the stranger hissed. His voice was deep and I figured his accent was French. 'I told you to get away from the hotel!'

'I *am* away from the hotel.'

'Don't be a wise guy. You know what I mean.'

'Who are you to tell me what to do?' I looked at the crowd surrounding Victor. 'Did you do that?'

'No,' the stranger rolled his eyes, 'it was just a strange coin-cidence.'

'You know, you remind me of someone.'

'I'm not messing around. You have to get free of those people before it's too late.'

'I'm free to leave whenever I want.'

'Oh, you're free but there just happens to be an armed guard accompanying you everywhere you go …'

'That's so the press don't get to me. Listen, I can walk away if I want, Shaw told me so.'

'Shaw? *Derek* Shaw?'

'I never caught his first name.'

'Lots of scars?'

'That's him.'

'Don't let him poison your mind, boy! He's as dangerous as they come.'

'Don't call me *boy* and Shaw just happens to be a really nice guy!'

'He's a murderer. You have to leave.'

'I'll be heading back home soon enough'

'I don't mean you should book a flight home. You have to *disappear*.'

'Disappear? Why would I do that? When I do decide to leave I assure you I won't be doing a disappearing act, I'll be going back home.'

'They won't simply let you leave. You have a *true* gift, they will never let you out of their grasp now that they've found you. They've been searching for someone like you for years. Why do you think they had that contest? Why spend millions on it? Do you think a man like Golding would give away millions because he's feeling charitable?'

'They can't stop me if I want to leave.'

'They have their ways.'

'You said I was in danger. In danger from who exactly?'

149

'The people around you but also…' The stranger suddenly shoved me aside and left through the rear door of the store. I turned to see Tsuyoshi pulling open the front door and stepping inside. He looked down at Victor, then at the ceiling, then narrowed his eyes at me.

'Er… I didn't do that,' I told him. 'Seriously, it wasn't me.'

'You're a little shit!' Victor moaned as we drove away from the store. He was sitting in the front seat holding a towel to his bloodied head. 'What'd you do that for?'

'I didn't. I swear I didn't do it. You should sue that place. You could have been seriously injured.'

'I *am* seriously injured!'

'I wouldn't say it's fatal.'

'It was you, I know it was. I've never done nothing to you. Just doing my job and I get a cracked skull for my trouble.' He looked over his shoulder and scowled at me. 'Nasty piece of work you are.'

'I didn't do it. Why would I?'

'I'm sure you had some childish reason.'

'Oh, stop being such a baby. It's only a bump on the head.'

'I'll bump you!'

'You're not supposed to be talking to me, remember?'

'You're not supposed to be dropping lights on people!'

'I told you it wasn't me!'

The bickering continued until we reached the hotel car park and once we got there I quickly left the car and made my way back to the room.

I felt so confused. Who was I supposed to trust? On one hand I had Shaw who had just made me a rich man, and was nicer to me than anyone had ever been, but he felt wrong somehow. On the other hand there was this crazed Frenchman with the same gift as me, who was telling me that I was in danger, but wouldn't say why.

I spent two hours trying to figure out what to do and who to trust, but couldn't come to a decision.

It was almost 7pm and I reckoned it'd be wise to have dinner with Shaw, so he wouldn't think anything was going on. When we finished having our meal I would either escape to somewhere far away from everything or book a flight back home. But first I wanted to try Gemma's phone again. I needed to hear a friendly voice.

All online and telephone conversations involving Golding Scientific staff are recorded and documented by Golding Scientific Security Division under the direction of Derek Shaw. The following discussion took place on the evening of 3 July. 6.46pm - 6.54pm and was remotely monitored by staff member Jason Moore.

TRANSCRIPT No. 183, 201

The content of this phone conversation is deemed legal under the terms of the Golding Scientific Security Division Act of 2004, Section 98, reference A-021, 'The director of Golding Scientific Security Division has the right to monitor the phone conversations of all Golding Scientific staff and those who he sees as beneficiaries of the corporation'.

(Internal investigation has commenced: Ross Bentley)

The following is a transcript of a phone conversation between Derek Shaw and Stuart Donald, an employee of Golding Scientific Security Division.

TRANSCRIPT No. 183,201:

Donald: I've just set up the bug on his mobile phone, but he hasn't made any calls yet.

Shaw: Well done, Stuart. Notify me immediately if he makes or receives any calls.

Donald: Hold on. He's making a call from his mobile right now.

Shaw: Do you have the number?

Donald: It's coming through now, it's another mobile, an Irish one … someone's just answered.

Shaw: Family member?

Donald: It's a girl called Gemma. They seem to be friends.

Shaw: Just friends or does it seem a little cosier than that?

Donald: Hard to say ... wait ... he's telling her how he can't wait to see her again.

Shaw: We may have a winner.

Donald: Seems that way, she's telling him how Maybrook just isn't the same without him.

Shaw: How touching.

Donald: You might want to get moving, Mr Shaw. Bentley has just said he has to get to the restaurant.

Shaw: Right, I want to get there before him. I'll be gone for a couple of hours, when I get back I want Gemma's full name, date of birth and home address.

Donald: No problem. We have some people in Ireland who can help us with this.

Shaw: This is all going perfectly to plan. Bentley will be all ours once we've taken care of little Gemma.

The restaurant was immense with a high, ornately-decorated

ceiling and numerous chandeliers. The floor was highly-polished wood and my runners made squeaking sounds as I entered. The room looked even bigger than it should have because there was only one table in it. The circular table was occupied by Shaw, who was sipping from a glass of red wine and waved when he spotted me.

'Hey, you decided to join me. I was just about to order without you. Sit here,' he said, pulling a chair from under the table.

A waiter came to the table when Shaw clicked his fingers and placed a menu in front of me and asked if I would like something to drink while I read it.

'Just a glass of water.'

'You want a real drink?' Shaw asked with a wink. 'I know you're underage, but I won't tell anyone. Promise.'

'Nah, I don't do alcohol.'

'Water it is then,' Shaw turned to the waiter, 'Get me another red wine, will you.'

I opened the menu and sifted through it. I hardly ever went to restaurants and didn't quite know what to order. 'What are you having?' I asked Shaw.

'I'm having a steak, juicy with loads of blood!' he laughed loudly. 'I don't go for fancy dishes myself.'

'I think I'll get the same.'

'You should probably get a starter too, though; you must have worked up quite an appetite today.'

'Yeah, the tests took a lot out of me.'

'I wasn't talking about the tests.'

'Oh?'

'I saw Victor's head and it's quite a mess. Lucky he doesn't have a fractured skull.'

'I already told Victor that I wasn't responsible.'

'It's all right to use the gift in that way, who am I to judge you? In all honesty, who wouldn't use it in that way? I probably would if someone was annoying me, and Victor can be a bit of a pain in the ass at times.'

'It wasn't me, honestly.'

'I somehow doubt it was just bad timing.'

I was about to tell him about the stranger and all that had transpired, but I was interrupted by Shaw's mobile phone.

'Who the hell is this?' Shaw grumbled as he searched his jacket. He plucked the phone from a pocket and stared at the screen. 'What the hell…?' He answered the call quite bluntly. 'What is it?'

I could hear there was a woman on the other end, but couldn't make out what she was saying. She sounded hysterical.

'You idiot!' Shaw shouted as he pounded the table with his fist.

I was stunned, by the ferocity of Shaw's temper and because he spoke to a woman so aggressively in front of me. I was always told never to raise my voice to, or intimidate, a girl.

Any guy who did was a coward.

'How could you be so stupid? I'm coming over there and you better have a good explanation for this or you'll be very sorry.'

Shaw's expression and tone completely changed when he hung up. 'You'll have to forgive me, Ross,' he said politely, 'I have to go.'

'Hope it's nothing too serious.'

'Just a minor problem. It's my job to sort out certain types of problems though.' He stood up from the table and pulled on his jacket. 'Have your dinner though, it's on the house.'

I now saw what the stranger had meant; Shaw wasn't the nice guy he portrayed himself as. There was something very dark inside him. I'd just caught a glimpse of it and was quite sure I didn't want to see any more of it.

I was also becoming curious as to what Shaw's job really was. He didn't seem to have any particular role in Golding Scientific. He seemed to hint that he was a trouble shooter of sorts which got me thinking. Trouble shooters for massive corporations like Golding's weren't likely to be very nice people. I would have to keep him at arm's length from then on.

Security Statement: 82,063
Date: 3 July
Statement by Derek Shaw

The content of this statement is deemed legal under
the terms of the Golding Scientific Security Division
Act of 2004, Section 16, reference A-001, 'The director
of Golding Scientific Security Division has the right
to eliminate any member of Golding Scientific staff,
excluding Paul Golding, who poses a serious and
immediate threat to the existence of the corporation'.

The following statement concerns Rachel Phillips, a member of Golding Scientific Communications
Division. Employee No. 251

SECURITY STATEMENT No. 82,063:

I received a phone call from Rachel Phillips on
the evening of 3 July, at approximately 8pm. Rachel
had been in charge of making all the video recordings
of the promising contestants of The Million Dollar
Gift, one of whom was Ross Bentley. When the contest
was officially concluded she remained on to record
all of Ross Bentley's tests. She had called to inform
me that she had apparently lost a laptop containing
copies of all Bentley's tests.

I quickly made my way to her apartment in west
London to question her further on this matter. She
said she had taken a laptop containing copies of the
videos so she could continue her editing work from
home. She had taken a bus and fallen asleep before

she reached her stop. When Rachel awoke she found her laptop had been stolen.

Taking the laptop from her workplace was in breach of Golding Scientific protocol and was reckless in the extreme. The Ross Bentley test videos could threaten decades of work done by members of this corporation. If those videos are to reach the mainstream media (the ones we don't have a direct influence over) it would be dangerous for us and we would have to cover our tracks, starting with Rachel Phillips.

I decided that the best course of action was to eliminate Rachel Phillips and to erase all records of her employment with Golding Scientific.

I have already disposed of the body and ordered a team of our best investigators to track down the stolen laptop.

Derek Shaw

Director, Golding Scientific Security Division

CHAPTER TWELVE -

Instant Fame

I'd lost my appetite and barely touched the meal. I handed the waiter a tip of twenty pounds and left the restaurant. I was accompanied by a new security guard, who watched me cautiously, and kept a safe distance from any overhead lights.

'Watch out for falling lamps while you're out here,' I said as I entered my room and left the guard in the corridor.

I sat on the bed and planned to spend the night surfing the web, only to find the laptop was not where I left it. I was convinced I left it on the pillows at the top of the bed, not at the bottom where it was now.

'Maybe I'm just losing my marbles … or maybe they were in the room while I was downstairs. Maybe that's why Shaw invited me.'

I turned the laptop on and searched for a broadband signal. There was one called *Free-Gold*. It instructed me to enter the code on the back of my room's electronic key card. Within seconds I was connected and was about to check my numerous social network profiles but a faint sound drew my attention to the window.

'Not again!' I thought. 'Does this man have no home to go to?'

I parted the curtains to find a sheet of paper pressed against the glass.

I AM SORRY IF I WAS RUDE TODAY!

This guy was weirder than I first thought! I opened the window, saw the stranger loitering on a nearby corner, and took the sheet inside.

I wrote: *There's no need to apologise. I was rude too, but you can't expect me to run away from here without telling me why I'm in danger and who intends to kill me.*

I flung the sheet out the window and used my powers to push it down the street and into the stranger's hand. Within a minute, a paper plane soared up the street and in through the open window. I unfolded it and read the message.

YOU ARE IN DANGER FROM THE PEOPLE WHO ARE KEEPING YOU IN THE HOTEL. SHAW WILL TRY TO EMPLOY YOU AND ASK YOU TO USE THE GIFT TO COMMIT CRIMES. HE MAY THREATEN YOUR LOVED ONES IF YOU RESIST.

THERE IS ANOTHER PSYCHOKINETIC WHO MAY TRY TO HARM YOU; SHE WILL SEE YOU AS A THREAT TO HER POSITION IN GOLDINGS CORPORATION. SHE EARNS A LOT OF MONEY FROM HER WORK WITH GOLDING SCIENTIFIC AND WONT ALLOW YOU TO GET IN THE WAY.

My thoughts turned to Dad and Gemma. I wouldn't be able to live with myself if my actions resulted in one or both of them being hurt. The desire to escape the hotel was growing in me. I wrote on the back of the sheet:

How can I escape this place? The hotel is full of armed guards!

I sent the sheet back to the stranger and a moment later another message came.

ESCAPE WILL NOT BE DIFFICULT. YOU ARE A PSYCHOKINETIC, YOU'RE MORE POWERFUL THAN A HUNDRED ARMED GUARDS.

I wrote on the back of the sheet:

I don't even know your name. I want to sleep on this, I'll make a decision in the morning. Will you come again tomorrow night?

Another paper plane flew into my hand after I sent the message.

I WILL COME TOMORROW NIGHT BUT I WILL NOT RETURN AFTER THAT IF YOU STILL INSIST ON REMAINING HERE.
ROMAND

I read the message and looked at the corner. Romand was gone. I tore the sheet up and threw the scraps into the small metal bin next to the bed. The stress of the situation was too much for me and my head felt light. I climbed onto the bed and quickly fell asleep, blissfully unaware of a storm that was starting to sweep across the world wide web. And I was at the centre of it.

My sleep was blighted by bad dreams and by 6am I was out of bed in search of something to do. I made myself a cuppa and sat at the mahogany desk to power up my new laptop. I instinctively went to Facebook when I connected to the net and was stunned when my profile page opened. Had I been hacked? There were over 91,000 friend requests, mostly from teenage girls. What the *hell* was going on?

I opened a second window and tried my MySpace page. 42,000 friend requests. My Bebo page had 76,000. Why were these people requesting me? I cursed aloud, thinking someone had finally recognised me from my Gotcha365 videos.

I opened yet another window and logged onto Youtube, but there was little or no activity on my personal channel. Something else caught my attention; on a side bar there were over twenty thumbnails of the most popular videos on Youtube. They included: *Ross Bentley, The magnificent Ross Bentley, Ross Bentley Test Videos, Ross Bentley the Telekinetic, Guy moves things with his mind, The Million Dollar Gift – Leaked Test Video of Winner* and *Ross Bentley is hot!!* The title of the last video brought a smile to my face. It faded quickly though.

These clips were footage of my tests. All of them. Even one from the initial interview when I had moved Dr Jones' cup of disgusting tea. That one video alone had over half a million views already.

I googled my own name and there were thousands of results. The top results led me to news websites in the USA and there were articles about the leaked test videos from the contest and that Ross Bentley could change the world, he could be the next step in human evolution and all sorts of crazy stuff. Apparently the videos appeared on a blogger's site the previous evening then spread to another blog, then it became an online wildfire. Within an hour of it appearing in the blogs it was on every paranormal forum in the UK. By midnight it had spread to almost every paranormal website in the world. It first showed up on Youtube at 2am GMT and had been spreading across the United States for the few hours since then and was growing faster now that Europe was waking up. The fascination with Ross Bentley was already out of control and the first television crews had appeared at the entrance to the hotel.

I rushed to the window and peeked through the curtains; there were at least ten news vans, with satellite dishes attached to their roofs, on the street outside and there were a number of people just hanging around. I felt light headed again. This was not gonna be a good day.

Suddenly someone pounded at the door to my room. It was *definitely* not gonna be a good day.

The door was pounded on until I opened it. Shaw was standing outside looking very flustered. He gazed over my shoulder and saw the laptop open on the desk.

'You on the internet?'

'Yep. Lot's of interesting stuff on it today.'

'Indeed, it looks like you're a celebrity now as well as a millionaire. You're having quite the week, aren't you?'

'You can say that again. Shaw, I was told that if someone won the contest their identity wouldn't be made public. How the hell did this happen? I'll never be able to walk down the street again without people asking me to … I don't know … to lift them up in the air or make their dog fly.'

'I'd be more worried about religious fundamentalists if I was you. They'll either want you to be their new messiah or they'll want to kill you because you threaten their beliefs.'

'You're really putting my mind at ease. How did this happen?'

'Our editor leaked the test videos yesterday, we don't know why she did it and it seems like she's now disappeared, probably off to some tropical island with a suitcase full of money.'

'Why would she do this?'

'Why do people ever betray each other? For selfish reasons, Ross. She was probably offered a lot of money to do it. I can't believe she could be so evil. I was very fond of that girl.'

'Who was the girl on the phone last night? She sounded frightened.'

'It was one of our employees. She called me when she discovered a laptop was missing from the lab. Why do you ask that?'

'No reason. So, what do we do now?'

'You do not leave this room until I come get you, under no

circumstance do you leave, understood?'

'I'm sick of being a prisoner.'

'Hold on, we've made you a rich man and now I'm going to use all my resources to clean up this mess, just so you can have a normal life. You can walk outside if you want but they'll eat you alive. It's your call.'

My instincts were telling me to get the hell out of there immediately, but did I really want to walk out of the hotel into a horde of reporters and strangers? I was now quite wealthy and I wouldn't have felt safe on the streets of London without protection of some sort.

'Well, what do you want to do?' Shaw pressed me. 'Ross?'

'I'll wait here.'

'Good. I'll try my best to make this go away, but if I can't, you might have to remain with us for a while. So we can *protect* you.'

Everything Romand had warned me about was coming true. It seemed I would never escape the corporation. I wished I'd taken his advice the night before and left. It would be virtually impossible now, because the security would be bolstered and the building was surrounded by the world's press.

'I'll be back in a few hours,' Shaw said. 'Don't look out that window! If they catch a glimpse of you, we'll never get rid of them.'

I went straight to the window when Shaw left the room. I stood by the curtain and looked out at the growing crowd.

More and more reporters and camera men appeared and the horde of onlookers grew as the morning went on.

I paced to the TV and put on the news channel. It didn't take long for a live feed from the hotel to be aired.

'I think we can go live to the Golding Plaza now,' the anchorman said. 'Yes, Katie is outside.'

'Hi, Tom. Well, this place is becoming a circus with the crowds that are gathering to catch even a glimpse of Ross Bentley, the teenager who has become an overnight global superstar.'

'Katie, how has this all come about?'

'It's alleged that Ross Bentley was one of the contestants in The Million Dollar Gift, which was held here,' she pointed over her shoulder at the building in the background, 'at the Golding Plaza Hotel. Somehow, and we haven't been able to trace the source as yet, his test videos were leaked yesterday. Understandably, the short videos have been watched by millions all over the world. Everyone wants to get a look at the boy who can move things with his mind!'

'These videos look very real, but is there a chance that this is all a big hoax?'

'I've already spoken to two independent video analysts and it's their opinion that the videos are genuine. This teenager could be a real life superman. It really is an incredible story.'

'There's also a lot of controversy about one of the tests?'

'There has been, yes. It would appear that one video, in

which Ross destroys a large piece of metal, he is being given electric shocks. This is raising all sorts of questions about the nature of the tests themselves, and what the purpose of them really was.'

'Very disturbing. And is it believed that he's still at the hotel?'

'It is yes, there have been reports, from a local shop and skateboard store, of Ross being around this area yesterday and he was accompanied by security personnel.'

'I heard there was a strange report, that he was involved in an accident yesterday.'

'Those are unconfirmed thus far, so I think we shouldn't really get into that one just now.'

'Is there anything known about him as yet?'

'There's very little information about him at this point, but it is believed he's Irish. We can't say much more at the moment.'

'All right, Katie. We'll check back in with you on the hour and do get in touch if the mysterious Ross Bentley makes an appearance.'

The live feed dissolved from the screen and the anchorman looked back at the camera and smiled. 'Is it a bird? Is it a plane? No, it's Ron Bentley. And now the weather with Martin…' He put his finger to his ear and frowned. 'Oh, it's actually *Ross* Bentley. Sorry, guys. And now the weather with Martin.'

I scowled at the screen. 'Amateur! Can't even get my name right. Ross – Ron, they don't even sound alike!'

I switched through all the news channels and every last one was featuring my story. Which meant the entire world knew my story.

My mobile phone started ringing and rolled my eyes. How was I going to explain this?

'Hi Dad.'

'You are dead when you get home! I can't even leave the house!'

'Why?'

'There are five reporters from the newspapers sitting in the front garden. I'm not going out there. I don't want my mug splattered across the front pages of the evening papers. "Here is the man who spawned the telekinetic." I'll never live it down.'

'Relax, this will all die down in a few days.'

'I don't want to be a prisoner in my own home. I landed myself a few days of work for this week!'

'Dad, I just earned more than you would in thirty years of working. I'll give you some money to make up for it.'

'I'll remind you that you said that when you get back. By the way, when will you be home?'

'I'm not sure.' I peeked out the window and the crowd had swelled even more. 'It could take longer than I thought. I don't know what's going to happen.'

All online and telephone conversations involving Golding Scientific staff are recorded and documented by Golding Scientific Security Division under the direction of Derek Shaw. The following discussion took place on the afternoon of 4 July. 10.18am - 10.32am and was remotely monitored by staff member Lisa Taylor.

TRANSCRIPT No. 184, 563 (Operation: White Dragon)
The content of this phone conversation relates to Operation: White Dragon, the ongoing operation being funded by Golding Scientific Security Division concerning employee S26, Marianne Dolloway.

The following is a transcript of a phone conversation between Derek Shaw and Paul Golding. This transcript is marked as top secret and can only be accessed by those with an A-7 security pass.

TRANSCRIPT No. 184,563:

Golding: How could this happen, Shaw? We have security checks for a reason.

Shaw: She slipped through. Nobody expected this to happen.

Golding: This was supposed to be the search for a new employee, not some sort of carnival for the press! After so many years keeping the **gifted** under wraps, keeping them out of the public eye, and now it's ruined. The entire world has not only found out about the **gifts,** but they also know Bentley's identity, and they know our method of testing.

Shaw: All's not lost. I have set a team of people to work on alternative test videos.

Golding: Alternative videos?

Shaw: We are amending the test videos, so that the objects don't move. We'll release them later today and make an announcement that the whole thing was a hoax, and that Ross Bentley was just a fake who failed every test we gave him.

Golding: Do you think it will work?

Shaw: This story will go away once there's any doubt in people's minds. We'll keep him confined to the hotel for two weeks and the whole thing will blow over.

Golding: And the violence test?

Shaw: We'll have to delay that for a few weeks; it wouldn't look good for us if his friend disappeared right now. I have all her details though, once the dust settles, we'll take care of her.

Golding: We have another problem though.

Shaw: Marianne?

Golding: Yes. She's certain to have watched these videos of Bentley, and she won't be fooled by doctored versions of the tapes. Once she gets wind of this she'll know we have a replacement. She'll turn up here at the hotel soon after that.

Shaw: I expect she will. I know her well enough by now to predict her actions though. She'll flex her muscles when she gets here. First, she'll infiltrate the building then attack me as a show of force. After that, she'll threaten you, thinking that you'll give in to her demands. When she's dealt with us, she'll go after Bentley.

Golding: Predicting her actions is easy, Shaw. Stopping them is the hard part.

Shaw: I'm already working on that. We should leave Bentley here in the hotel, but double the amount of armed guards on the premises. You and I should move to the Laberinto across town. It's a smaller building with fewer access points. It'll be easy for me to set a trap up for her.

Golding: What if she moves against Bentley first?

Shaw: She won't. Not while there are so many reporters around.

Golding: I wonder if the publicity will resurrect one of our longer standing problems.

Shaw: Marcus Romand?

Golding: Yes.

Shaw: I wouldn't worry about him. He's never had the bottle to take us on. He won't show his face around here, he's too frightened that we'll catch him. Marianne is the dangerous one, let's concentrate on her for the moment.

Golding: I have a bad feeling about all this, Shaw.

The crowds surrounding the hotel grew during the course of the afternoon and I figured there were thousands now filling the street out front. I didn't need to look out the window anymore because there were over twenty news channels airing non-stop coverage. Shaw had been right about the religious nuts, they were there in abundance. Many had placards. Some read, *He has returned!* Others weren't so worshipful; *He is the devil's boy!*

There was a new group of people who had started arriving though, the girls. There were hundreds and hundreds of them gathered, looking at the windows for me to appear. This was not such a bad thing in my opinion. Female attention is never a bad thing.

The whole atmosphere changed at 5pm though, Golding's people had released doctored tapes and they appeared on all the news channels. The coverage became thinner after that and they started to feature regular news again. The crowd outside shrank too, and as night fell there were only a few stragglers and a couple of news vans. It seemed Shaw's plan had worked and I would still have a chance at a life without fame.

I left the window open as the night went on and occasionally popped my head around the curtain to see if there was any sign of Romand. He was nowhere to be seen though.

At midnight, after I'd climbed into bed to get some sleep, a post-it note hovered past my face and rested on the pillow.

IT IS TOO RISKY FOR US TO TALK THIS EVENING.

I WILL RETURN TOMORROW WHEN THESE PEOPLE HAVE GONE.

It was early morning and I stirred in my bed, I opened one eye then licked my lips. I hadn't quite woken up yet and wrapped the pillow around my head. I couldn't drown out the sounds though.

'What's with all this noise?' I moaned.

I flung the pillow aside and sat up. There was an almighty racket coming though the open window. It was people chanting, 'Ross! Ross! Ross!'

'What the hell is going on now?'

I jumped from the bed and glanced out the window. The crowd was ten times bigger than it had been at any time on the previous day. There were hundreds upon hundreds of news vans and thousands of screaming girls.

'How did this happen?'

Suddenly the door was kicked in and Shaw stormed into the room. 'What do you know about Gotcha365?' he shouted.

'Crap,' I sighed. 'Only that he's a really good skateboarder ... no?'

CHAPTER THIRTEEN

A Skeleton in the Closet

'We'll never live this down now!' Shaw hissed. He walked through the room to the window and inspected the sea of faces below. 'How am I meant to sort this out? Every news channel in the world is giving this round-the-clock coverage. You're the most famous person on the planet now.'

'Why are you so bothered, Shaw? I can walk out of here in a couple of days and it's no longer got anything to do with you.'

'We had hoped you'd come and work for us, remember?'

'Why would this stop me from working with you?'

Shaw came close to me and lowered his voice. 'Because we deal with very sensitive matters, Bentley, and we can't have you dealing with them if there's a hundred reporters following you around.'

'*Sensitive* matters?'

'I'll explain it for you some other time. Now, gather your things, we're moving you to the penthouse. It's not for your added comfort. It's for security reasons only.'

'Guys,' Shaw turned to the broken doorway where a team of security men were waiting. Victor was among them and sporting a white bandage on his head. 'Escort him to the penthouse suite. I want all elevators shut down and the stairwells manned. Nobody moves between floors of this hotel unless I've given them personal clearance. Is that understood?'

'Do I get an iron mask?' I asked.

'You've got a real smart mouth and you're ungrateful, you know that? I had such high hopes for you, but you seem intent on ruining those hopes.'

'Sorry to disappoint you.'

'I've got a meeting to attend. I'll speak to you later, and don't go doing anything foolish.'

I was in no doubt about Shaw now. He was a villain and it was starting to show. I guessed there were more than ten burly security guys, led by the small, muscular woman with the lemon sucking face, and they surrounded me on all sides as we made our way to the top floor of the hotel. I was shown inside a magnificent penthouse suite, which I figured was bigger than my house, and was left alone. They bolted the door from the outside, which made me extremely uncomfortable.

I really was a prisoner now. Romand had been right about it all. Why hadn't I listened to him? Entering the competition was one big disaster. I traded being under Reynold's thumb to being under Shaw's. There had to be a way of escaping though.

I switched on the TV and turned to a news channel. I was

shocked by what was on the screen: it wasn't just the street outside that was packed; every street for two blocks was crammed with people. The heavy whirr of a helicopter thumped past the window and I shot to my feet.

There were three helicopters circling the building, sirens wailed from below, police officers with hi-vis coats lined the streets and the people just kept coming. What had I gotten myself into?

I went back to the TV and they were showing my old skateboarding and free running videos. There was an interview with one of the world's top ranking skateboarders, and he was full of praise for me.

'Personally I think he's the best thing since sliced bread. I'm currently number one in the rankings but I'd love to meet Ross Bentley so he can teach me some new moves!'

'Do you think your number one status maybe under threat from him?'

'Hey, if he ever decides to join the circuit we're all going to be in serious trouble. I don't think he will though. I just want to wish him the best and hopefully shake his hand.'

After the interview, pictures from Maybrook Avenue appeared on the screen. There were reporters all over the place and gangs of young girls with home-made 'Ross Bentley' posters. There were a lot of people in my front garden and the morning's highlight was when Dad stuck his head out of an upstairs window and shouted down, 'Get off my lawn! I don't want to talk to you people!'

This was followed by, what the news channel classed as a *shocking revelation*: It was Reynolds standing outside his supermarket.

'I believe he's unstable. He has serious psychological problems, possibly as a result of his freakish powers. I would go so far as to say he's dangerous. My advice for the London metropolitan police would be to lock him up and throw away the key.'

I sat on the bed and the most dangerous feeling imaginable took me: boredom! It just came on me out of nowhere. I scanned the room but there was nothing to occupy me. Suddenly I couldn't draw my gaze from the window the balcony beyond it...

All official meetings involving Golding Scientific staff are recorded and documented by Golding Scientific Security Division under the direction of Derek Shaw. The following meeting took place on the afternoon of 5 July. 1.02pm - 1.41pm and was monitored by staff member Julia Smith.

TRANSCRIPT No. 183, 237
The content of this meeting relates to the ongoing

investigation into Ross Bentley and Operation: White Dragon.

In attendance:
Paul Golding, owner of Golding Scientific (All divisions).
Derek Shaw, director of Golding Scientific Security Division.
Helen Greene, director of Golding Scientific Communications Division.

TRANSCRIPT No. 183,201:

Golding: We are being put under immense pressure to make a public statement regarding Bentley and the contest. We'll probably have to make an announcement of some description within the next twenty-four hours.

Shaw: Bad idea. We should remain silent, it's the best course of action. As long as we keep him hidden and quiet, they'll lose interest. The media are fickle, they'll move onto something else soon enough.

Greene: Are you nuts? Honey, this isn't some scandal about a B-list celebrity who slept with the nanny! This is big news! Ross Bentley is the first person to have superpowers, the press will hound us relentlessly until they get an interview with him. There has never, ever been a story like this before. It won't go away even if we stick our heads in the sand.

Golding: But it doesn't serve our interests to make it public, Helen. We wanted him to work for us, the more exposure he gets the less use he is to us.

Greene: It's already public. His face has been seen all over the world, Paul.

Golding: Is there any way to salvage the situation?

Greene: Salvage it? You should be taking advantage of it. Announce it now, make it public and cash in. Sign him up to deals and control his image rights, you could make billions from this.

Golding: Perhaps this will not be a total loss. We could actually make a lot of money out of him.

Greene: More than a lot. We should do it as soon as possible though, strike while the iron is hot. And before anyone else gets to him.

Shaw: We have a few separate matters to deal with before we can do all this.

Greene: What? What could be more important than this?

Shaw: It's none of your business, Helen. Let's just slow everything down for a while. I'd like a couple of days without any new revelations, so we can draw up a definite strategy to … What? I got something on my face?

Golding and Greene were looking over Shaw's shoulder at a small muted TV that was mounted on the wall behind him.

Shaw: I'm gonna kill him.

The news channel was broadcasting live pictures from the Golding Plaza hotel. Ross Bentley was standing on the penthouse balcony waving to the crowds of people on the streets below. The crowd chanted his name.

Shaw: That little muppet. We were better off with Marianne. She's dangerous, but at least she has a brain.

Incoming call (Derek Shaw's mobile).
Inaudible conversation lasting 32 seconds.

Shaw: That package has just arrived at the airport, Mr Golding.

Golding: We should get moving then. Immediately. Helen, a very pressing matter has just come up and I'm not going to be around for a day or two. I would like you to deal with Bentley for the moment.

Greene: Leave it with me, Paul. I'll have Bentley sign all of his rights and even his soul over to you by the end of the day.

Golding: Just sort this mess out. I can't deal with Bentley anymore, he's become a disaster zone.

CHAPTER FOURTEEN -

Marianne Dolloway

All official meetings involving Golding Scientific staff are recorded and documented by Golding Scientific Security Division under the direction of Derek Shaw. The following meeting took place on the afternoon of 5 July. 3.07pm - 3.29pm and was monitored by staff member, James Brent.

TRANSCRIPT No. 183, 252
The content of this meeting relates to the ongoing investigation into Ross Bentley and Operation: White Dragon.

In attendance:
Paul Golding, owner of Golding Scientific (All divisions).
Derek Shaw, director of Golding Scientific Security Division.
Thomas Cameron, Security Chief of the Laberinto, London.

TRANSCRIPT No. 183,252:

Cameron: I have put in place all the measures you requested, Mr Shaw. The building is totally secure.

Shaw: Good. Just make sure your men are ready, they'll need to be on their toes when this kicks off.

Cameron: They'll be ready.

Shaw: Good work, Thomas. You can leave us now.

Cameron nods to Golding and Shaw then leaves the room.

Golding: You invest far too much faith in men who are only trained to deal with military situations, and not with combating the gifted.

Shaw: They'll do all right. They're the best men we've got in the corporation.

Golding: Ordinary people are no match for the gifted.

Shaw: I remember doing all right against one when I was young!

Golding: How dare you mention that in my presence?

Shaw: My apologies.

Golding: You forget your place at times, Shaw. It doesn't make me feel very secure.

Shaw: You're perfectly safe here. There's no need to worry.

Golding: How can you ask me to stop worrying? The most dangerous person on the planet wants me dead and you're going to let her into this building. Into this very office ...

Shaw: I have the situation under control.

Golding: You can't control any situation she's involved in, Shaw. I fear she'll uncover this ambush of yours. We should just have her shot once she enters the lobby and be done with it.

Shaw: No. She'll see straight through that, it's far too obvious. What we need is subtlety. And I have set three traps for her, not just one.

Golding: You only told me about one. What are the other two?

Shaw: I have over one hundred of our finest men scattered throughout the building, once she reaches this office they will gather in each of the two stairwells, then close in on her. If she wants to evade them, the only way out will be the roof and I've a very special surprise waiting up there for her.

Golding: A surprise?

Shaw: Barega is on the roof.

Golding: Barega! You shouldn't have involved him in

this; he's one of my most prized assets. He is the only person alive who has the gift of warping.

Shaw: Is he more important than getting Marianne out of the way? She'll never make it out of this building alive.

Golding: Will **we**? I'm more concerned about that.

Shaw: Have I ever let you down?

Golding: I guess not ... Do you have any idea where she is now?

Shaw: No. My men lost her outside the airport. She probably went straight to the hotel, but used her other gifts to sense we weren't inside. She'll guess we're here and should be on her way.

Golding: I don't like this. You know, Bentley's not working out like we had planned, perhaps we can negotiate with her, offer her more money? If we get rid of her, we'll have no psychokinetic. We need a psychokinetic in the corporation. We've always had one.

Shaw: We can always begin another search.

Golding: There aren't any more like her.

Shaw: You said that when I suggested we set up The Million Dollar Gift. Besides, her financial demands are outrageous and untenable. We've been paying ten million every time she uses her gift to damage one of your competitors. That was bad enough but now she wants fifteen million a time! It's simply not profitable anymore. We'd be spending more on her wages than we gain from her services. She knows you have a replacement lined up and she'll be very insulted, and you know how violent she gets when insulted. Marianne is far too unpredictable to work with. This is the wisest course of action. We should probably get rid of Bentley too; he's almost as unpredictable as her. I don't like unpredictable colleagues.

Golding: No. Greene was right about Bentley. Judging by all the screaming girls, we can make a fortune on promoting him. He'll turn out to be a golden hen.

Shaw: And that's another reason to get rid of Marianne. She likes to be number one, she won't take kindly to Bentley being such a big fish. She may even decide to come out and go public with her own gifts. After all the illegal jobs she's done for us, we can't allow that to happen. She's a liability. We **need** to get rid of her. When she does turn up just try to remain calm and focused. Remember, she's an emotomagnet.

An abandoned vehicle was blocking a busy street in London's docklands. The engine was still running, the radio was blasting out a tune, and the driver's door was left wide open. Odd considering it was a new Maserati; who would ditch an expensive car like that? The car meant nothing to the person who had forsaken it, though. Marianne Dolloway had stolen it at the airport just because she didn't like to take taxis. Once she'd neared her destination she stopped in the middle of the street and continued on foot.

Her destination was the Laberinto building. It resembled the many office blocks in the city, but internally it lived up to its name; it was constructed as a fall-back position if Golding ever got into trouble while in England and it was designed as a labyrinth. It was a five-storey building with no elevators, just two tight stairwells on either side of the structure. Once she ascertained that her employer was no longer at the Golding Plaza hotel she knew he'd be hiding out at the Laberinto.

Marianne strode along the street as if she hadn't a care in the world. No one would have guessed by looking at her that she was about enter a life-or-death situation.

She was in her mid-twenties, but most people struggled to guess her exact age; she had one of those faces that sometimes seemed full of youthful vitality, but at others betrayed an entire lifetime of memory. It was a face that was attractive yet stern. It was a face that expressed the enigma that lurked behind it.

Her athletic build was partially hidden under a white fur jacket and black leather trousers. She was average height, but her high heels made her seem quite tall. Her fingers, wrists, neck and ears were covered with silver rings that jingled as she moved along the pavement and gave her an almost robotic look. The most striking aspect of her appearance, though, was her hair. It was as white as snow and styled in long, very well-maintained dreadlocks that were tied up above her head. Her make-up was just as extravagant and her thick eyelashes were as white as her hair.

She paused on a street corner and fixed her gaze on the entrance to the building across the street – the Laberinto. There was no visible activity in the lobby but she sensed heightened levels of anxiety in those who occupied the offices above. One of Marianne's gifts was emotomagnetism; she could pick up on the emotions of others, even from a considerable distance, but she would need to enter the Laberinto to find out what was making the occupants so anxious.

There was no point in delaying the inevitable; she had to get inside the building to find Golding. Waiting around to scope out the place was pointless. She cracked her neck on both sides then paced across the road to the revolving glass door. As she passed through the entrance she saw three uniformed guards watching her from behind a counter. Their anxiety levels went through the roof when the caught sight of her. She liked evoking that reaction. Marianne loved to intimidate people, men in particular. Mostly because the majority of men couldn't accept that they could ever be outmatched by a woman. She chuckled as she walked across the marble chequered floor of the lobby.

There was dead silence as she approached the counter. She used her emotomagnet gift to assess the guards' emotions and to uncover the thoughts giving rise to those feelings. She tried to hide her amusement; each of the guards was waiting for one of the others to do the talking.

'What's wrong boys?' she asked, her accent an elegant mixture of English and American.

'Aren't you going to ask me why I'm here?'

Marianne knew she already had them eating out of her hand. She sensed they had been warned about her and they knew she was dangerous, but they were also very attracted to her and instinctively wanted to be nice. Deep down each of them could have overlooked the menace she represented if they thought they could get her phone number.

'Well? Isn't this when you ask for identification?'

'They're expecting you,' the oldest of the guards said. 'They're on the top floor, room 415.'

'Who is waiting for me?'

The guards looked at each other, but none had an answer for her.

'There was a message left by the lads on the early shift.' The older guard actually made a point of placing the sheet of paper on the counter top so Marianne could read it for herself. 'Have a look if you don't believe me.'

Marianne Dolloway – Employee S26
(Girl with white hair)
is expected in room 415. No security
check is needed.

This was an unexpected, but clever, move. Her employers knew she was an emotomagnet so they hadn't let the lowly security staff in on their plan, they knew Marianne would immediately sense it in their minds.

She grinned as she picked up the sheet and rolled it into a tight ball. Only Derek Shaw could be so devious. He'd always been able to keep her on her toes. He was a repulsive individual on so many levels, but Marianne did like the way his mind worked.

She tossed the ball of paper over her shoulder and turned away from the counter then headed for the nearest stair. She'd been in the Laberinto once, a couple of years before, and remembered there were only two stairwells, each of them tight and dimly-lit. They were perfect for an ambush, but this didn't phase her. Marianne was one of the most powerful humans who had ever walked the earth and she felt indestructible. Many had tried to kill her in the past, even when she was a child, but none had even come close to defeating her.

She climbed the metal steps slowly. All the while she was reaching out with her emotomagnet gift, trying to pick up on any feelings from others in the building. There was that same anxiety she'd been sensing since she neared the Laberinto, but it was coming into focus. It was mainly radiating from one person. It was Golding. She knew the scent of his fear.

When she reached the top floor she entered a long and

narrow hallway. The floor, walls and ceiling were completely covered in black marble that reflected the light from the bright overhead lamps in strange ways. It was difficult to see properly and she struggled to focus on the other end of the corridor; it just appeared to go on and on forever. It was an optical illusion though, designed to disorientate any intruders, and as she advanced the opposite end became clear. There was another entrance down there to the only other stairwell. It was identical to the one she'd just come from.

She paused for a moment. It was too quiet. It *had* to be a trap. She knew they would have set up some sort of ambush for her even before she decided to enter, but she still couldn't sense how they intended to kill her. It made her more than a little uneasy, but there was no turning back now. This matter had to be resolved without further delay. They had tried to replace her while she was on vacation. This simply would not do. This was a serious insult. Made even worse by the fact they'd chosen a reckless teenage skateboarder to take her place. She continued along the corridor until she reached room 415.

She took a moment to assess the situation. The door might have been booby-trapped, but she was now sensing that Golding was in the room. They wouldn't put him at risk. Under any circumstances.

She tapped the door with the rings on her left hand and waited for a response.

'Please come in, Marianne.' It was Shaw. She'd know his

voice anywhere. 'The door is unlocked.'

Marianne pushed the door open and took a step into the room, a spacious office with a long window opposite the only doorway. She scowled at the two men, Golding and Shaw, who were sitting behind an oval mahogany table, as she entered and closed the door behind her.

She glanced at a flat-screen TV on the wall and grimaced. The news channel was showing images of Ross Bentley at the Golding Plaza Hotel. She tapped into her psychokinesis gift and the TV suddenly rattled on its hinges then fell to the floor and went dead. She walked slowly to one end of the room, instinctively distancing herself from the window, and leaned against the wall. Her attention first went to Shaw. He'd insulted her many years before and she'd flown into a rage and hit him with a glass table. His face had been cut badly and the scars were still horrendous.

'Hey, Derek. How's the face?'

She knew the remark would make him furious and she took pleasure in watching him hold back his rage.

'It's not quite what it was before you hit me with that table, but it's not as bad as it has been in the past. The twitches have stopped now, since I had my nineteenth visit to the surgeon.'

'Sounds like quite an ordeal with all those operations.' She smiled maliciously at him. 'You should be more careful with your choice of words in future. Some people don't like to be insulted.'

'Maybe some people need to learn to control their temper.'

'Shut your mouth, you gorilla,' she snapped, 'or I'll shut it for you! Permanently!'

Her expression had changed and was no longer attractive; her face was contorted into a vicious frown. 'I should have made sure one of those shards cut your tongue out so I wouldn't have to listen to your crap.'

'Okay, let's not get into this *very* old argument again,' Golding interrupted. 'What can we do for you, Marianne? I thought you were on holiday? Tahiti, wasn't it?'

'Ah, yes, my holiday.' Marianne laughed sarcastically. 'Of course I needed some time off after that last nightmare you two dropped me into. So, picture this: me, sitting by the pool yesterday morning, sipping on a cocktail and relaxing in the sunshine. Then my relaxation is broken by a buzzing sound. Everyone around me is *buzzing*. They keep repeating the same two words over and over again. "Ross Bentley, Ross Bentley, Ross Bentley," So, I ask this very fat man wearing a very small pair of briefs, who keeps saying that name, what the buzz is all about. And he looks at me like I'm a talking crab. "What rock have you been living under, darling?" he says. "You should go look at the news," he says. So, after he inexplicably fell off his sun lounger, I went to the hotel bar to order another cocktail and watch the TV. Lo and behold, I see some little twerp doing very familiar tests.'

She pushed herself away from the wall and slowly moved

forward. 'I can tell you now that I won't stand for this. I won't be replaced by some snot-nosed teenager. If that *is* your intention, I'll have to take matters into my own hands.'

'Meaning?' Shaw asked.

'Meaning I'll have to rip Bentley's head off his shoulders.'

'He isn't intended to be your replacement, Marianne.' Golding told her. 'He's just an extra hand to be around in case of emergencies. If you're on vacation and we need something done in a hurry, we can call on Bentley so that you're not disturbed. We all know that no one could *ever* take your place.'

'Come off it, Golding. I know how you work. I've already made my position clear on this and I want an immediate answer. Either you make him disappear or I will.'

'You're the most important person in the corporation,' Golding replied. 'Bentley is a maggot. We'll step on him for you.'

Marianne circled the oval table, her heels making dull knocks on the marble floor. 'Make sure that you do. Do it quickly, I don't want—' she paused, then looked at both men and grinned. 'You two gentlemen do remember that I'm not just a psychokinetic. I do have *other* gifts.'

'Of course we remember, Marianne,' Golding said. 'How could we forget?'

'What do you call it, Shaw…? Ah, yes. An emotomagnet. I can sense strong emotions from those around me, then tap into the thoughts that fuel those emotions. I'm picking up very strong feelings from you both right now. Golding, you are very afraid. I see that you fear I might kill you. That's natural enough I suppose. Shaw, I'm sensing that you're very wound up. You're oozing nervous excitement.' She stalked around the table and approached him. The sunlight pouring in from the window made her silver neck rings gleam and her blue eyes were as bright as neon. 'Ah, you're feeling anticipation now. I was wondering how I got in here so easily. You've set a trap for me, haven't you?' She moved to the back of his chair and placed her hands on his shoulders. 'Let me read those dirty little thoughts of yours.'

She straightened all of a sudden and her expression went blank.

'There's interference. Someone else is feeling anxious. Someone outside—' Marianne sensed there were people in the building across the street who were monitoring activity in the office. She bolted to the window and placed her hands on it. The glass instantly frosted over.

'Damn it,' Shaw cursed. 'Nothing's ever easy, is it?'

'The sniper you placed in the building across the street hasn't got a target now,' Marianne said. 'He can't see into this room and if he fires a shot he could hit either of you.'

'There's more than one sniper out there, in fact there are eight of them, and the instant you take your hand off that window, the frost will disappear and they'll blow your head off. They're armed with the most powerful rifles ever built, and they're all set to automatic. I bet you wish you were a precog now, then you would have been able to deflect the bullet.'

'I *can* deflect bullets.'

'Not from a high powered rifle you can't. You're in quite a pickle there, aren't you?'

'Not quite...'

Marianne knew she had to take matters into her own hands; they probably had more than one ambush set up. She reached out towards Shaw with one hand, releasing a burst of energy out of her body and sending him hurtling across the room. He clattered into the wall and collapsed to the floor.

'It doesn't have to be like this, Marianne,' Golding pleaded. 'We can still renegotiate your contract.'

'I don't negotiate with people who try to kill me.'

She ran from the window and the glass suddenly cleared. A volley of bullets blasted through the window and whizzed into the room, tearing the mahogany table to shreds. Marianne threw herself to the ground and slid under the remains of the table. The bullets cut the room to ribbons. Glass and splinters rained down on her, but she remained unharmed. She bolted for the door as soon as there was a pause in the attack. Another flurry of bullets dashed against the marble floor, but she was quick enough to evade them all. She continued through the doorway and slid into the hallway where she sensed a massive a surge of anxiety.

She heard Shaw stumbling around in the office behind her. 'I'll kill her!' he roared. 'Where's my gun. Give me my gun.'

'Leave it,' Golding shouted at him. 'Your plan has failed.'

'Shut up, Golding. Get me my gun!'

Marianne hurried along the corridor, but soon came to a halt. The fear she was sensing was getting stronger and she now saw where it was coming from; a man dressed in full body-armour entered the hallway from the stairwell ahead. He pointed a SCAR automatic rifle at her and began to fire. She flung herself through a door as bullets ricocheted around the corridor and landed on the cold marble floor of another office. This one was dark and there were no windows. She tried to break the wall with her psychokinesis, but it refused to collapse. There was only one material that could withstand her power.

'Clever boys,' she whispered. 'A building made of Metali-glass.'

Marianne got to her feet and drew in a deep breath; she would have to do this the hard way. She summoned a residual anger that she kept hidden deep inside. Her body swelled with power. She turned to the doorway and was ready to kill all who stood in her way.

She ducked back into the hallway; there were a number of armed men making their way towards her. They pointed their weapons, but Marianne raised her hands first. The hallway lights flicked off and when they came back on the men were all lying on the ground, dead. More followed from the stairwell. She spun around and ran toward the other end of the hallway. More armed guards appeared at the opposite stairwell. They had cut her off completely; both stairwells were blocked with armed guards, the back of the building had no windows and was made of Metaliglass, and the front was covered by snipers. She wasn't giving in to them, though. Not without a monumental fight.

She slid to a full stop, raised her hands in front of her chest and her body became rigid. She tapped into her third gift, the power of metallisiring. The guards closed in from both sides then opened fire on her. The noise in the tight corridor was thunderous as hundreds of rounds flew at Marianne. None reached her though. The bullets simply evaporated as they neared her. The armed guards stood motionless for a few seconds, stunned by what she'd just done. When she finally made a move they fanned out and took up positions of cover in the many doorways and started firing again.

Bullets were flying around the corridor, but Marianne was unscathed; every bullet that was fired got incinerated before it reached her.

'You're firing regular rounds!' she heard Shaw roaring at his guards. 'I told you to use rubber bullets. She's a metallisir, you morons. She can melt any type of metal.'

She saw Shaw stepping into the hallway and firing at her. The bullets flew straight through the metallisir shield she had created. One bullet missed, another cut off one of her dreads and the last grazed her over the collar bone. Marianne fell to the floor clutching her injured shoulder; blood tricked through her fingers and stained her white fur jacket. He'd outsmarted her. He was using flexible plastic bullets and the metallisir gift had no effect on them.

Shaw laughed wildly, 'Not so cocky now are you, Dolloway?'

A rage took control of Marianne and there was an immense surge of energy around her body. The walls either side of her trembled and shattered. She stood, outstretched her arms and the armed men at both ends were all blasted violently into the air.

Shaw had avoided the terrible energy wave by stepping back inside Golding's office. When he leaned back through the doorway he fired another burst of shots at Marianne. She used her psychokinesis to shatter them in mid flight.

'You'll need more than bullets, Derek.'

'We've got more than just bullets,' he shouted back. 'Bring up those RPGs!'

Two guards clambered from the stairwell with shoulder-mounted rocket-propelled grenade launchers. They rushed upward and fell to their knees on entering the corridor. The men at the opposite end of the corridor had disappeared and were replaced by two more men armed with rocket launchers. They aimed directly at Marianne.

'Take her out,' Shaw screamed as he ran for cover.

Four rockets shot along the corridor and Marianne focused all her concentration on her psychokinesis; she had to grab hold of the rockets and throw them off course while creating a cocoon of energy to shield herself from the inevitable explosion.

There was an almighty blast, powerful enough to shake the foundations of the building. She had used the rockets to her own benefit. She had been powerful enough to deflect them and to send them hurtling into the floor of the hallway. That created a gaping hole between the third and fourth floors of the Laberinto. Before the dust had settled she'd slipped through the blast hole into a large office below.

Within moments the emergency air filtration system kicked in and the clouds of smoke were sucked away.

She heard Shaw shouting at his men, 'She's still alive. All guards converge on the third floor. Shoot at anything that moves!'

Marianne was always one step ahead though. She was making her way through the vast office area that was partitioned into numerous small work stations. She sneaked from one station to the next, sending any guard she came across into the air with violent bursts of psychokinetic energy.

It wasn't long before she had reached one of the stairwells and cleared it of guards.

Her way out was cut off though; there were more and more armed guards pouring onto the metal steps from the ground floor. She could not continue to fight them all off; sooner or later another bullet would get evade her gifts.

'The only way is up,' she said as she quickly climbed the stair.

Moments later she blasted her way through a heavy metal door onto the rooftop. Before trying to flee she melted the hinges and lock so that she couldn't be followed. Marianne thought for a moment that she'd escaped the trap Shaw had set for her, but as she turned from the door she realised the battle had only just begun.

Standing in the centre of the roof was someone she knew all too well. She'd worked with him many times before. He was a thin man in a smart, grey suit and she could not read any emotions from him. It was Barega. He was a little older than her, an Australian aborigine with dark, piercing eyes. Marianne knew that he had the gift of warping, one of the fifteen true gifts. He was no faster than any other person, but he could manipulate the fabric of time around his body in short bursts, which meant he appeared to move at impossible speeds. Marianne knew she could not let him get within twenty feet of her. If she did, he would move at her so swiftly that she wouldn't even see his attack. Barega was the most perfect assassin nature had ever created.

'Hello, Barega.'

'Marianne.' He smiled and nodded courteously. 'Been a while.'

'Three years I'd say. So, they included you in this little game of theirs. I thought the world's only warper would have been far too valuable to fling into a violent conflict like this.'

'They pay me a lot of money.'

'Believe me, it won't be worth it this time.'

Barega took off his jacket, folded it carefully and placed it on the rooftop. The door at Marianne's back was being hammered from inside; Shaw and his guards would break through soon enough. She was running out of time.

'I'm sorry to do this, Marianne.'

'It is I who must apologise, Barega.'

She sent a shockwave towards him, but he moved away from it at blinding speed. He grinned at her and took an obsidian knife from a scabbard attached to his ankle.

'Is that all you've got?'

'Try this on for size!'

Marianne directed a burst of energy into the air that crashed down on the rooftop so powerfully it would swatted an elephant. Barega appeared a few metres away with his hands on his hips.

Marianne summoned her rage and sent numerous blasts of energy at him, but Barega darted between them and was unhurt. He was incredibly fast. She sent blast after blast at him, slowly eroding the surface of the roof, but she could not catch him, and she was finally beginning to tire. Barega on the other hand wasn't even out of breath.

It would take every last bit of Marianne's abilities if she was to survive; she would need to use all three of her gifts together and at their maximum output. She focused her power of emotion on her opponent, sensing for any slight change, for any sign of when he would come at her. She was already using her psychokinesis to weaken the concrete beneath his feet. Most importantly she was draining all her metallisir gift to soften the platinum in the Metaliglass panels of the roof. The door behind her was breaking apart. It was now or never.

Barega shifted slightly and she sensed it a fraction of a second before he moved. She melted the platinum in the roof then cracked the concrete. The ground caved in under Barega's feet and not even he was fast enough to escape. A gaping hole appeared under him and he fell a full twenty feet to the floor below. Slabs of the roof came crashing down up on him and he screamed in agony.

Marianne took a deep breath then walked to the hole and gazed down. Barega was lying on the floor, his spine broken, his legs crushed. She didn't get time to revel in her victory as the door behind began to come apart and two guards pounded it open. Shaw stood in the shadows of the doorway and pointed a handgun at her.

'Goodnight, sweetheart,' he laughed before firing a single shot at her.

Marianne waved her hand and the bullet ricocheted in mid-air and struck Shaw in the forehead. He was dead before he hit the ground.

'I warned you not to call me that.'

The stairwell was clogged with guards but they posed no threat to her after she had melted the barrels of all their guns. They fell over each other trying to get out of her way as she walked casually down the stairs and back onto the fourth floor.

Within a few moments she had returned to room 415 to find Golding cowering in a corner. His eyes almost popped out of his head when she entered the room.

'Don't kill me, Marianne,' Golding pleaded. 'It was all Shaw's idea. It was his plan. I swear it was.'

'He won't be making any further plans *and* you just lost the only warper in the world.'

'You killed Barega?'

'No, but he'll need a very good wheelchair if he's to continue making money from his gift.' Marianne dragged her employer off the floor and pushed him into a leather chair. 'You made a big mistake here today.'

'I'll offer you whatever money you want. You can even take Shaw's job if you want it!'

She raised a leg and pressed one of her sharp stilettos against his chest. 'I don't want Shaw's job, Golding. That would mean I'd have to spend a lot of time with you, which isn't a very appealing prospect.'

'What do you want?'

'Double the pay increase that I asked for.' A smile grew on

her face. 'Will you agree to that?'

'Of course, Marianne.'

'Good. Now, what about this Bentley character?'

'We can't touch him. Every news channel in the world is watching him now.'

'We'll have to get rid of them.'

'How?'

'I can make him look like a fake.'

'You can?'

'Of course I can,' Marianne chuckled deviously. 'Tell your PR people to arrange a press conference, and make an announcement that Bentley will publicly display his powers to the cameras of the world.'

'But that will only heighten the press attention.'

'Trust me, when that press conference is over, no reporter in the world will ever want to hear the name *Ross Bentley* again. Then after the crowds have disappeared, I'll take great pleasure in killing him.'

CHAPTER FIFTEEN -

Going Public

I sat on a chair in the penthouse surrounded by a wall of security guards. There'd been an order given by Victor that I wasn't to be allowed near any windows for the rest of the day; it was creating hysteria in the streets surrounding the hotel. I promised them I wouldn't show off again and those in the room allowed me a little space, just enough so I could watch the TV.

The news channel was repeating my stunts from earlier in the day and experts from around the world were debating how I could have developed such powers and what the repercussions could be for society in general. I thought the whole thing was hilarious, but tried my best to hide my amusement from the guards in the room.

As the afternoon wore on I grew tired and was nodding off in my chair – suddenly, I was snapped out of it by one of the security guards gasping, 'Lord Almighty! That's the boss' building!'

I pushed the guards aside and saw the news channel was

featuring images from a building called the Laberinto. There was a huge hole in the roof and black smoke was billowing from many of the windows below.

'Authorities have blamed a gas explosion for the damage,' the reporter said. 'The Laberinto has suffered serious structural damage and a number of the people who work inside the building have lost their lives.'

'Do you have any confirmed numbers regarding those who have died?' an anchorwoman asked.

'Nothing definite, but it's been hinted that over thirty people are dead, more are missing.'

'It truly is a shocking story. But Liz, there's a strange twist here, isn't there.'

'There certainly is, Amanda. This building is owned by none other than Paul Golding, the man behind The Million Dollar Gift that has been all over the news for the last few days. The authorities aren't making too many comments right now, but there are rumours that this could have been a terrorist attack linked to the exposure that Ross Bentley is getting. As you know, his gift has caused a lot of uncertainty and anger among religious organisations, with a number of extremists issuing threats.'

'Paul Golding wasn't in the building was he?'

'It's believed he actually was, but escaped unharmed. A number of his closest colleagues were killed in the blast though. There are truly awful scenes here, Amanda, reminiscent of the terror attacks we've seen in recent times. I think everyone is just hoping that this is simply a tragic accident.'

'Will the authorities be making any further statements tonight?'

'They're not expected to. They'll be conducting a full investigation, starting later this evening, and I'm sure we will be hearing more about what happened here, but we don't expect any facts to emerge for a few days.'

I caught Victor staring at me from across the room.

'I didn't do that, Victor!'

'I know you didn't,' he grunted. 'But do you now see why we didn't want you showing off in public?'

I hung my head. Was it really because of me? Had my actions caused the massacre? This had to end! I was in the middle of a tornado without so much as an umbrella. I thought I'd lose my mind if I didn't escape the Golding Plaza soon.

I stared at the screen, showing bodies wrapped in sheets being removed from the rubble. All the security guards were now watching me. Nobody said a single word, but it was obvious they were blaming me for the disaster at the Laberinto. I held my face in my hands and tried to hold back tears.

'Hey, hey, hey,' a kind voice said.

I looked up to see a small woman with a kind face entering the penthouse. She put her hand on my shoulder and smiled down at me. 'Why are you so upset, honey?'

I pointed at the TV. 'They said it was a terror attack and it could've been because of me.'

She looked at the horrific scenes but simply shrugged, as if she was looking at an episode of *Desperate Housewives*.

'It had nothing to do with you. I've just been speaking with Mr Golding on the phone and he assured me it was a gas explosion, and *he* was in the building at the time so he should know. The media do this, they say *terror* to get people stirred up.'

'Who are you?' I asked.

'I'm Helen Greene and it's my job to look after you now.'

'Do you work for Golding?'

'Not quite … I'm mostly independent.' She looked to the guards. 'Outside! All of you. You included, Victor. I want to speak with my client alone.'

'I'm under orders to keep an eye on him,' Victor argued. 'He's not to get out of my sight under any circumstance.'

'He's not Golding's property!' She pointed at the door. 'Out!'

When the room was cleared Greene closed the door and sat next to me. 'Now, that's better isn't it?'

'What did you mean when you said *client*?'

'I'm one of the world's leading agents. You need someone like me, Ross. This whole thing has been handled horribly! If I'd been your manager from the start none of this would have happened. You'd be sitting at home watching skateboard videos or on a beach on some tropical island right now.'

'I think the press would even find me on a remote tropical island. What am I supposed to do now? I can't spend the rest of my life in this goddamn hotel!'

'I'll get you out of here soon enough. First, we have to straighten all this out, and start planning for your future. Ross, you could be the richest man in the world if we market you in the right way. You say they'll bug you on a tropical island, I can make you so rich that you'll be able to *buy* your own tropical island!'

'Money's no use to me.'

'You say that now but in a few months all this will have changed. Drastically! You have to make the right decisions now if you're going to secure a lucrative future for yourself and your family.'

'What do you suggest I do?'

'What I suggest *we* do is hold a press conference. There are millions of young ladies around the globe who want to know more about you, so let's give them the opportunity. These are the girls who'll buy a lot of Ross Bentley merchandise.'

'You make me sound like a poser from a boy band!'

'We're not just doing this for the girls, Ross. All the young guys are going to want to be like you! Ross Bentley runners, Ross Bentley skateboards...'

'Maybe I could design my own boards ... I'd be really good at that.'

'You see, now you're getting into this. You could have your

own clothing line, your own brand of hair gel. "Get the Bentley look!" Can you imagine it? We can get you interviewed on the major networks in the US. You know how much money the networks will pay you to do shows like that?'

'A lot?'

'A hell of a lot! We can even produce our own shows, like David Copperfield used to do, and auction them off to the highest bidder. The possibilities are endless.'

'Okay,' I said. She seemed to know what she was talking about and I didn't feel suspicious of her, in the same way I was of Shaw. 'Can you organise this press conference for me?'

'I already have, in the restaurant downstairs; they're setting up the stage as we speak. It starts at nine.'

'That's like three hours from now!' I bawled. 'I'll need to write a speech or something.'

'No. You just be yourself and they'll love you. I promise. Maybe move something around, just to whet the public's appetite?'

'I don't really feel right about using my gift in that way.'

'This won't work out if you don't show them the talents you've got, Ross.'

'I guess you're right.'

'Of course I'm right,' Helen said, clapping me on the back. 'It's my job to be right about these things. Trust me, Ross, this will go off without a hitch.'

Marianne staggered along the hall to her apartment door. She leaned her weary body against it and fumbled in her pockets for the key. She rarely used a key, as she could manipulate any locking mechanism with her psychokinesis, but she was too tired to use her gifts.

She unlocked the door and took a cautious step inside. It was dark and she'd never used the light switch before. Normally she just thought of light and the lamps came on. She had to preserve her strength though so she ran her hand along the wall until she found the plastic switch.

'How do people live like this?' she wondered as she kicked the door closed. 'Must be awful having to do everything manually.'

The apartment was enormous but appeared even bigger than it actually was because there was little or no furniture. Marianne had earned millions from her work with Golding but her life was spartan. Material possessions meant little to her; she valued knowledge more than anything else and there were piles of books and magazines everywhere. Her pursuit of knowledge, particularly knowledge of the true gifts, was more important than anything else.

She kicked off her boots and threw down her jacket, which was dashed with blood. Her shoulder was going numb from the injury Shaw had inflicted. The bullet had only grazed her but the force of it had damaged her shoulder muscles. It wasn't only the injury that had drained her; she'd extended herself to the limit during the battle of the Laberinto. It had been a monumental achievement though, she'd faced and defeated not only a small army, but also Barega, who was one of the most dangerous of all the gifted in the world. Her gifts had been growing in strength since childhood and had now reached their peak.

Even the most powerful need a rest though and Marianne headed straight for the bathroom to fill the tub with hot water.

She removed her clothes and walked to the mirror where she gazed at her reflection. The wound on her shoulder wasn't serious, but there was a lot of bruising, some dried blood and she couldn't move her right arm without wincing. She couldn't allow the injury to get in the way of her plans, though. She'd just have to take a bath, clean and bandage the wound and take the pain.

She stepped into the tub and soaked her lower body for a while. She'd spent twenty hours sitting on a plane before the battle with Golding's guards. She would have loved to spend the entire evening in the bath, but time was not on her side.

Her dreadlocks began to unravel then bloated out. Marianne had so much control over her gift of psychokinesis that she could control her hair and create, and keep in place, any sort of hairstyle. The bloated dreads formed one massive globe of white frizz then fell into a perfectly straight, silky white mane that splashed into the steaming water around her chest.

Her thoughts were filled with what was to come. Within hours she would confront Ross Bentley. Within days she would kill him. Marianne had no problem with killing people, even those who were gifted like her. Bentley was a little bit different though, he reminded her of someone who was once very special to her. In fact, he reminded her of the only person who had ever been special.

A painful memory was being uncovered and Marianne's anger spiked. The tall mirror on the other side of the room suddenly cracked and fell from the wall.

'Seven years bad luck,' Marianne snorted. She'd accidentally destroyed hundreds of mirrors throughout her life. Enough to give her bad luck for a millennium.

'Too much bad luck for one person,' she sighed. 'Far too much. I'll have to pass it onto someone else. Poor little Bentley won't know what hit him.'

She spent almost an hour soaking in the tub before drying herself off and heading to the bedroom. Her usual extravagant clothes were all in the wardrobe, but she went to a humble wicker basket instead that stood in the corner. This was where she kept her modest dresses and sweaters. She was instinctively a flamboyant dresser but often when she was working she changed her appearance, so she wouldn't draw attention to herself. Shaw used to call it the *baby-sitter* look.

The clothes inside the basket looked like they belonged to

an older person; all shapeless, colourless and cotton. She rummaged around then took a long grey skirt, a green cardigan, a pair of brown tights and a white shirt. She continued sifting through the basket in search of a beret but stumbled upon something else. She took a photo in a tarnished frame from the jumble of clothes.

She gazed at her teenage self, arms wrapped around a handsome young man with scruffy brown hair and innocent eyes. They were smiling. Not just for the camera though, these were two very happy youngsters who were deeply in love. The young man's resemblance to Ross Bentley was uncanny. She threw down the photo and it landed on its front. There was some writing scribbled on its back: *Peter, 2001.*

'One day,' she hissed. 'One day, my love, I will avenge you. Romand cannot hide from me forever.'

Flames of rage burned behind her eyes. If she could not make Peter's killer suffer then someone would have to take his place and suffer her anger. Others had been taking his place for years. Ross Bentley would just be the latest in a long line of Marianne's victims.

'Ross, it's time,' Helen Greene said as she poked her head into the penthouse suite.

I felt my heart sink; I really hated being the centre of attention and my stomach was doing somersaults. She took my hand and led me towards the door where her PR team was waiting. I'd only been famous for a couple of days but most of Helen's staff, although very experienced, seemed star-struck by me. I didn't like the way they stared at me, like some sort of side-show freak. My fame was fast losing its charm.

'Remember what I told you, Ross,' Helen said as we took to the stair. 'Just let me do most of the talking, even when a reporter directs a question at you.' She stopped for a moment and sucked in a deep breath. 'Damn stairs! Why did they have to shut down the elevator?'

'For security reasons,' Victor said.

'Shut up, Victor, I wasn't talking to you.'

I was getting very nervous as we entered the lobby and the security shielded me on all sides. They led me through a service corridor that ran round the back of the restaurant then I was then taken to a metal door and told to wait.

Greene placed her hand on my shoulder and smiled. 'Stop fretting. You'll be great. Just be yourself.'

Could I really be myself though? This wasn't me. The real me was a loner who hated shallow people, like the ones who were now surrounding me because they thought I could make them rich.

There was someone speaking on a PA in the restaurant, the voice was muffled by the walls and it was hard to hear what he was saying until he raised his voice, 'It's my pleasure to introduce you all to the incredible, the magical, the one and only, Ross Bentley!'

Before I knew what was happening I was bundled through the door, along a canvas tunnel and onto a stage. There were about a thousand people in the room and I was almost blinded by the flashing bulbs of the cameras. Reporters were falling over each other, all trying to be the first one to ask me a question. Security was pulling people who were a little too excited out of the crowd and the noise was deafening.

'Please! Please, everyone!' the MC cried. 'Settle down or we'll have to cancel this. Come on, this won't work if it's not orderly.'

It took more than ten minutes to get the room under control, but the cameras never ceased flashing. I was sitting at a long table with Greene on one side and Victor on the other. More guards lined up behind me and there was another wall of them in front of the stage.

'You in the front, with the blue shirt,' Greene said into a microphone, pointing at one of the nearest reporters. 'You may put your question to Ross.'

'Peter Banks from international news. Hi, Ross. I guess I should ask what's on everyone's mind: how long have you had this power?'

'Keep it brief,' Greene whispered in my ear. 'Come across as an innocent; don't say you killed the neighbour's cat or anything like that.'

I nodded and tried to focus on the reporter but it was

impossible with all the flashing cameras. I put my hand to my forehead to shield my eyes and began.

'I probably had it my whole life, but I only found out about it seven years ago.'

'It just happened out of the blue?' the reporter asked.

'Not exactly…' I thought back to the day when Mam died and the terrifying rage that had built up inside me, my bedroom tearing itself apart. 'My mother passed away suddenly. It was a heart attack …' I'd never talked to anyone about what had happened and surprised myself by how open I was to such a large crowd. Tears filled my eyes as I recalled the moment I was told of her passing. 'I was very close to her, it just killed me inside, you know. I lost control of myself and some things in my room moved by themselves.'

Helen Greene leaned over, 'Brilliant, you already have them eating out of your hand. Don't say anymore about this story, save it for the Piers Morgan interview.' She turned to the crowd and spoke into her microphone. 'Let's move this along,' she pointed at a blonde woman three rows back. 'Your question?'

'Alison Lennon, The Independent Press. Ross, how powerful are you? We saw some extraordinary stuff in your test videos, but can you move cars, trucks, buildings …?'

Helen leaned over and whispered in my ear again, 'I don't know if you can move buildings or not, but don't tell them you can.'

'I don't think it's possible to move buildings,' I said to the room. 'I can move some larger objects but there's not much call for me to move cars or trucks around.'

'What are you going to do with the money from the competition?' another reporter asked.

'I haven't really given it a lot of thought. I'll probably go on a holiday or something, or buy my dad a new car.'

'Is your father your only family?' another asked.

'Yeah, it's just the two of us.'

'And how is your relationship with him?'

Helen Greene pressed the palm of her hand over my microphone then addressed the reporter. 'I'd rather we didn't talk about his personal life at this time.' She pointed at a young man to the side of the stage. 'Next question.'

'Vincent Bates, NCC News. Ross, could you display some of your powers for us?'

'Yes, he can,' Helen proudly announced before I could say a word. 'Just give us a few moments to rearrange the stage so you can all get a good look at his abilities.'

Marianne appeared at the front entrance of the hotel after spending twenty minutes working her way through the crowd. There was a wall of security guards blocking her way and they weren't entertaining anyone who wanted to get inside. Marianne wasn't like everyone else though.

'Could you let me in please?' she asked the nearest guard, making her voice polite and squeaky.

'Sorry, love. There's about ten thousand other girls who've asked that question and you're gonna get the same answer they got: press only!'

'But I *have* to get in there.'

'Not a chance!'

A more senior member of the security team came approached when he noticed her. 'What's your name, darlin'?'

'Marianne.'

He turned to his colleague and spoke quietly to him. 'I just got a phone call from Golding himself, saying that a girl with white hair, calling herself Marianne, is to be allowed inside. Nobody is to get in her way, or lay a finger on her no matter what she does.'

'That's a bit strange.'

'A bit? Get on the radio and make sure all security staff are aware of Golding's instructions.' He turned to Marianne. 'You can go inside, darlin'.'

'Don't call me that, I told you my name was *Marianne*.'

'Whatever.'

She was tempted to tie a knot in his intestines, which was one of her torture techniques, but she didn't want to create a scene.

'Thanks,' she sneered before brushing past him into the lobby. Once inside the hotel she went straight to the restaurant where the crowd had gathered. She stood at the back of the room and watched as staff removed the long table from the stage.

Her nemesis was standing at the centre of the platform with Greene and the security people on both sides of him. There were hundreds of press people between her and the stage, but that wouldn't pose any serious problem for her.

I was tapped on the shoulder by one of Helen Greene's PR people who handed me a leather football. I held it in my hands then turned to the crowd and smiled. It had gone very quiet and all eyes were on me. A thousand people were watching me, but one person stood out from the crowd; a girl with white hair who was standing at the back was staring at me and her expression was far from pleasant. There was something really sinister about her eyes, but I tried to ignore her gaze as much as I could. I *had* to give the crowd of reporters what they were looking for.

I threw the ball into the air and it landed on my foot. I volleyed it a few times then sent it above my head again. The ball almost came to a stop in mid-flight then very slowly fell onto my shoulder where it came to a dead stop before rolling down my body. The crowd was stunned, some clapped, others cheered, the cameras flashed incessantly. It hadn't taken much to please them. I was only just getting started though; I planned to put on a really explosive show.

I took the ball in my hands, smiled to the crowd then threw it into the air. I'd intended to make the ball levitate over the crowd, but my gift failed and the ball bounced off a reporter's head. I lot of them laughed; others started to frown and whisper to each other.

'Sorry,' I shouted. 'Let me try that again ...'

One of Greene's staff handed me another football and I tested its weight before I threw it over my head. I tried to make the ball stop in mid-flight, but again my gift failed and the ball came crashing down on the table behind me. I was starting to panic and the crowd was jeering me.

'Ross!' Greene hissed at me. 'What the hell are you doing?'

I couldn't give her an answer. I couldn't explain why my gift was failing. Then I remembered that another psychokinetic could counter my gift, like Romand had done a few nights before. But I knew it wasn't Romand who was doing this, it was someone else. I looked out over the crowd who were starting to disperse. The girl with the white hair was gazing at me and smirking. I knew she was responsible; she *must* be the person Romand had warned me about.

Helen Greene shoved another football into my hands. 'Try it again. You're losing them! Hurry!'

Again I tried but I couldn't control the ball. It fell onto the stage and bounced away and onto the restaurant floor. The remaining reporters left their seats and flooded out of the room.

'Your million dollar gift just became a hundred dollar gift. Good luck, kid,' Greene said before she exited the stage and followed the crowd out of the restaurant.

I caught one last look at the white haired girl before she left. She ran her finger across her throat then pointed at me. I knew it meant I was in for big trouble.

I no longer had a choice. I *had* to escape the hotel. My life *was* in danger; if she could counter my gift, it probably meant she was more powerful than me and I wouldn't be able to defend myself against her. I needed to disappear and fast.

CHAPTER SIXTEEN

The Getaway

'**W**ill you people give me some space,' I shouted at the security and public relations people.

I slammed the door and left them in the hallway outside my penthouse room then went straight to the bathroom to soak my face in cold water. I felt stunned and needed to snap out of it. I was still somewhat bewildered by how the day had developed and I needed to clear my mind. I'd just been made a laughing stock in front of the world's media; millions, if not billions, of people were probably laughing their asses off me. All thanks to that demented-looking blonde.

I lifted my face from the sink and went to the main room and switched on the lamp by the bed. I almost died with fright when the room was lit – Romand was sitting in a chair by the window.

'Are you nuts?' I hissed at him. 'What are you doing in here? I could have gotten undressed in there … you know … I could've come back out here in the nip!'

'I can assure you I am not a pervert. I did not risk my life so

I could see you without clothes.'

'I'm not so sure.'

'Believe me, you are not my type.'

'How did you get in here?'

'It was quite simple. There was no security up here while the press conference was on. I walked straight in, the door wasn't even locked. I sat right here and watched the press conference live on your TV.'

'Good for you. I'm glad you made yourself at home.' I sat on the side of the bed and sighed. 'What do you want, Romand?'

'I just wanted to say that you truly are an idiot! I felt the need to say this to your face.'

'No, you came here to say *I told you so* ... in your silly French accent.'

'What do you mean? I do not have a silly accent.'

'Sounds silly to me.'

'You are the silly one. I told you to leave, but you have remained. You said you were in control and that you would go home and it would all be peachy! It has not quite worked out that way. You get yourself into more trouble every day. You need proper supervision.'

'All right. I should have listened to you,' I admitted. 'How was I supposed to know you were right? You were just a stranger on the street with weird hair!'

'I showed you that I also have the gift. That should have been enough for you to put your trust in me ... and I don't have weird hair.'

'After today I will never trust another person who has this gift. I wish I never came to this place. Everyone has their hooks in me. Why won't they leave me be, Romand?'

'What did you expect? You are a powerful psychokinetic; you have one of the rarest gifts known to man. Did you think that they would admire it, give you some money and wish you farewell? There are people in this world who would do almost anything to control you and the powers you possess. And there are others who will kill you for having this gift.'

'This other psychokinetic who wants to kill me, is it a girl with white hair?'

'Yes, her name is Marianne Dolloway and she's been working for Golding most of her life. I feared she would assassinate you because she might have thought you were intended to be her replacement. What she did today though was most unexpected.' Romand raised a hand to his face and rubbed the stubble on his chin. 'Or perhaps not, considering what transpired at the Laberinto.'

'The gas explosion?'

'The gas explosion was to cover up what really happened.'

I left the bed and pulled a chair across the floor. I sat next to Romand and my mind was buzzing with excited curiosity. 'What really happened there?'

'Marianne happened. She has been doing work for Golding for years but she is out of control. That is why they set up that ridiculous contest; they wanted to find a replacement for her. She went to the Laberinto to force Golding into killing you.'

'Obviously it didn't go according to plan.'

'Shaw must have set up a trap for her but it did not work. Those who died today were not office workers, they were Shaw's best security operatives, and Marianne killed them.'

'And Shaw?'

'Dead.'

'Jesus,' I breathed. 'I only spoke to him this morning.'

'He got what he deserved. He lured Marianne there to kill her, but like most, he underestimated her. She is the most powerful psychokinetic that has ever lived and she is also a strong metallisir and an emotomagnet. All three gifts combine to make her virtually indestructible. Add to that a vicious temper and no inhibitions about killing people, even innocent people, and you've got a weapon of mass destruction. You see now what you are dealing with? And there are more threats against your life from religious nuts. You need to leave this place. Now that they have discredited you, they will most likely kill you.'

'Back up, what's a metallisir and emotomagnet?'

'They are two of the true gifts. There are fifteen in all. Marianne has three. I have two, and from watching your test videos, I would say you also have three.'

I was finding this hard to take in – I really wasn't alone, there were lots of gifts and some people had more than one.

Even *I* might have more than one …

'Tell me more about these gifts.'

'Now is not the time. We have to find a way out of here.'

'We?'

'I told you I would come back one more time. You won't get this opportunity again. Once I leave, you will never see me again.'

I barely hesitated. I could not let Romand leave and let my only chance at getting the answers I wanted evade me forever. I had to follow him.

'How are we gonna get out of here?' I asked.

Romand stood and towered over me. He lifted one hand and clicked his fingers. A spot of white light appeared above his hand and it grew and grew until it was an orb of piercing light that was about the size of an orange.

'What the hell is that?' I wondered. 'It looks dangerous.'

'Stand up and touch it.'

'No way!'

'I promise you will be unharmed.'

I got to my feet and reached out tentatively at the white object. My fingers were only centimetres from the orb but there was no heat radiating from it. I took a leap of faith and plunged my hand inside the white sphere. It passed harmlessly through.

'It is only light,' Romand said. 'A simple trick really.'

'How did you create it?'

'With gift of light-tuning. You see, I am not only a psycho-kinetic, I am also a light-tuner.'

'A light-tuner?'

The orb blinked a few times then disintegrated. 'A light-tuner has the ability to manipulate light in certain ways. My powers are limited though and I cannot maintain my control over light for very long. But perhaps long enough to get us out of here.'

'How can you get us out of here by creating balls of light?'

'A light-tuner can do more than that. I can refract light around both of us, so that we will be practically invisible to the guards outside.'

'We're not prisoners. Can't we just tell them we're leaving?'

'They will think of a reason to keep you here, Ross, and they will shoot me on sight.'

'Why would they do that?'

'They view me as an enemy, but there is no time to explain. I will make us invisible but I can only do it for perhaps a minute. That gives us sixty seconds to get past the guards, down the corridor and to the elevator. We must be swift.'

'The lifts aren't working, they shut them down. We'll have to use the stairs.'

'No. They have armed men on the stairs and I would like to avoid a shootout. We must use the elevator.'

'I just told you the lift won't be working!'

'We will make it work! We can control it with our minds.

Start using your head for a change.' He leaned forward and tapped my temple with his finger. 'Are you ready?'

'I need to get my stuff.'

'No. We must be invisible, that means we must also be silent. If you bring your *stuff* they will hear us.'

'Okay. How do we get through the door?'

'We open it like anyone else would, or did you have some special door opening technique in mind?'

'You're a real funny guy, Romand.'

'Thank you.'

'I was being sarcastic.'

'Be silent.' Romand grabbed hold of me, threw his arms around my chest and held me close to his body.

'You sure you're not a pervert?'

'Shut up!'

We stood next to the door and Romand tapped his knuckles on it. A strange haze surrounded us and I looked at my hands – they were rippling like a mirage. The door opened and two security men walked into the room, straight past us as if we weren't there.

'Where is he?' one asked.

'Must be in the bathroom.'

Romand dragged me from the room and into the corridor where more security men were standing. One of them seemed to be staring right at me, but I realised he was just day dreaming. None of them noticed us quietly treading along the hallway. Romand forced me to walk faster and faster until we turned a corner into another hallway.

He fell to his knees and we were visible again. He was out of breath and looked in physical pain. I reached down and tried to get him on his feet.

'Romand, are you all right?'

'Yes. It takes a lot out of me to do something like that.' He struggled to his feet and used the wall to push himself forward. 'Quickly, they will soon realise you are not in the bathroom.'

We hurried through the corridors until we reached the elevator doors.

'Open them,' Romand ordered.

I used my gift to part the metal doors and I looked down into the dark emptiness of the shaft. Romand took a few deep breaths and stood next to me.

'Put your hand onto my shoulder,' he said.

I eyed him with suspicion. 'Why?'

'Just do it! When two psychokinetics make a physical connection they can combine their gifts. Concentrate on raising the elevator.'

Once we made a physical connection, I found that I could read some of Romand's thoughts.

'I can feel—'

'Yes, we also make a psychological connection when we join our gifts.'

It was so strange. I could sense some of my companion's

thoughts and could also grasp his motives and character. There was nothing malicious in him and he was genuinely concerned for my safety. There was a great deal of fear behind his wall of strength and courage though; it was almost as if I had touched a new world that was much more dangerous than the one I was used to. Now I understood his urgency.

'Concentrate, Ross. We have little time.'

We both gazed into the shadows below and transmitted our powers together. Metal clanked and the thick wires began to move. Within seconds the elevator was in front of us and we stepped in then used our gifts to make it move down, towards the basement of the hotel.

'I'm sensing danger, Romand. Something's going to happen when the doors open … a gun … they will fire on us …'

'You are using your precog gift. How many guns are you sensing?'

'Two. Right outside these doors.'

'*You* must deal with this, Ross. Use your gifts together.'

The elevator bumped as it reached the basement levels and the doors parted. I reached out and two guns flew into my hands. Romand stepped outside and punched a guard who had been waiting for us, knocking him unconscious. The owner of the other gun was Tsuyoshi who was slowly backing away from us.

'Hello, Tsuyoshi,' Romand said with a short nod. 'I'm sure you remember how dangerous I am when I need to be. Don't make me kill you. Bring us to a car and get us out of here.'

Tsuyoshi didn't respond. He didn't even flinch.

'Tsuyoshi,' Romand demanded. 'Don't make me hurt you!'

I knew we were running out of time so I took matters into my hands. I walked up to Tsuyoshi and directed both guns at his face. 'Maybe this will get you moving?'

The BMW rolled up the ramp to the metal barrier that was manned by two security guards. Tsuyoshi brought the car to a halt and pulled the handbrake.

'Remember that there's a gun pointed at you,' Romand whispered.

One of the guards indicated for the driver to pull down his window. He stooped and looked at Tsuyoshi then in the back. He couldn't see Romand and I, sitting in the back seat pointing guns at him, we were masked by Romand's strange gift of light-tuning. It was faltering though; he could not hold it for very long once it was extended beyond his own body.

'Lift the barrier,' the guard said. 'The car's clean.'

Romand's powers collapsed as the car passed out of the building and through a crowd of people who were being held back by police. Luckily for us, the car had tinted windows and no one noticed us. We were finally free of the Golding Plaza Hotel.

Once we got a few blocks from the hotel we switched from the

BMW, with Tsuyoshi tied up in the boot, to Romand's more cramped, and very old, Citroen. We then took to the road leading us to the city limits.

'Where we headed, Romand?'

'It is best if you do not know.'

'You don't trust me?'

'I trust *you,* but not your age and inexperience. You may give our location away and not even realise.'

I didn't argue. I knew Romand didn't mean me any harm and I sank into the passenger seat and rested my cheek against the cold window. I was about to drift off when the car skidded to a halt.

'What's going on?' I asked, straightening up in my seat.

'Did you leave your mobile phone in the hotel?'

'No. I have it here.' I took the phone from my jeans pocket and showed it to Romand. 'Why? You need to make a call? I don't have much credit.'

'Give it to me.' Romand snatched it from my grasp and left the car. I watched him through the window as he walked to the side of the road where he dropped it on the ground. He raised his boot and was about to smash it into the tarmac.

'Hey, be careful with that!' I shouted as I pounced from the car.

'It's more than likely bugged or got some hi-tech tracer installed on it. They could use it to track us.'

'I need that phone to stay in contact with my dad. He has

no other way to get in touch with me.'

'You'll be putting him at risk by being in contact with him.'

'I can't simply disappear, Romand. I'm not that type of person and I won't do that to the old man.'

'You *must* do it. Simple as that.'

'You smash that phone and I'm walking back to the Golding Plaza.'

Romand sighed then picked up the phone. He threw it at me then told me to ring Dad and to tell him I wouldn't be available for a few weeks.

'He won't buy into that, Romand.'

'You need to sort this out before we leave London. We are running out of time, Ross. They're probably already looking for us.'

'Okay.' I punched my dad's mobile number into the phone. 'You're going to help me though.'

'No,' Romand hissed. 'I am no good on the phone.'

'You *must* do it. Simple as that.' Romand didn't like me using his lines and his face went very red. I was starting to find it all very amusing though. I put the phone on speaker when I heard the dial tone.

'Ross! Where have you been?' Dad sounded well ticked off. 'I'll kill you when you get home!'

'Calm down, calm down,' I replied. 'Listen, you won't be able to contact me on this phone for a while. The press got hold of my number and I've been swamped with calls and texts. I have get rid of it *and* I'll be lying low for a few weeks. If I return now the house will be surrounded by thousands of reporters and screaming girls who are madly in love with me. Do you really want that?'

'Can't say it sounds too appealing.'

'No, it's not. Can you do without me for a few weeks? When I get back we can head off on a nice holiday somewhere in the Mediterranean.' Dad was a real sun worshipper. We'd always gone on annual holidays to Spain or Portugal when I was younger, back when we had money.

'A holiday...'

'Yes. You know, since I'm now a millionaire I was thinking I might even buy you a villa in the south of Spain. Somewhere you can retire and enjoy the good weather.'

Romand gave me a thumbs up for creativity.

'That sounds nice...'

'You deserve it, Dad.'

'I do. After all, I have been looking after you all your life. You do owe me.'

'You're right, Dad. You are so right.'

'But why don't you just get another number, rather than all this messing around?'

'The press are a pretty crafty bunch. They'll find out my new number and they could be recording our conversations. I'm sure you don't want that!'

'Of course I don't. How do I know you're not lying to me

though? You could be going off on that European tour you always dreamed about. The one where you free style in every capitol city of Europe.'

'It's called free-running.'

'I don't care what it's called. How do I know you're not lying to me?'

'You can talk to Mr Romand if you like. He's the er ... head of ... publicity at Golding hotel group...'

Romand furiously waved his fists at me.

'Mr Romand?' I said, trying not to laugh. 'My father wishes to speak to you.'

'Hello, Mr Bentley,' Romand said after a couple of deep breaths. 'I can confirm Ross is perfectly safe and that we are doing everything we can to keep him away from the press. He will be well looked after and should be home with you after the media hype has calmed down a little.'

'I think I should just come over there,' Dad replied.

'Unwise,' Romand replied instantly. 'The reporters would follow you and locate Ross and neither of you would have any peace. We are deeply sorry for this inconvenience and would also like to reward you for your patience regarding this matter ... by compensating you with ... fifty thousand pounds. How does that sound?'

'Fifty thousand pounds for my patience?'

'Yes.'

'Does that amount increase the longer my ... *wonderful*

son is kept from me?'

'It will of course.'

'Keep him as long you like, Mr Romand. Sorry, I meant: keep him safe and I will look forward to talking to you again.'

'Right, Dad,' I butted in. 'I'm going to call it a day. I'm real tired. I'll speak to you in a few weeks.'

'Look after yourself, son.'

'I will.'

Romand snatched the phone from my grasp before I had a chance to hang up and threw it on the ground. He stomped violently on it until it was shattered into a thousand pieces.

'Crap!' I shouted. 'I needed to make one more call. I told Gemma I'd get in touch.'

'Your sweetheart?'

'What business is it of yours?'

'Is she the love of your life?'

'What are you on about, Romand?'

'Is she the love of your life? The one and only? A person you cannot be apart from?'

'No, she's just a mate.'

'Then you'll both be able to live without each other for a while.'

He went back to the car and climbed into the driver's seat. 'Let's get going.'

'You're cunning, Romand. Real cunning … I hope I *can* buy my dad that villa, and pay him that compensation. I'd hate him to think I was lying to him ...'

'Someone in my group will arrange for money to be sent to him, now get into the car.'

I grudgingly returned to my seat and we were soon on the move again. It was now past midnight and the city was behind us. I had no idea where we headed, but I trusted Romand. When our minds had joined at the hotel I sensed there was no malice in him; he only wanted to protect me. I actually felt safe for the first time since I'd arrived in England.

CHAPTER SEVENTEEN -

The Hideout

I was in that strange place between the world of reality and the world of dreams when the car hit a bump and snapped me out of it. I opened my eyes to see the beam of the headlights scanning the grey stonework façade of a farmhouse. Romand parked the car in the front yard next to an old 4x4 then shut off the engine. I had a quick look around as I stepped from the car and noticed we were in the countryside; there was nothing but darkness beyond the stone boundaries of the property.

The farmhouse looked old, but was well maintained and, with its hanging baskets full of flowers, had a certain charm to it. This place looked homely and was a welcome change from the emotionless architecture of the Golding Plaza. There were small windows deeply set in the weathered stonework; all were dark apart from one on the ground floor, which I figured was a sitting room. The grand front door, which looked robust enough to withstand a tsunami, was ajar and I could see a shadow moving in the hallway.

'Who lives here?'

'It is the home of a very good friend of mine. She is taking a risk by allowing you to stay here so you should try to be nice.'

'I'm always nice.'

'Like hell you are.'

We stepped from the car and Romand smiled at me. 'Oh, make sure you show respect to the dogs at all times.'

'Not really a dog lover, me.'

I didn't like the way Romand laughed. I followed him towards the house and monitored the yard for any sign of vicious sheepdogs. As we neared the house I looked in through the front door to a warmly-lit hallway with a glossy wooden floor and large portraits on the walls.

As we were about to cross the threshold, two giant shapes appeared from a room inside. I immediately jumped behind Romand and used him as a shield.

'What the hell are they?' I gasped. 'You said *dogs*, not polar bears!'

'They are *dogs* and I told you to show them respect.'

'Are they civilised?'

'They are more civilised than you or I.'

I peered round Romand's strong shoulder and spied two enormous hounds with short tan coats, enormous black faces and fangs as long as my fingers. I'd never seen dogs as big as them, not even a Great-Dane would come close.

'Hello, doggies,' I said quietly. 'I'm showing you respect,

please don't bite me.'

'That's better.' Romand said. 'A little respect can go a long way.'

He smiled and shook the paw of the older of the two dogs. 'These are Pepe and Bebe, Kurdish kangals. They are the largest and strongest breed of dog in the world. They are also very intelligent ... particularly these two.' He looked at the younger of the two, who was slightly smaller than the other, but was more lively and seemed very excited to see him. 'Am I right?'

The dog nodded at him as if it had human intelligence. It then looked in my direction and seemed to narrow its eyes at me.

'Am I still dreaming?' That dog just nodded at you, no dog is that smart!'

'You've left the world of the blind behind you, Ross. You need to open your mind if you are to survive in the *real* world. Most people are blind to what really exists and to what is possible. You cannot be so short sighted from now on.'

'Are you trying to tell me those dogs can understand what we're saying?'

'Yes and no.'

'You know, you're very vague!'

'You'll have all the answers in time. Let's get inside. I'm hungry.'

The colossal kangals left the house and allowed us to pass.

Before I entered the hall I noticed that both dogs lay down outside and closed their eyes. It was all very, very strange … I never thought the world could be so colourful and I had a feeling that much more was to be revealed to me. I'd taken a first step into a world that ordinary people knew nothing about.

The house was cosy and tidy inside and I followed my companion down the hallway into a large, two-tier kitchen. We walked through the cooking area that was framed with old wooden counters to a lower level that was dominated by a rectangular mahogany table where we sat. There was an old-fashioned kettle boiling on the stove and the room smelled of chicken soup and freshly-baked bread. It was so different to the hotel room I'd spent the last few days in, and also Romand's car, which wasn't very comfortable and stank of cigar smoke.

'Do we help ourselves?' I was practically drooling at this point; I hadn't eaten all day. 'I'm starved.'

'We are guests, and guests always wait for their host before they eat. It's called manners.'

'I was only asking. You make me out to be some sort of spoilt brat. There doesn't seem to be anyone around, so I thought—'

'You thought exactly what a hungry teenage boy should think,' a woman said.

I turned to see her entering the kitchen. I guessed she was about sixty years old, but she looked strong and alert despite the late hour. She had long grey hair elegantly tied in a loose plait that hung over her shoulder and her clothes were colourful without being gaudy.

'Have you eaten at all today, Ross?'

'No, but I wouldn't want to put you out. It is quite late and—'

'And your mother once told you never to fill your stomach so late at night, didn't she?'

'How did you know that?'

'No need to get defensive.'

'I'm not. I'm just curious how you knew.'

She smiled at me and made a point of crossing the room and gently squeezing my arm. 'All mothers tell their sons that. It was just a lucky guess.'

'This is June Atkinson,' Romand said, smiling. 'She is our host and my very dear friend.'

She turned to smile and curtsy.

'This is Ross Bentley,' Romand added.

'Oh, I know who he is. He's been on the news all week and in every newspaper. He's all the young girls in town talk about.'

I was a little embarrassed, which wasn't helped by Romand reaching over the table and pinching my cheek. 'You are so dreamy, Ross!' he jeered.

'Get off, Romand!'

'How are you dealing with your newfound fame, Ross?'

'I haven't been. I've spent the last week in hotel rooms on my own.'

'Sounds awful,' June said. She was pouring tea for us both and laying bowls and cutlery on a large tray. 'You're with friends now though. Would you like a hot cup of tea and some food?'

'Big time!'

'Romand?'

'Yes, please.'

'Oh, yes, please, Mrs Atkinson.' I had forgotten my manners and I got a nod of approval from Romand.

'No need to be so formal. You can call me June.'

She brought two cups to the table then poured some soup for us both and took a loaf of fresh bread from the oven. When she had brought everything from the counter she sat at the head of the table and smiled.

'Tuck in. Come on, before it goes cold.'

After we finished our meal, Romand poured himself a glass of red wine and told June how we had escaped Golding's men. She seemed very entertained by it, not at all shocked, as I was expecting. After an hour or so, he told her that I had been in a foul mood ever since he destroyed my phone. Romand certainly had a strange sense of humour.

I wasn't impressed and told him he should have destroyed the SIM card instead of breaking a perfectly good phone.

'You can never be too careful,' he shrugged.

'This comes from the man who sat watching TV in my room while there were armed guards outside who wanted to kill him!'

'It's late and emotions and fatigue don't make good bedfellows,' June said, interrupting the heated discussion. 'I think it's time you both got some rest. Romand, you go on upstairs. I'll show Ross to his room in a few moments.'

Romand drained the wine glass and said goodnight to us both before leaving the kitchen. I heard his heavy footsteps on the stair and asked June how she knew him.

'It's a very long story. I'm sure he'll tell you about it in time. He's a little difficult at times, but Romand is a loyal friend and he would risk his life to save those he cares about. Just like he did for you today.'

'But he doesn't even know me.'

'Even more reason for you to cut him some slack.' She stood up and said, 'Come on, I'll show you which room is yours.'

She led me up the creaking staircase and along a very narrow hallway with rooms on both sides. I passed one room with an open door and saw Romand sprawled across the bed, fully clothed, and snoring like a rhino.

'Poor Romand,' June laughed, 'he's barely had a wink of sleep all week and that wine must have gone straight to his head. The room at the end is yours. Hopefully she's already—'

The door swung open and a girl, about the same age as me, stepped into the hall with a large bag over her shoulder.

'I don't see why I have to give up my room for *him*!'

'It's only for a few days, Cathy,' June said, giving her a scolding look. 'Ross, this is my daughter. You'll be staying in her room for the next while.'

'And I have to sleep in the dusty old spare room!'

'Sorry …' I said, 'I don't want to put you out …'

I stared at her as she moved towards me. She was utterly stunning, impossibly perfect in every single way. She had extremely long red hair, pale skin with a peppering of light freckles across her button nose, large green eyes and strong cheek bones. She was quite tall, almost my own height, and athletically-built. It was difficult to draw my gaze from her, even though she was scowling at me.

'Don't go rummaging around in my stuff!' she said as she moved past me and dragged her bag down the stairs. 'I know where I left everything.'

'Pay her no mind, Ross. She'll get over it.'

'Hopefully. I really do appreciate all this, June.'

'Think nothing of it. Sleep tight.'

I took a step into the room and closed the door. I was about to leap onto the bed but froze halfway across the floor. One of the kangals, Pepe, the younger of the two, was in the room and sniffing around under the bed. I turned around and opened the door.

'Er, June? That dog is…' There was no one in the hallway and the lights were off. I turned back. 'Out you go, doggie.

Come on. Out.'

The kangal was still sniffing around the room blissfully unaware of my presence. I liked dogs and this one seemed cheer-
ful enough, but I didn't want to be sharing my room with one.
Especially one this big. I kept the door open for about five
minutes, but the dog wasn't interested in leaving.

'Out! Don't have me to—'

Suddenly the dog's mood was completely altered. It turned
to me slowly and let out a low growl. It stopped panting and
became very still.

'Okey-Dokey … but I better not get fleas from you!'

I closed the door and edged nervously into the room as the
dog watched me very carefully. I gave him a wide berth and
carefully got into the bed. The dog sat beside the bed, tower-
ing over me. It was only inches from my face and the gaze
from its large black eyes deepened.

'Stop looking at me.'

He continued to watch me.

'You're weird. You must be Romand's dog.'

The lights went out and I nestled my face into the pillow.
I was so tired, but it wouldn't be easy to sleep; the dog was
panting right beside me and Romand's snoring was like a hurricane in the house.

I focused on the light switch and the overhead lamp came
back on. The dog was still watching me.

'What do you want? I have no food. I have nothing for

you.' I was getting seriously irritated at this point. 'Get lost or I'll—'

The dog growled again. It was going to be a long night.

Romand kicked the bed and I leaped in the air and screamed, 'What is it? What's going on?'

'Breakfast.'

'Are you for real? You could've given me a heart attack waking me like that.'

'It was funny though.' Romand turned to the doorway. 'Don't keep us waiting.'

Pepe was still sitting next to the bed, it seemed to me like he hadn't slept or taken his eyes off me the whole night.

'Don't you sleep?' I mumbled as I got out of bed.

I stood in the centre of the room wearing just my boxer shorts and stretched my weary limbs; the journey in Romand's beat-up Citroen had stiffened up my joints. I became aware then of the kangal. It wasn't just staring at me now. It was looking me up and down in a way that made me suspicious and also made me feel downright uncomfortable.

'You're a real weird dog, Pepe!' I snapped and quickly put on some clothes.

I cautiously rounded him and walked along the hallway. Pepe was right behind me all the time, but I didn't dare threaten him again like I had countless times during the night;

he had growled at me every time I told him I'd make him fly out the window. I decided that ignoring him was the best course of action.

When I entered the kitchen I found June and Romand both sitting at the table and eating. There was a pot of tea, a stack of toast, marmalade, butter, boiled eggs and some ham. I took a plate and heaped as much as I could onto it.

'Leave some for the rest of us,' Romand grumbled.

'Oh, Romand,' June sighed, 'stop harassing him, boys his age have big appetites.'

I smirked across the table. 'Yeah, Romand.'

The dog had followed me and was now sitting by the table. It was so big that we were practically face to face. The stink of its breath *almost* put me off my breakfast.

'I see you and Pepe are getting very attached,' June said.

'You could say that.'

Pepe did the same thing I had seen him do the previous night; he lay on the floor, closed his eyes for a moment, then got back up. He was now acting like a normal dog and was sniffing at the kitchen table and wagging his tail like crazy.

Romand snorted into his mug of coffee.

'What's so funny?' I asked.

'Someone likes you or doesn't trust you.'

'What's that supposed to mean?'

'Oh, nothing.'

I noticed that he and June were grinning at each other.

Something odd was going on and they weren't sharing it with me. I'd get to the bottom of it sooner or later though. I didn't like mysteries.

Cathy breezed into the kitchen a few moments later. 'Hi Mum. Hi Romand,' she said before she sat opposite me. She took some toast and a single egg then poured herself a cup of tea.

'Cathy…?' her mother said.

'Morning, *Ross*. Sleep well? I know I didn't.'

'Can't say that I did, what with Pepe staring at me and Romand "The Hurricane" over there with his snoring.' I looked up at her and smiled. 'The bed was really comfortable though.'

She scowled at me and took a vicious bite from her toast.

'I'm done,' Romand said. He lifted his plate and cup and brought them to the sink and washed them. 'Time to get busy.'

'Busy?' Cathy asked.

'Yes.' He looked at me and grinned deviously. 'Training starts today.'

Cathy took her plate to the sink. 'This I have to see. I'm in need of a good laugh.'

'Training?' I asked, with my mouth full of half-chewed toast. 'You don't mean dog training, do you?'

Cathy and Romand looked at each other and shared a smile that was full of devilry.

CHAPTER EIGHTEEN -

Psychokinesis For Dummies

Romand led me from the back of the house, through a colourful garden and across a field of long grass. He'd kept the plans for the day to himself, but I guessed he was heading towards a tall barn, a few hundred metres down the field, for *training*. Cathy followed us from a short distance, flanked by Pepe and Bebe.

I glanced over my shoulder to see her strolling through the long grass with her red hair dancing in the breeze. She was so beautiful and carefree, now that she wasn't scowling at me. I had a feeling she was watching my every move so I tried to walk in a macho way, like Romand. Not that anything was ever going to happen between us. She obviously hated my guts! I did feel the need to impress her, though, which was making me nervous about what Romand had planned. I didn't want to make a fool of myself in front of her.

I hurried alongside Romand and tugged at his shirt. 'I'd prefer if she,' I nodded at Cathy, 'wasn't around while I'm doing this.'

'Are you afraid you'll make a fool of yourself in front of her?'

'No … Okay, yes. I tend to get a little anxious around girls. Especially good-looking ones … Not that she's good-looking or anything!'

'*Marianne* is a girl and you could not afford to be nervous in her presence. And she is attractive is she not?'

'Marianne?'

'Yes.'

'I guess she's kinda cute in a demented way, but certainly not my type. What's she got to do with this?'

'There may come a day when you have to face her and when it does, it would be wise not to hesitate just because she is a member of the opposite sex. Cathy stays. She'll help you conquer your fear of women. She might even come in useful during some of the exercises.'

'It's not a *fear of women* … hang on – exercises?'

'Do not fear, I will not ask you to do any sit-ups.'

'Good. Because I don't need to do any. Bit of a six-pack going on here,' I patted my stomach, 'you know.'

'You're skin and bone, Ross.'

I rolled up a sleeve and flexed my bicep. 'Check it out! That look like skin and bone to you?'

Romand lifted his shirt sleeve and flexed his right bicep. It was three times thicker than mine. He didn't say anything, but his smile spoke volumes. I kept my thoughts to myself after that.

We entered the immense barn that had cement block walls and a corrugated metal roof. There were hundreds of hay bales in the back and a number of tables up front with an assortment of items on them.

'You need more control over your gifts,' Romand said as he sat on the edge of one of the tables. 'Everything you will require is in this barn. I have designed a number of exercises to help you attain more skill and power.'

'Where do we start?'

He told me to stand a few metres away and to lift a pencil that was next to him on the table.

'This is a bit simple in all fairness, Romand.'

'It is not a training exercise. This is just to limber up.'

I focused on the pencil and used my power to seize it before I lifted it a few feet off the table.

'Allow the pencil to fall, take a moment then lift the lead weight next to it.'

'I don't need to take a moment,' I scoffed. 'It's like Yoda said: "There's no difference between a rock and a ship".' I tapped my temple. 'Only different in your mind!'

Romand hopped off the table and flicked me on the temple.

'*T'es stupide*! This is not *Star Wars*! Of course there is a difference! To move a pencil is easy, to move a rock can leave you drained, to move a truck can kill you!'

'Really?'

'Yes! Let's skip the limbering up.' He turned his back on

me and went to the table. When he reached the first table he shouted, 'Lesson one,' then fired a golf ball at my face. I'd sensed it before it left his hand and instinctively reached out and caught it cleanly.

'Uh, oh,' Cathy laughed. She was leaning by the entrance; she shook her head at me and giggled uncontrollably.

'What are you doing?' Romand snapped, furiously waving his arms in the air. 'What do you think this is?'

'I caught it! What was I supposed to do with it? Eat it?'

'You were supposed to deflect it with your thoughts. I'm not training you to be a handball player.'

He took two more golf balls from the table and fired them one after the other. I easily deflected the first, but the second almost caught me out.

'You're very slow,' Romand muttered. 'You will need to be much faster than this.'

'It's half seven in the morning and I only got about three hours sleep last night because of that stupid dog, not to mention your snoring!'

'Look sharp!' Cathy threw a tennis ball at me.

I deflected it then sensed another golf ball hurtling towards me from Romand's direction. I deflected that too and it bounced off the tennis ball.

'Better,' Romand said before he spun round and shouted, 'Again!'

They spent over an hour throwing all sorts of objects, from

golf balls to old kettles, at me, and although some came close, none hit me. When there was nothing left to throw Romand told me that the warm up was over and I could have a short break.

This was just a warm up? Romand was a slave driver, even worse than Professor Foster!

He patted me on the back when I sat next to him. 'Not bad for a novice. You do have great potential. I want to see how good you are with fast-moving objects before we move onto more complex training techniques.'

'What's next for the novice?' Cathy asked, she'd cheered up – slightly – since the morning, probably because she'd gotten the chance to throw things at my face.

'Have you ever played paintball?' the tall Frenchman asked her. He had a cheeky grin that I didn't like one bit.

'No.'

'Would you like to?'

She looked at me she flashed her teeth. 'I'd *love* to!'

I put my hands on my hips and frowned. 'Why do I get the feeling that I won't have a gun in this game?'

Romand pulled a case from under one of the tables and opened it. He took two guns and gave one to Cathy then loaded his own with a magazine full of paintballs. 'Let's see how fast you *really* are.'

I was ordered into the vast maze of hay bales in the back of the large barn and was followed in moments later by Romand

and Cathy. The objective was simple: avoid being hit. I hid near the rear of the barn and tapped into my precognitive gift. I tried my best to sense when they would attack. It started out well and I evaded every attempt by my opponents, but Romand was obviously an expert with a firearm and his agility (along with the auto-fire option) outdid me. During the first session I was hit seven times, including a particularly painful hit in the back of the neck from Cathy.

'Focus,' Romand told me as we prepared for the next session. 'Use your two gifts as one. You are better than this!'

I hid at the back wall of the barn and listened for their approach. I sensed danger to the left and raced away from it. Cathy caught me somewhat off guard and fired a volley of paint balls in my direction. I raised a hand and the balls scattered away from me and dashed the hay bales. I blew her a kiss which infuriated her even more.

'I'll get you right on those stupid lips of yours!' she cried. She reloaded and ran after me into the hay bales. When she caught up with me I deflected her shots and laughed.

'Bang, Bang!' Romand said as he pressed his gun against the back of my head.

'Crap,' I sighed.

'Very crap if you ask me. I told you to focus and here you are having a laugh, which clouds your concentration and diminishes your powers. I walked up right behind you and you didn't even sense me. Try again. Harder this time!'

I avoided them both for the first five minutes of the final session. Romand ultimately found me, but couldn't manage to shoot me, I had mastered the game and my trainer soon ran out of ammo. That left Cathy and I amid the vast maze of hay bales. She crept around as quietly as possible, but couldn't catch me off guard; I sensed her every time she got close.

Eventually the game was brought to an end when I used my telekinesis to draw the gun from her hand and into my own. I pointed it at her and when she ran away I shot her twice in the backside.

'You're not supposed to shoot me!' she screamed. 'That's not part of the game.'

'Nobody told me the rules!'

'That bloody hurt.' She rubbed her bum cheek and limped back to the front of the barn. 'I hate you, I do!'

'I just acted out of instinct and shot at the first thing that came to mind.'

I winked at her and she almost broke a smile, but fought off the urge and stormed out of the barn. Pepe followed her, but the older dog, Bebe, remained in the entrance, watching everything Romand and I did.

'You've shown that you can predict and deflect fast moving objects so you might just be able to protect yourself against an attack from another psychokinetic.'

'Aren't you getting a bit carried away, Romand? It's not like there's a team of people with superhuman gifts trying to kill me!'

'You still don't get it, do you?'

'Get what?'

'Marianne is probably already searching for you. If she ever finds this place, she will try to kill you!'

'I find that hard to believe.'

'You saw what she did at the Laberinto. She could fight off a legion of police officers. Marianne can do whatever she wants.'

It finally dawned on me that my life was in jeopardy and probably always would be. I really did need to be better prepared.

'I need to get serious about this,' I said and Romand nodded at me. 'What's next? Bring it on.'

'That's the attitude you need,' Romand said smiling. 'Offensive training. How fast can you propel an object?'

'Dunno. Can move my skateboard pretty quickly,' I said proudly. 'Maybe a hundred miles per hour.'

'That's pitiful! You will need to be able to move objects at the speed of sound.'

'That's pretty fast.'

'It's over 1,200 kilometres per hour.'

Romand took two large metal cases from the floor and placed them on the table. They contained parts to a strange looking contraption that reminded me of the laser machine used in Professor Foster's tests. When Romand had assembled it though I could see it was very different. It had a hard-drive, a thick base, and at the top there was a metal cylinder with hundreds of small red lights inside it.

'What the hell is that?'

'It's a chronograph of my own design.' He stood back and presented it with his chest puffed out. 'What do you think?'

'Very impressive, Romand. You've outdone yourself.'

'*Merci beaucoup.*'

'Just one thing…'

'Yes?'

'What the hell is it?'

'*Imbecile!*' he cursed. 'You shoot something through the cylinder and its speed is calculated by a series of lasers. The precise speed is shown here,' he pointed an LCD screen on the hard drive. 'See?'

'I see. What do I fire?'

'This,' Romand handed me a playing dart. 'I want you to place it in the palm of your hand and send it through the cylinder into the hay at the back. And watch your aim; I don't want to be picking it out of my face.'

'I'm quite good at darts for your information!'

Romand outstretched his hand towards the cylinder. 'Show me.'

I took my time, gathered energy from my body and sent the dart whizzing through the chronograph. The speed was quickly calculated and the screen flashed. 442kph.

'I thought you said you were good…'

'That's just a warm up shot.' I retrieved the dart and prepared myself for a second attempt. 'You just wait and see!'

I gathered all my power and fired. 822kph.

'Not bad. Keep trying.'

After four attempts the best I could manage was 995kph.

'I can't do it,' I panted.

'Give me the dart,' Romand demanded. He took some deep breaths then launched it. Before it reached the cylinder there was a boom and white flash. The screen read 1,525kph.

'That's incredible,' I gasped. 'Absolutely *incredible*!'

'Especially incredible seeing as I am nowhere near as powerful as you.'

'You're not?'

'No. I have the gift, but I cannot master it like you and Marianne can.'

'But I can't break the sound barrier, so how could I be more powerful?'

'I have my suspicions. I want you to try one more time.'

I took the dart and held it in the palm of my hand then stood in front of the chronograph. I took a moment and focused on the small projectile then stared carefully at the cylinder.

'You do realise how ridiculous she made you look at the press conference, right?' Romand said unexpectedly.

'No, she didn't!' I barked – every time I thought of that press conference I felt embarrassed and enraged.

'You looked like the silly fool that you really are. You can't even complete the most basic of training exercises.'

My temper boiled inside my chest and I swung round to him, 'Oh, really? You just watch *this*.'

I spun back and launched the dart with all my rage. The dart flew into the air and there was a deafening boom that shook the metal roof of the barn. The small screen on the hard-drive flashed: *1,768kph*. I was stunned by what I'd just done. I couldn't really understand it at first.

'It's as I suspected,' Romand said thoughtfully. 'You have the purest form of psychokinesis.'

'What do you mean by *pure*?'

'A psychokinetic like me can summon energy from the body and use it to move objects. You can also do this but, you see, the body's energy is limited. Those with the purest form can suck energy from their environment and use it to move almost anything. When someone with the pure gift feels extreme anger or happiness or sadness they can suck in huge amounts of energy. Just like you did moments ago. This is what makes Marianne so powerful; she is very troubled and is *always* angry. She can summon immense powers at will, making it almost impossible to contend with her.'

'Anger is the key to matching her abilities?'

'Strong emotions are the key.'

'Happiness can be as useful as anger?'

'Anger is very immediate and tends to be one of the most effective emotions. Panic is the most powerful emotion to use but it is unpredictable and cannot be easily replicated in tests or training.'

I sat on the table and thought back to when I'd smashed the concrete pillar in Dullbrook, I'd felt intense panic just before I did it. Everything Romand said was making sense. While I was pondering my gift I saw Bebe lie down in the entrance, close his eyes then spring back up and walk away from the barn. I looked at Romand, who was dismantling the chronograph.

'What's the deal with those dogs?'

'Deal?'

'You know what I'm talking about, Romand. Some times they're just like normal pets, bouncing around the house and sniffing out food. Other times they act *real* suspicious. The old dog is listening to every damn word we say and the younger one is watching me like a hawk … and I won't even tell you about *how* it was watching me when I got out of bed this morning … but it was *pretty odd*!'

'They *are* normal dogs, Ross.'

'I want to know what's going on,' I demanded. 'You're keeping way too much from me.'

'All right. I guess you are old enough to comprehend it.'

He took a briefcase from a drawer under one of the tables, thumbed a combination into the locks and opened it. There was a block of sheets inside, around two hundred, and the title printed on the front read: *A Study of True Gifts by Marcus*

Romand. 1992.

Romand unclipped a metal binder and took three of the A4 sheets from the front of the block and handed them to me.

'Read this. It will open your mind to the real world and may answer some of your questions. As for your curiosity regarding the dogs, I think you will find the second last entry very informative. It may also explain my comment at breakfast.'

'Which comment was that?'

'You'll have to figure that out for yourself.'

We got back to the house at 5pm and I was told by June that I had two hours before dinner was served. Cathy was sitting on the edge of her chair by the table; she refused to even look at me. I figured she'd get over her delicate injuries though and made my way upstairs to my temporary bedroom. I locked the door then sat on the bed and read the first paragraph.

I took a deep breath. What the hell had I gotten myself involved in?

CHAPTER NINETEEN

The True Gifts

I had to read the first paragraph a few times over before it sank in. Romand was right about me taking a step into world that most are blind to. It was hard to believe this stuff really existed. I read over it once more before moving on to a number of paragraphs that looked like dictionary entries.

There are over two hundred known gifts. These have been documented throughout history and have recently been brought together in a paper by Professor William Davidson of the Golding Scientific Center in California. They include extraordinary abilities in the areas of mathematics, physical capabilities, artistic talent, etc. The paper was not intended for publication and the only physical copy exists in the vault library of the Golding Scientific building in Pittsburgh.

I am an employee of Golding Scientific so I have had the opportunity to study the paper for many weeks and have decided to write my own on the subject, focusing

primarily on the 'True Gifts', of which there are only fifteen. The search for more true gifts is ongoing, but to
date only fifteen have emerged.

The existence of these true gifts has been veri-
fied under laboratory conditions by Golding Scientific. There have been many reported instances of true
gifts in the distant past. These cannot be scientifically
proven, but some are considered to be reliable accounts
based on government records and historical texts that
have been studied by the staff at Golding Scientific.

Below I have numbered the reliable instances of
true gifts recorded throughout the centuries; there
could be many more people who hid their gifts, for var-
ious reasons.

Although some would argue there is a sixteenth
true gift, this has yet to be backed up with any significant scientific evidence. The fifteen true gifts are as follows:

Gift 005. (First reported: Mesopotamia, 3,245 BC.)
Prophet / Seer / *Propheta* /
An individual who has visions of future events. There
have been thousands of reported cases, the vast majority of which are unconfirmed. Most individuals with this
gift suffer serious emotional difficulties as a result of their
visions. The nature of this gift means only traumatic events

are predicted. This relates to the belief that surges of strong emotion reverberate through time and can be detected by certain humans (Prophets).

Most noted Prophet: Michel de Nostredame / Nostradamus (1503 - 1566 AD.)

Gift 044. (First reported: Macedonia, 1,574 BC.)
Psychokinetic / Telekinetic / *Pyrya Domina* /
An individual who can move objects at a distance by paranormal means.

This phenomena was first recorded in Macedonia in 1,574 BC. Subject was said to be able to move pottery from distances that equate to more than ten metres. There have since been sixty-one recorded cases.

At the time of writing, there are only two confirmed cases: Marcus Romand and Sarah Golding.

Most noted Psychokinetic: Ala Qush, general in the Mongolian Army.

Gift 078. (First reported: China, 1,202 BC.)
Fire-Starter / Pyrokinetic / *Ignis Incipere* /
An individual who can set alight any combustible material without physical contact. There have to date been over two thousand recorded cases of individuals with this gift. The gift is closely linked to strong emotions and is typically unstable. Most individuals with this gift

do not live beyond their teenage years, as the onset of hormonal changes in the body leads to unpredictable mood swings that often result in the individual setting themselves on fire. Spontaneous Human Combustion is blamed for most of these deaths.

Most noted Fire-Starter: Li Chang. (1899 - 1915 AD)

Gift 083. (First reported: Egypt, 981 BC.)

Precog / Precognitive / *Futura Videre* /

Persons with this gift can sense the actions of other humans seconds before they encounter such actions. It is believed that humans emit emotion and thought as they perform dramatic physical actions and that these thoughts and emotions are powerful enough to transcend time. As when a pebble is dropped into a pond, the ripples travel outward (into the past and the future). Precogs are the only humans who can detect these ripples. Contrary to popular belief, precogs cannot predict specific events like prophets; they can only sense strong actions and in most cases cannot interpret these actions in any coherent way. The boundaries of their senses are never more than two minutes into the future or past.

Most noted Precog: Peter Connolly. (1677 - 1731 AD)

Gift 099. (First reported: Greece, 512 BC.)

Metallisir / *Lique Ferro* / για την τήξη μετάλλων /

One of the most obscure of the fifteen true gifts. There have only been three recorded cases, the first being in Athens, Greece. The individual can melt any known metal. In each case the gift took a different form: the first individual known to have it needed physical contact with metal to use her powers. The second needed to be fully immersed in water. The third needed only to see the metal in order to liquefy it. There has not been a recorded case of Metallisiring in over two hundred years.

Most noted Metallisir: Gregory Antall. (1743 - 1788 AD)

Gift 146. (First reported: Spain, 218 AD.)

Ink-seer / *Videns Verborum* / Leer Libros Ciegos /

Ink-seers are rare; there have only been fifty-seven reported cases. They have the ability to consume incredible amounts of information in short periods of time. In most cases they can touch the cover of a book and within seconds have read every word contained within it (without needing to turn a single page). They were treasured by many societies through ancient times, but in recent decades they have failed to reappear. The last recorded case was in 1967, the United States, (John Brant, CIA operative who was executed in

East Germany when found guilty of espionage charges). Most noted Ink-Seer: Robert Sorenson. (1878 - 1931 AD)

Gift 154. (First reported: Britain, 32 AD.)
Warper / Time-Warper / *Tempore Continere* /

An extremely rare gift that was first reported by a scholar travelling with a Roman Legion on the south coast of England. One of the indigenous warriors displayed astounding speed in battle and slaughtered many of the Roman troops. He was captured and displayed the gift numerous times while imprisoned, before his subsequent execution. Since then, there have only been two recorded cases: a German girl in the seventeenth century who was burned at the stake after being accused of witchery, and more recently a teenager found in Australia who has displayed an exceptional ability to warp. His Aborigine name is 'Barega', meaning 'The Wind'.

It is thought that these individuals can manipulate the fabric of time that surrounds their body. In most cases they can slow down the flow of time that affects them physically, which allows them to move faster than the world surrounding them.

Most noted Warper: Barega. (1979 - present)

Gift 157. (First reported: Turkey, 48 AD.)

Emotomagnet / Psychic / *Motus Legere* / Kafasında Okuyucu /

The most common of the true gifts. There were many unconfirmed reports of this gift throughout history, but the earliest reliable account came in the first century. Since then there have been almost ten thousand emotomagnets.

These individuals can sense the emotions of others, no matter how well hidden they are. Once the individual picks up on a definite emotion, they can track that emotion back to its source: the thought processes that inspired it. This is the closest thing to being able to read the minds of others.

Most noted Emotomagnet: Linda Lucas. (1942 - 1983 AD)

Gift 159. (First reported: Mongolia, 77 AD.)

Spacerupter / Magician / *Magus* /

One of the rarest of all gifts, yet the most famous of all. There have been hundreds of thousands of reported Spacerupters throughout history; all but eight of them were most likely false.

These individuals had the power to open gaps in the fabric of the universe. All people see the world in three dimensions, but it is speculated that there is a fourth dimension that can be manipulated. Spacerupters are the only humans who can do this. They can tear the fabric of the universe and pass through it, seeming to disappear, then tear through the fabric of the universe and re-enter what we know as reality.

Most noted Spacerupter: Tsu Yang. (1452 - 1498 AD.)

Gift 167. (First reported: Scotland, 199 AD.)

Electro-psych / *Magister Electricitatis* /

All humans interact with electricity, but we have very little natural control over it. These individuals can control all types of electricity with incredible accuracy. This phenomenon was most famously recorded in 1666 when an English man, Thomas Farynor, drew a number of lightning bolts into his body then discharged them in one orb that started a massive blaze (igniting the great fire of London – subsequently covered up by the British government).

There have been seventeen recorded cases.

Most noted Electro-psych: Thomas Farriner. (1621 - 1670 AD.)

Gift 172. (First reported: Siberia, 578 AD.)

Mageleton / *Dominus Aqua* / для контроля воды /

There have only been six recorded cases of this gift. Individuals with this gift use magnetic forces to control liquids. There are virtually no limitations to the gift, those who have it can stop rivers, reverse tides, raise lakes and empty clouds. As with most of the true gifts, Mageletonia is very dangerous in the wrong hands. Humans are made up mostly of water and Mageletons can drain other humans of all fluids in an instant (resulting in death). This was infamously exploited by Anton LaVerharre, a Belgian who lived in the late eighteenth century. It is documented that he killed over two hundred people in his lifetime, using his gift in every murder.

There are no current recorded cases of this gift.

Most noted Mageleton: Anton LaVerharre (1749 - 1791 AD.)

Gift 174. (First reported: Sudan, 661 AD.)

Light-tuner / *Lux Mutante* /

Light tuning has been recorded twenty-three times to date, mostly in Africa. These individuals can manipulate light in numerous ways, but most commonly in creating light orbs, which can become so bright that they blind anyone who looks at them, and by 'body refraction', making themselves invisible for periods of time. Body refraction is created by the individual bending light rays around their body. Body refraction can be maintained for up to an hour, it can also be extended around numerous individuals and objects, but only for very short periods of time.

Most noted Light-tuner: Olajide Adebayo (1901 - 1942 AD.)

Gift 179. (First reported: Greece, 750 BC.)

Siren / Σειρήν / *Pitch Shifter* /

Most commonly occurs in females. Sirens can alter sound-waves in numerous ways, but are most noted for inducing hypnosis with their voice. It is believed they can reach a series of notes that shut down a person's brain, thus putting them into an almost comatose state. They can also drown out any sound and increase any sound to a deafening volume. There have only been three cases in the twentieth century.

Most noted Siren: Laura Aston. (1898 - 1917 AD.)

Gift 183. (First reported: Norway, 855 AD.)

Mind switcher / *Dominus Mentem* /

Possibly the most intriguing of all the true gifts. These individuals can actually transfer their minds into the brains of others. It is quite rare and often runs in families. It is possible for people with this gift to transfer their thoughts, and to control the actions of others, but this cannot be maintained for very long, usually no more than ten minutes. They can, however, transfer their minds into the bodies of animals and maintain the gift for many hours, even days. The mind of the host is numbed while the switch is held, their conscious and subconscious minds become comatose and when they wake they have no recollection of what occurred while they were under control. There are many fascinating aspects to mind switching – the most powerful of their kind can also add or remove thoughts in the minds of others, thus influencing their actions and their beliefs. One such case related to Miriam Tompkins, who could remove violent tendencies in other humans. Another case involved James Fanning who could tame wild beasts.

Mind switching, like all other true gifts, can be very dangerous in the wrong hands. They can enter the minds of almost anyone, albeit for only a brief time. They cannot for reasons yet unknown take control of the minds of those who possess any of the other true gifts.

There have been eighty-nine reported cases throughout history and fifteen in the twentieth century. Most noted Mind Switcher: Franz Matelle (1840 - 1880 AD.)

Gift 198. (First recorded: Mexico, 1952 AD.)
Time Scanner / Vidente /

This is the most recent of the true gifts to be discovered, October 1952. Since the discovery, there have been four recorded cases (all in the Americas). These individuals can transport their minds in the future or past of a particular object. It is an unpredictable gift, searching too far into the past or future leads to a stroke which usually proves fatal. The gift only works with inanimate objects.

Most noted Time Scanner: Pedro Sanchez. (1966 - 1982 AD.)

There are many cases in which individuals display more than one gift. There have been eleven instances of individuals having three gifts. It is hypothesised that if an individual has four true gifts and can use them simultaneously, that the sixteenth true gift appears in them. There have only been two reported cases: Bali, Indonesia, 1989 & Egypt, 2,100 BC. These are unconfirmed. It is thought that this sixteenth gift is the most—

'Damn it!' I hissed. The last paragraph ran into the next page, which Romand hadn't given me. 'Did he purposely leave me with a cliff-hanger or did he not want me knowing about his mysterious sixteenth gift?'

I looked over the explanation of the mind-switcher again, the entry Romand had referred me to, and it all started to make sense. The two kangals were obviously being used by mind-switchers, and that gift can be hereditary. I realised that Cathy and June were controlling the dogs. That would mean one of them had been controlling Pepe the previous night. My instincts told me it was Cathy! But why would she want to keep an eye on me?

I remembered Romand's words that morning: 'Someone likes you or doesn't trust you.'

I guessed it was because she thought I'd be rummaging in her room but a part of me wanted the real reason to be because she liked me. I really didn't have time to be thinking about girls, but Cathy was exciting in so many ways. And she had a gift, which made me want to know her better, even if the attraction wasn't mutual.

I read over the pages a few times then slipped them under the bed and went downstairs. As I reached the bottom of the staircase, Cathy brushed past me and pulled open the hall door.

'You not having dinner?' I asked.

'I have to go into town to pick up some stuff.'

'Hey,' I said, taking a step towards her, 'I'm sorry about shooting you today. I didn't mean to hurt you.'

'It's okay,' she said with a shrug of her shoulders, 'wasn't as painful as I made out. I'm sorry for shooting you in the neck.'

'I barely felt it,' I lied.

'I was actually going to shoot you in the ear, but changed

my mind for some reason.'

'Thanks.'

'I'll see you, Ross.' She grabbed hold of the door and took a step outside.

'Later, Pepe.'

Cathy poked her head back inside. 'What did you say?'

I winked at her and walked to the kitchen where the table was set and June was busy by the stove.

Romand was sitting on a wall by the back door smoking a cigar and looked round, giving me a questioning look. I nodded to him then asked June if she wanted any help.

'I'll tell you what I told Romand a million times: stay out of my way while I'm cooking.'

'All right,' I said. 'I'm not much of a cook anyway.'

'It's a big world, isn't it?' Romand said when I sat next to him on the wall over-looking the picturesque farmland.

'Bigger than I ever imagined. It's like cryptozoology or something; you hear about some of this stuff, but never actually think it's real.'

'Everything in that paper is real and most of it is quite dangerous.'

'Dangerous in what way?'

'Never mind. Did you read up on mind-switchers?'

'Yes. Cathy and June control the dogs, don't they?'

'They do,' Romand chuckled. 'It's incredible, isn't it?'

'It messes with my head! To think that they can actually live in the body of another being! That's nuts ... but really cool too!'

'Cool if used in the correct manner.'

'How do you know all this stuff, Romand?

'Come inside. We can talk about it over dinner.'

We sat opposite each other and June took the seat at the head of the table, I figured it was some sort of tradition, and after all, it was very clear that June was the boss of the house. There was quite a selection of food laid out: roast beef, mashed and roast potatoes, mixed veg, Yorkshire puddings and ham. I helped myself to as much of it as possible.

While we were eating Romand told June that he'd given me some pages from his paper on the true gifts. She didn't raise her eyes from her dinner and said very little. As if she knew this would mean a difficult conversation was to be had. One she'd rather avoid.

'He has also figured out your trick with Pepe and Bebe,' Romand said with a nervous grin on his face.

'Has he now?' She finally looked up and smiled at me. 'Cathy and I use the dogs for security. You see, having a true gift means that your life is in constant danger. People are searching for the gifted, for all the wrong reasons. We chose the kangal breed because of their power, agility and size. Once we control their bodies we can outmatch any human who may pose a threat to us.'

'What happens to your body, your actual body, when you

transfer your mind?'

'It becomes still, as if unconscious, but we remain inside our own bodies on a subconscious level. If we sense danger to our actual bodies we can snap out of the mind switch.'

'That's freaky!' I gasped. 'How can your mind be in two places at once?'

'All human minds are split in two, Ross.' Romand added. 'There is the conscious and subconscious. The majority of humans cannot separate these two sides to their minds though. Mind switchers can.'

I nodded at him like I actually knew what he was going on about.

'That's not quite accurate, Romand,' June said. 'In fact all humans split their minds each night when they dream. The conscious mind takes a break and the subconscious takes over and vice versa when the individual wakes. Most humans don't have much of a grasp on how it happens and have very little influence over it. It's simply instinctive for most people. Mind switchers manage both sides of their minds very well. This allows us to transport the conscious part of ourselves into another body.'

'That's a pretty cool gift,' I said. 'Something is bothering me though: why are gifted people always in danger? Surely we should be cherished by the rest of the world.'

'We *are* cherished, in a way, by those who know of us. But greed is a trait that runs in most people and those with the true gifts can generate an awful lot of money. Especially for people like Golding.'

'That's another thing I wanted to know. I read up about psychokinetics and in the paper it said there were only two: you,' I pointed at Romand, 'and Sarah Golding.'

'The paper was written twenty years ago,' Romand said.

'I know. But,' I see-sawed my hands in the air, 'Sarah Golding is a psychokinetic, Paul Golding organised the contest. It seems like more than a coincidence to me that they both have the same name. You know, it's not exactly a common name.'

Romand looked to June and she pushed her plate to the centre of the table and folded her arms.

'I suppose you should know how it all came to this,' she said. 'Sarah was Paul Golding's older sister. She was a psycho-kinetic of immense power and her brother was a brilliant busi-ness man. Together they created a vast fortune in the seventies and eighties; he made investments in large corporations, she would use her gift to secretly damage competitors. For exam-ple he once set up an airline, a few months later his sister used her incredible moving abilities to rip a wing off a plane from a competitor airline as it was about to take off from a runway. Customers flocked away from the competitor, thinking their crafts were unsafe, and *Golding's* airline took on all these new customers. That one incident earned him millions of dollars. It is but one of many examples I could give you. Golding owns shares in thousands of companies around the world. Share prices went sky high in every company he invested in. In 1983 the Goldings set up Golding Scientific, they hired over a hundred top scientists to search out and investigate superhuman gifts. The ultimate goal was to locate and hire other people who had the gifts.

'Professor William Davidson discovered that there were fifteen true gifts and he found a number of people who displayed the powers that you have read about. One was a young French lad, Marcus Romand, who had two gifts. You see, Golding was greedy and wanted more and more money and power. He intended to use the gifted to attain the wealth he desired, but he realised he would need gifted people without morals, people who didn't mind murder being part of their job description. This wasn't an easy task and when he could not find gifted people who were naturally evil, he tried his best to make them bitter and twisted.'

'How could he do that?' I asked. 'You can't change a person's nature.'

'Unfortunately you can,' Romand said sombrely. 'He found a way.'

'How?'

'He found that by murdering a relative or a spouse of a gifted person he could make them desire revenge, which leads to retribution and also to psychological damage and can make a person instinctively violent.'

I looked across the table at Romand. 'Did he do that to you?'

'Yes ... I do not speak of it though.'

June rested her hand on Romand's. 'And you don't have to speak of it now.' She turned to me. 'Romand didn't give in no matter how hard they tried to hurt him. He remained a good man with a clean conscience. Others weren't so lucky though.

'Golding's most powerful employee was always his sister, but she had limits to what she would do for money. And so, in 1993 he had her husband murdered. She was in London at the time and Golding's men paid a young thug to carry out the despicable act. A few days later, Golding gave his sister the name and address of the teenage brute and allowed nature to take its course. She went to a run-down flat with the intention of tearing that kid to shreds. She never left the flat. The teenager did though.'

'He had a gift too?'

'No. Only a gift for killing and violence. He somehow outsmarted her and stabbed her to death in the kitchen with a steak knife. Golding was quite infuriated, as you can imagine, but was so impressed by what the thug had done that he hired him as his personal bodyguard. The boy grew into a man and he injected even more malice into Golding's activities.'

'How could anyone do something like that?' I wondered. 'That's the most disgusting thing I've ever heard! He actually *hired* the man who murdered his sister.'

'Yes,' Romand said. 'Golding's desire for money was much powerful than his love for family. Golding saw a killer instinct, a ruthlessness, in the youngster that he believed could make the corporation money, or at least protect it from losing money.'

'Who was this youngster?'

'His name was Derek Shaw.'

'The same—'

'The very same,' Romand said. 'They intended for me to take Sarah Golding's place, but I managed to escape them with the help of June and her late husband who was a talented electro-psych.'

'We,' June said, 'are part of a network of gifted people from all over the world. We help each other and we keep our eyes open for others with the true gifts and try to save them before Golding, or someone worse, finds them.'

'Where does Marianne Dolloway come into all this?' I wondered.

'She was discovered when she was eight years old,' Romand said, 'in 1994, living rough and alone on the streets of Birmingham. There had been strange reports that a child had attacked a group of teenage skinheads, killing three of them and seriously injuring the rest. No one really believed it, but someone had killed those men, so the police were investigating. Golding thought the story pointed to a gifted being involved and his people picked her up before the authorities could find her. I was still part of Golding's corporation at the time and was one of the first to meet her. She was exceptionally powerful even at such a young age but displayed the gift in sinister ways ...'

'What do you mean?'

'She could do things that took me, and even Sarah Golding, years to learn. It seemed that she had already been trained by people who knew much more than us about the true gifts. She knew how to use her metallisir gift to melt moving objects like bullets, she had already started to use her emotomagnet gift, which most don't until they're almost in adulthood, and her psychokinesis appeared to be most developed in combat scenarios.'

'But who could who train her better than Golding's staff?'

Romand and June looked at each other worriedly and didn't give me a direct answer.

'We have no idea,' June said finally. 'But she was everything that Golding had been searching for.'

'Which meant I was surplus to requirements,' Romand added. 'That is when I escaped. Shaw and his men hunted me like a dog until June found me and hid me here.'

'Marianne became the most powerful psychokinetic there has ever been,' June told me, 'and she had a violent streak in her. This was exploited when she was fifteen years old and had fallen in love for the first time. Shaw killed her boyfriend, a boy called Peter if I remember correctly, and she became a flesh and blood weapon. Unfortunately Marianne's emoto-magnet skills were still underdeveloped at the time and she could not read Shaw's emotions and see that he was the true killer. She might even have been saved if she'd discovered the truth back then. Alas, Golding and Shaw poisoned her young mind and she is now forever blind to the truth. She has grown bitter towards all others who have true gifts.'

'Why?'

'Shaw told her, and provided false evidence to *prove*, that Romand had murdered her boyfriend. Shaw is a snake. A despicable human being. He told her that Romand had been jealous of Peter, and that was why he murdered him. Romand had been Marianne's mentor and only friend up to that point. The sense of betrayal shattered her fragile mind and formed her into the monster she is now. After that deception she was capable of committing horrendous crimes: she brought down a plane full of passengers, tore down an office building, sank a ferry in the North Sea and maybe even worse. She has become an abomination.'

'She's practically a hired killer!' I muttered.

'The worst there has ever been,' Romand nodded.

'She's exactly what Golding always wanted, but in recent years she has caught his own disease: greed. She has demanded more and more money for using her gifts. This inspired them to set up The Million Dollar Gift to find a replacement.'

'You know the rest,' Romand said.

'Not quite,' I replied.

'Oh?'

'Tell me about the sixteenth gift.'

'You'd be better off not knowing,' Romand said. He grew quite agitated and poured a glass of wine for himself and took a mouthful. 'It is little more than a myth.'

'But it's mentioned in your paper. There was an incident in 1989.'

'You already have a lot to ponder,' June said. She began gathering cutlery from the table. 'Forget about that story. You need to focus on improving your skills. These are dangerous times for us; you need to be able to protect yourself if something bad was to happen.'

'Does Golding have other gifted people on his payroll?' I wondered.

'You have enough to think about for now,' Romand said. He blew a cloud of smoke over the table. 'In time, we will tell you more.'

'In time… how long will I have to stay here?'

'At least for the summer. You're still all over the TV and in the newspapers.'

'Can I give you some money,' I said to June. 'I don't want you guys paying for me like this.'

'You don't have any money,' Romand snorted.

'I have a lot of money, Romand.'

'But you can't access it. ATMs have cameras built into them;

you would lead Golding's people right to our doorstep if you withdraw any cash.'

'You mean I'll never be able to access the prize money?'

'You have no need for money right now. When the public attention has died down, I will help you get your money from the bank.'

'You know, Romand, it was never really about the money. I just needed to prove something to myself. That's why I entered. I wouldn't have even considered it if I'd known the trouble it would cause.'

'I know, Ross. When we joined our gifts and moved the elevator together our minds connected. I read your thoughts. I know there is no evil in you.'

'You sneaky—'

'I had to be sure about you before I brought you here.'

'And are you sure?'

'Yes. He is,' June answered. 'We are all very happy to have you as part of our family, Ross.'

My mind was racing that night and I didn't get much sleep. Although they kept telling me I was in peril, I felt very at ease, as though I'd discovered my true purpose in life. I'd found the right road after so many years wandering through obscurity and confusion. I was ready to face my fate.

Everything I used to be meant little to me now and even those I had once been so attached to seemed very distant and almost meaningless. I didn't want to return to my old life; the new life I was exploring was full of excitement and discovery and nothing could compare to it. Romand was like the big brother I never had, June was like the mother I had lost so long ago and Cathy was more and more alluring as the hours passed in the peaceful English countryside.

How could I ever go back to Dullbrook and be content? How could I ever turn my back on the true gifts and have peace of mind? There was so much to learn and experience, I would never be able to drag myself away from this new world I'd entered. This was the life for me.

One thing did bother me though: Dad. Even though I'd managed to reassure him for the moment, if I stayed here all summer, he'd be going out of his mind with worry, but I was under strict orders not to contact anyone close to me. I couldn't leave the old man like that though, I'd have to find some way of contacting him again and letting him know I was all right.

CHAPTER TWENTY -

Kingfisher

Eight days passed quickly at the Atkinson house and I trained night and day with Romand. He kept referring to combat training and advanced techniques, but all he was teaching me were the basics, which was beginning to infuriate me.

As the days went by Cathy seemed to warm to me and we often shared jokes over dinner or poked fun at Romand's accent. She still wasn't happy that she was staying in the pokey little spare room, but her mother insisted that I was to be made welcome, and was to get a good sleep each night.

On my ninth morning with the Atkinsons I moped down the stairs and fell into a seat by the table. Romand had pushed me hard the previous day and I felt like my head was made of stone, but I straightened and tried to look as vigorous as ever when Cathy joined me at the table.

'Morning,' I said, grinning like a fool. 'Sleep well?'

'You trying to be smart?'

'No! It's polite to ask people how they slept ... isn't it?'

'Bit of a stupid question if you ask me.'

June put some toast, eggs, bacon and a box of cornflakes in front of us and I tucked in immediately. I was expecting the usual scolding from Romand, but the room was quiet. He was nowhere to be seen.

'Where's Romand?' I wondered. 'He's usually nagging me to finish my breakfast by this time of the morning.'

'He had to go to London,' June said. 'Bit of urgent business, don't expect he'll be back until late evening.'

'What about the training?'

'He said you could take the day off.'

'A day off …' A smile grew on my face. I looked at Cathy and caught her smiling and staring at me, as if the news that I'd be at a loose end for the day pleased her. She quickly looked away and continued eating.

Later that morning I went to the training area in the barn and practised some of the techniques I'd been taught. I also spent over an hour trying to open the briefcase containing Romand's paper on the true gifts, but to no avail. I'd have given my new fortune to read the rest of the pages.

'Goddamn it! I need to know what the rest of paper says. Curse Romand and his secrets!'

The case would not open and boredom got the better of me at midday so I went strolling around the boundaries of the property, listening to music on an iPod Cathy had lent me. I was surprised by how good her music library was, it was almost as good as my own. Almost.

It was so peaceful and I was able to clear my mind of all anxieties about my gift, my home and the danger Marianne and Golding represented. I had left Dullbrook in search of a busy place to fit in and, ironically, I found myself feeling at home in the quietest location imaginable.

I went roaming and as I walked along the eastern fence of the property, beyond which was a yard filled with old tractors, cars, vans and machinery, I felt my precog gift awakening then sensed someone was approaching. I turned off the iPod and looked over my shoulder to see Cathy and Pepe walking through the field.

The big kangal suddenly rushed forward and jumped on me, he was as tall as me, and started vigorously licking my face. He looked like a killer, and probably could have killed me, but he was as playful as any young pet dog.

'Get him off me, Cathy!'

'Say "please"!'

'Come on, tell him to get down.'

'Magic word?'

'Please,' it killed me to say it, 'get him off. Quick, he just licked my eye!'

'Down, Pepe,' she commanded. The giant dog immediately leaped away and started running around us in circles.

'You look bored, Ross.'

'No, not really. I was just looking at this ... junk yard.'

'It wasn't always a junk yard. It used to belong to Mr Barnes, he used to sell farm vehicles to the local farmers. He died three years ago and nobody has ever showed up to take this stuff away. Kinda sad really, he was a lovely man, but he was totally alone in life. No family and hardly any friends.'

'At least he spent his years here,' I said, looking over the sprawling countryside. 'It's a beautiful place, you know. You must love it here.'

'I guess. It's a bit quiet though, I'd like to spend some time in a city, just for a change.'

'I was like that too until recently. The place I grew up is old-fashioned and nothing ever happens there. I spent most of my life wanting to live in a big city, then I spent one week in London and I'd had enough!'

'You're rich now! You could probably buy a place like this of your own if you wanted.'

'True. Maybe I could buy Mr Barnes' place. We could be neighbours.'

'Oh God, that would mean we'd always be bumping into each other.'

'Very funny.'

'I thought so.' Cathy smiled at me. 'You know, it wouldn't be so bad having you around … Kinda.'

'Wow. That's the nicest thing you've said to me since I arrived.'

There was a silence between us for a few moments before

Cathy said, 'How about some training?'

'I've had enough of those boring exercises that Romand comes up with.'

'I wasn't talking about Romand's beginner course. How about we have a go at something more challenging?'

'That would be cool,' I nodded. 'That would be *really* cool. Anything in mind?'

'Follow me,' she said playfully.

We headed out into the fields and I expected her to go to the barn but she took to a dirt path that led away from the house and down a sloping field and into a small woodland. When we were surrounded by the thick, old trees she searched out a small clearing and said, 'This place is perfect.'

'Perfect for what?'

'*Combat training.*'

'You aren't qualified to teach me combat training.'

'Oh, there's a university where people study combat training for the gifted?'

'Smart ass! You know what I mean.'

'Romand likes to keep his skills up to date and I usually help him out with his combat exercises.'

'Really?'

'Yeah.'

'I wanna do the same training that he does.'

'You might not be up to it …'

'Shut up! Bring it on, *Cathy*.'

'Right, *Ross*. You see the fallen tree trunk behind you?'

'Yeah.'

'Use your gift to lift it and stand it upright.'

'What's that got to do with combat?'

'Just do it!'

I took a long look at the dead tree, that was still very robust and looked very heavy, then focused my powers. I sucked in a sharp breath and the tree rolled over before one end was raised into the air. When it was perfectly upright I turned to Cathy. 'What's next?'

'You have to hold it in that position no matter what happens.'

'I can do that.'

'Take one last look at the tree before we begin.'

I did and when I turned back around Cathy was sitting on the ground, her eyes closed and her chin resting on her chest.

'Are you okay?'

She didn't answer.

'*Cathy*?'

Suddenly there was a deep growl coming from within the trees. It shook me to my bones when I heard it and the tree almost fell. I maintained my focus as best I could, but the growling continued and got louder and more aggressive. Then Pepe emerged from the shadows between the trees. He was not the passive dog that I had gotten used to, he was now a snarling, giant beast with black eyes full of murderous intent.

The kangal stalked into the clearing and showed his fangs. I was nervous, but now that I was looking out for it, I soon realised that I wasn't facing a vicious dog; I was facing Cathy who was just using the enormous canine as a vehicle for her mind.

The dog rushed forward and lunged at me with his jaws snapping. I leaped out of his way and rolled across the dirt. I saw the tree leaning to one side. I focused, but the dog snapped at me and caught hold of my sleeve.

I managed to escape by unzipping my hoody and freeing my body from it. Pepe ripped the hoody up, then came at me once again. I fired a slight blast of energy that jolted the dog backward. It didn't do much good because it only further infuriated the kangal, or Cathy, I couldn't quite figure it out.

Again I summoned a power from deep within myself and the dog was flung into the air and crashed into the bushes by the base of a tree. I was winning so far; the dead tree was still upright, but I was getting tired and didn't know much longer I could carry on.

Pepe emerged from the bushes looking aggravated. He bolted out of the undergrowth and charged right at me. I sent out a nudge at it, but it wasn't enough, the dog latched onto my trouser leg and wasn't letting go. It swung its head and I fell face first in the dirt. The dead tree rocked and almost fell.

I felt a sliver of anger and sent out a shockwave. The dog toppled over the dirt, but stood and growled, unharmed and undeterred.

Romand was right when he said these were the toughest dogs in the world. Pepe was unstoppable.

I rose from the ground, inspected my torn jeans then taunted the dog.

'Come and get me!'

The kangal got ready to charge, but before it did I had a moment of inspiration. Pepe raced forward, raising a cloud of dust in its wake then jumped at me. I pointed my hands at the ground, channelled all my powers downward and I was lifted into the air. Pepe slid to a halt and snapped at my heels, but I was over eight feet from the ground, levitating.

I looked at the dead tree. It was still standing. I was starting to realise that anything was possible!

Pepe abruptly sat down, shut his eyes then trotted off to sniff at the base of a tree. Cathy opened her eyes and got off the ground. She looked up at me and laughed, 'You're good. You're *real* good. Romand can't even do what you've just done.'

I slowly came floating back to earth and the dead tree crashed down behind me.

'I can't believe I just did that.' I looked at her and we both laughed from the excitement and exhilaration of using our gifts against one another. 'I didn't appreciate you chewing up my good jeans though! If you want to see me without them you only have to ask.'

'Don't flatter yourself,' she snorted, shaking her head. 'I've seen you in your boxer shorts already.'

'What?'

'The first night you were here ... Pepe was watching you getting into bed ...'

'You dirty little—'

'You'd have done the same if you were a mind-switcher!'

'Oh-my-god!' I said incredulously. 'I am truly shocked!'

'No you're not. You're a boy. Get over it.'

'I have to keep my eye on you in future.'

'You've been keeping an eye on me since you arrived, mister.'

'What do you mean?'

'I catch you looking at me.'

'Now, who's flattering themselves?'

'I have to flatter myself, no one else will.'

'Well ... I think you're kinda ... nice.'

'Okay ... that almost sounded like a compliment.'

'You're face is ... not bad for looking at. I mean ...'

'You're not too good at this, Ross, are you?'

'Oh, give me a break.'

She laughed then took the shredded hoody from the dirt and handed it to me. 'I think we've had enough combat for one day. Come on, let's find something to do.'

I followed her without question through the thick forest, down an incline and to the bank of a small, lazy river with long reeds on the opposite side.

'I come down here a lot,' she told me. 'You know, when I need some time away from my mum and Romand. I do my own training here too.'

'How can you train yourself using a river?' I asked, making a funny face at her.

'There are a lot of ways. Hey, are you good at this?' She stooped, took a smooth circular stone and fired it at the calm surface of the water. It skipped four times and she jumped and cheered. 'What do you think? Not bad, eh!'

I shrugged and picked up a stone. 'Let's see if I can do any better.'

I spread my feet apart took a very dramatic stance and threw the stone. It skipped five times across the river, then changed direction and continued skipping in an ever decreasing circle before it finally sank beneath the surface. 'Twenty three skips,' I bragged.

Cathy grinned ruefully at me. 'That's cheating! You and your bloody psychokinesis!'

'I can't help it. Just comes naturally to me.'

'I've an idea!' she said excitedly. 'This way!' She took me by the hand and hurried along the river bank until we reached a clear sloping patch of dirt to the side of a large oak. There was a tyre swing hanging from one of the thickest branches.

'You're on pushing duty,' she said.

'I can do that,' I replied as she climbed into the large tyre. 'How high do you want to go?'

'Real high! But don't you dare send me into the water. If you do, you will die!'

'I won't. Promise.'

I stood back from the river and gently summoned some power into my mind. I pushed the tyre and it swung slowly out over the river then back up over the bank. I sent more power towards it and Cathy screamed with excitement.

'Higher, Ross.'

Her joy was infectious and I felt an immense level of energy entering my body. I'd never been that content in my whole life and my strong positive emotions were drawing in an enormous amount of energy. Moving Cathy and the heavy tyre swing was like flicking a feather. I'd never felt so powerful, even when I'd smashed the block of Metaliglass during the tests.

The tyre swing was extended to its fullest and she roared with giddiness. It was dangerous, but I had total control over the situation, I figured I could have uprooted the giant oak if I'd wanted to. I swung her for as long she could laugh before her sides hurt.

'You have your uses,' she said as she jumped out of the tyre. She was unsteady on her feet and had to sit down. She removed her shoes and dipped her toes in the cool water. I sat next to her and we looked out over the peaceful waterway.

'Look,' I whispered, pointing at the opposite bank. 'It's a kingfisher. I've never seen one in the flesh before.'

'There's lots of them around here.'

'He's beautiful.'

'How about a closer look?'

'I'm not a good swimmer.'

'You don't need to be.' She closed her eyes and hung her head then transported her mind. The little bird sprung from the reeds and fluttered into the air. It glided fast over the river's surface and flew over my head.

It darted around the trees then hovered close to me before it landed on my forearm. I laughed and gazed at its glittering blue wings and bright eyes. It hopped up my arm and stood on my shoulder, chirping a tune. I laughed again; the bird was chirping the opening bars of *VivaLaVida* by Coldplay.

I laughed uncontrollably. 'Wow! That is the coolest thing ever!'

The bird hopped further up my shoulder and went silent. It watched me very carefully then tapped my cheek very gently with its beak. I was speechless and the kingfisher flew off across the river.

'You see how I do my training down here?' Cathy said suddenly.

'I do. You're incredible, really incredible.'

'So are you. I've met some gifted people in my life, but you're the best.'

'You're embarrassing me now.'

'I'm embarrassing you *again*, you mean. You went very red in the face when the bird gave you a peck on the cheek.'

'No comment.'

Cathy looked down at the white earphones hanging from my trouser pocket. 'You wanna listen to some music?'

'Wouldn't be very sociable for me to do that …'

'I meant we share the earphones.'

'Oh, I knew that. I was just joking.'

'You're silly.'

She took one earphone and pressed it into her left ear and I thumbed the other into my right. I searched for a good song, but she swiped the iPod from my hand. She flicked at the screen until she found a song she liked and pressed play.

'I love this band!'

'Me too.'

When the song was over, the iPod randomly went to another. I took a deep intake of breath and my eyes searched the river for anything I could comment on; it was a real lovey-dovey song!

'Shall I change it? Bit smoochy isn't it?'

'Leave it,' she replied. 'I think it seems appropriate in a way.'

'You do?'

We looked at one another and I felt her hand wrapping around mine. I leaned close to her and kissed her softly. Her arms swept over my shoulders and mine wrapped around her waist. I felt as if I was drawing energy into my body; I hardly noticed that we were both rising into the air and hovering out over the river.

'Don't let me fall,' she said, holding me tight.

I didn't know how I was making it happen. It was subconscious. It was like there was too much energy flowing into me because of how much joy the kiss had brought me. I didn't care though, it felt amazing! We were practically flying!

'Don't let me fall!'

'I've got you,' I replied confidently. I kissed her again. 'I'm not letting go.'

I don't know if it was just a coincidence or if it was something to do with Cathy's gift, but suddenly we were surrounded by a flock of birds that circled us over and over again. It was the most magical moment of my life.

Romand was sitting by the back patio doors when we returned. He was eyeing us very suspiciously, and I was thankful he wasn't an emotomagnet; it could have been awkward if he knew we had kissed.

'Hey, Romand,' Cathy said. 'How was the trip?'

'Not as productive as I had wished.' He looked at me and pulled a seat from under the table. 'Sit. Cathy, give us some privacy.'

When she left the kitchen I reluctantly sat. I felt like a child who was about to get an earful for not doing his homework.

'You two seem…'

'We talked, that's all.'

'Make sure it stays that way. Here,' he said, taking a few sheets from the table, 'take these and read them tonight.'

'More pages from your study on the gifts?'

'Yes. This may make up for the time we lost today.'

'Thanks, Romand. I want to thank you for all the things you've done. Without you I'd be still in that hotel with the vultures.'

'Try not to forget it.'

'I'll try my best.'

CHAPTER TWENTY-ONE

Advanced Techniques

I got under the bed sheet and turned off the overhead light, leaving just the bed-side lamp on to read the text Romand had given me. There were only three pages, numbered: *49, 50, 51.*

Fighting Strategies Using The Gift of Psychokinesis

Translation of Mongolian Texts, circa 13th century

These texts were found amid ruins on the eastern border of the Gobi desert that were excavated in 1923 by Sir Alfred Tompkins.

The author of the original material is believed to be Ala-Qush, a noted chieftain of Genghis Khan's.
Most of the text was destroyed. The following is what was salvaged.

I discovered my gift when I first left my mother and

began to travel with the men. Our caravan became lodged in loose dirt during heavy rains. I managed to lift the caravan, two horses and four grown men from a flooded section of the road using my will alone. News of what I had done spread quickly across the lonely plains of my homeland, and I was soon summoned to the tent of our tribal leader, who did not believe any man could have powers that only a god should have. He demanded I display this strange power so he could witness it for himself. My hands were bound and a sword was put to my neck. If trickery were employed I would have been put to death. My good name was upheld when I lifted his four sons from their chairs with my mind. Within weeks I had been drafted into the army, under the service of the great Khan.

I mastered its use on the battlefield. So skilful have I become that I do not arm myself with any conventional weapons during ground warfare. While on horseback I continue to use my trusty bow but I use my mind to direct any arrow I fire. I now have a rank of Chief and my days of frontline fighting are behind me. This has afforded me many hours to study this rare power. The results of my studies are contained within these pages.

Ala-Qush.

I found it amazing that I was reading the works of another

psychokinetic who lived eight hundred years ago, a man who fought alongside Genghis Khan! To think I had something in common with such a man.

I read on and the next two paragraphs were explaining the powers he had and what he was capable of, parts of which seemed quite familiar to me.

On the second page there was more enlightening text. It was arranged into three sections and had simple diagrams accompanying them.

Methods of increasing my power

1. Name given by Ala-Qush: Tornado
(Modern phrase by Alfred Tompkins: Spin Technique)
Spinning the body creates slight confusion within the mind, a subconscious panic over a perceived loss of control. Panic makes me extremely powerful for a brief moment. When I complete a spin I channel energy into my body, through my shoulders, arms and finally my hands. In the battle of Zhangjiakou, I managed to kill or maim a grouping of more than fifty soldiers of the Jin Dynasty using this technique.

2. Name given by Ala-Qush: Waking Nightmare
(Modern phrase by Alfred Tompkins: Power from false memories)

I have found this to be most effective while preparing for battle. I have created a waking nightmare: my wife and children being slaughtered by Jin spies. The fictitious scenario sends my emotions into turmoil and I can summon great energy for an extended period of time.

3. Name given by Ala-Qush: Pain Clouds
(Modern phrase by Alfred Tompkins: Mass Neurological Disruption)
I have recently invented this technique. It can be achieved by drawing large amounts of energy into my body then releasing it without any direction whatsoever. This leads to, what I call a cloud of pain. A large area is affected by this cloud and anyone in that area has their brain functions interrupted resulting in loss of muscular function and severe pain.

Killing techniques

1. Name given by Ala-Qush: Spirit Sword
(Modern phrase by Alfred Tompkins: Decapitation Slice)
This is the quickest and most humane method of killing. First I must draw in negative energy, saving it in my chest, then I swing one arm with all my strength, in a chopping motion. This seems to create an invisible disk

of energy which slices through the opponent resulting in them being severed in two. Death is instantaneous.

2. Name given by Ala-Qush: The Spear
(Modern phrase by Alfred Tompkins: Energy Shot)
This is a very similar attack to the slice, but the movement of the body is different. The energy must be channelled into the chest then both arms must be quickly stretched out in front with the index fingers touching. This releases a very precise bolt of power. The effect on the body of the enemy is deplorable and almost always fatal.

3. Name given by Ala-Qush: *Stone Swarm*
(Modern phrase by Alfred Tompkins: Small Projectile Firing)
Very effective when outnumbered in a ground battle. Small stones or other light projectiles require very little energy to move, even at incredible speeds. Pebbles can be fired so fast that they pass straight through the body of an enemy. I have perfected the technique of firing multiple small objects, and in different directions which can prove a very successful attack against a large number of men.

Defensive Manoeuvres

The Emperor Xuanzong has long been aware of my powers and has been scouring his lands for someone with similar powers. In the battle of Yangtze, 1219, three Chinese soldiers emerged from the main Chinese force and targeted me directly. They all had the gift of moving. They had not honed their skills though and I defeated them quickly. The incident inspired me to develop defensive moves, in case a more powerful mover is ever found by the Jin.

1. Name given by Ala-Qush: Floating Falcon
(Modern phrase by Alfred Tompkins: Levitation)
Most effective in one-on-one situations. This technique is extremely difficult to master. One must draw energy from the earth itself then channel that energy back towards the ground, resulting in lift. Positive emotions work best when attempting levitation but this takes great discipline while in combat.

2. Name given by Ala-Qush: Air Shield
(Modern phrase by Alfred Tompkins: Deflection)
The easiest and often the most effective defence when under fire from arrows and throwing weapons. Short bursts of energy must be sent at the objects but calmness of mind is required. Once perfected, deflection can protect against projectiles of almost any size.

3. Name given by Ala-Qush: Wave

(Modern phrase by Alfred Tompkins: Energy Pulse)

All energy must be sent out of the body in a pulse. This results in a shockwave that surrounds my body and travels outward in all directions, protecting me even from a barrage of arrows.

I turned to the final page and there were only two short paragraphs, this disappointed me deeply; I could have read the combat techniques of this great warrior for hours and hours. I was starting to learn that the possibilities were endless.

I am now in the twilight of my life and illness is the opponent that I battle from day to day. My gifts cannot defeat this new and insipid enemy that slowly conquers me from within.

In life, rage was my only weakness. Pure rage can summon so much power that I kill or injure as many of my comrades as enemies. This happened twice in battle and I regret that over three hundred of my countrymen have died by my own hand. I see this strange power as a gift but without a sound mind it can become a terrible curse. My greatest fear is if this power was to fall under the control of a demented mind. It could lead to butchery on an unimaginable scale.

The next day began early and with Romand in bullish mood. He woke me at 6am and only allowed to me to have two slices of toast for breakfast. Once I finished the scant meal we left the house and headed across the fields to the training barn.

'What's on the cards today?' I asked, trying my best to keep up with the older man who was cutting through the long grass with great strides.

'We need to fine-tune your gift. You require much more precision when you force energy from your body and you must also learn to calm your mind. After that we will introduce some violence into the exercises.'

I considered telling him about the combat training that Cathy and I had done the day before, but decided against it. He seemed to be in a foul mood and would probably blow a fuse if he knew his training regime had been meddled with.

'Did you look at the text I gave you?'

'Yeah, it was an incredible read.'

'He was an incredible man, but alas he has been forgotten by history. If the world only knew what he achieved in life. It is their loss though, I only lament that most of the original manuscript was destroyed by the ravages of time.'

'Has Marianne read about Ala-Qush?'

'She studied all the works of military psychokinetics at the Golding Scientific vaults. She knows all the techniques and can produce them at will.'

'I really hope we don't ever have to fight her!'

Romand was about to say something, but held back his words and continued his march towards the barn.

'What is it?' I asked.

'Nothing.'

'Romand!'

'It's nothing that can't wait for another day.'

I had learned so much in my time at the Atkinsons, but I knew Romand was still keeping a lot of information from me. There was something being hidden, something dark and very serious. I wasn't really sure if I wanted to hear about it and I didn't pester Romand any further.

'You must learn how to manage your psychokinesis better,' he told me when we reached the barn. 'I have devised an exercise that will help you greatly in achieving higher control.' He held out a pencil with a string attached to it and a blank sheet of paper then placed them on the table top. 'You will write your name on this page in a legible manner.'

'I'm not allowed to hold the pen, right?'

'Right.'

I sat a few feet from a table and the pencil floated upward then the lead point fell against the page. It moved in a fluid motion for a few seconds, but what was on the page looked more like *4C53* than *ROSS*.

'Try again, but hold the end of the string.'

'What good will that do?'

'It creates a physical connection with the pencil.'

'But isn't this about *not* having a physical connection?'

'Yes, but it's also about training. Using your gift and having a physical connection means you will have more control. When you've done it with the string, you can try without it again.'

'This is confusing.'

'Your mind is making something simple into something confusing. Think! What object have you been able to control the best?'

'My skateboard.'

'An object that you move with your mind, but also touch with your feet.'

'Ah, now I get it.'

'No. When you have written your name, legibly, you will have *got it*.'

It took five attempts to write my name in a way that anyone could read. First it looked like *4C55*, then *4055*, *R055*, *R0S5* then finally *ROSS*.

Romand patted me on the shoulder and actually smiled for a change. 'Excellent. I had expected that it would have taken most of the day for you to get it right.'

'You underestimate me.'

'Don't get too cocky! Now try without holding the piece of string.'

It took me over an hour to get it right without a physical

connection with the pencil. My signature wasn't very neat, but I'd learned the lesson Romand was trying to teach me. The power was much more accurate when any type of physical connection was made.

We then tried a similar, but much more difficult exercise. I was to write my name on the wall of the barn with a spray can. This required much more concentration; I had to elevate the can but also had to have precise control over the button on the cap. I failed miserably until Romand tied a piece of string to the can. I held the other end and passed the test after ten attempts. I couldn't do it without the string, no matter how many times I tried.

I was greatly disappointed, but Romand told me it was one of the most difficult tests he'd ever invented, and he couldn't even complete it himself. I didn't like failure though; I promised him that I would try every day until I got it right.

'Let's leave this one for today,' he said. 'We should move on to something new.'

'Do you have anything in mind?'

'Yes. Let's try to kill one another.'

'What?'

CHAPTER TWENTY-TWO -

Combat

We both put on fencing masks, stood twenty feet from each other then Romand threw a pebble in the air and it froze, six feet from the ground, between us. It was perfectly round, about the size of a marble, and was rotating very slowly.

'Couldn't you've picked something a little more intimidating than a pebble?'

'It's as dangerous as a bullet when it's travelling at the speed of sound.'

'I take your point.' I remembered the entry in Ala Qush's text about small-projectile firing and how precarious it was. 'How do we do this?'

'The pebble is under my control,' Romand announced. 'I intend to hit you with it. You must deflect it, avoid it or steal it.'

'Doubt we'll ever see this in the Olympics.'

'Focus! You can pick up very nasty injuries during this exercise.'

'I'm ready.'

I was expecting the pebble to be shot directly at me; instead it flew straight though the open entrance of the barn and into the open air. I wouldn't see the attack coming. I would need to use my precognitive skills if I was to avoid being hit.

There was a bang on the roof of the barn as the pebble broke through and it came towards me at incredible speed. I sensed it just in time and jumped from its path. The projectile clattered the ground and whizzed back outside again.

I straightened myself and saw Romand grinning confidently at me through the mesh of his mask. Meanwhile the pebble was flying around the outside of the barn again and was picking up speed. There was bang at the end of the barn and the pebble came straight at my face.

Just before the impact I managed to conjure up an outward wave, the defensive technique I'd read about, and the pebble bounced away and rattled around the floor. I tried to seize control of it, but Romand was too quick for me and sent it shooting out through the entrance once more.

I sensed danger from behind and rolled across the floor as the pebble burst through the corrugated metal of the barn and cracked off the ground. I watched it ricochet into the air and then focused my precog gift. I predicted its flight-path and reached out with my psychokinesis and took control of it.

I slowly stood and laughed at Romand who was looking very nervous as he caught sight of the pebble whizzing through the entrance and back out into the open air.

'I hope you had your Weetabix this morning, Romand.'

'Give it your best shot.'

'I intend to!'

The pebble penetrated the roof and came shooting down at Romand who used a simple deflection manoeuvre to avoid being hit. The pebble clattered around the barn like a pinball for a few seconds then shot through some hay bales. It was headed for Romand, but he used the outward wave to protect himself. The pebble rolled across the floor then stopped dead in its tracks. Romand had taken control of it once more.

I focused my power on it and we both tried to gain sway over the pebble. It was wobbling and was spinning erratically through the air. It zigzagged around the barn as we both attempted to take total control over it but neither of us could outmatch the other. I'd never actually experienced something like this before. There were two psychokinetic forces trying to dominate the pebble and instead of feeling weaker, I felt stronger, as if some of Romand's power was being transferred to me.

'Both of our gifts are occupying the same space and time,' Romand shouted to me. 'Does it feel like your power has doubled?'

'Yes. Feels like I have too much power and not enough control.'

'Be wary of situations like this. The added power can make

you complacent but be warned, this is when you are most vulnerable to your opponent.'

'How?'

'You have created a channel of energy between your body and the pebble. My power surrounds that pebble. I can force all my power along your path of energy and into your body. This will kill you.'

'I'd rather you didn't do that.'

'Never do something like this in a real fight with one of the gifted. If they are knowledgeable about the gifts they will use your channel to take your life.'

'Shall we continue or is it too dangerous?' I shouted. We were still fighting for control of the pebble.

'For the sake of the game, we can continue.'

I remembered that Romand had said he didn't have the purest form of the gift, that he could never summon as much energy as I was able to. That meant I *could* defeat him. I realised that anger was the key to winning. If I made myself angry I'd be able to win.

I thought about all the bad things in my life: Reynolds, my mother dying, Marianne stealing my thunder at the press conference, Shaw's manipulative ways, the gang who used to shout at me in Dullbrook.

I felt power radiating from the atmosphere around me. I sucked it in then directed it at the pebble. I held my hand out and the pebble flew into my grasp.

'I think that would decide the game,' I said. 'Or do you want me to fire at you using all of my anger?'

'I would rather you refrained from doing that,' Romand panted and he pulled off his mask.

He was visibly shaken and his face was damp with perspiration. 'I applaud your skills.' He sat on one of the tables and sucked in heavy breaths. 'You may have a chance of defending yourself from other gifted people after all.'

I took off my mask and threw the pebble through the entrance it landed harmlessly in the long grass. 'Will it be enough?' I asked.

'No. We also must train in more realistic combat … although I am not looking forward to it after this exercise.'

'I'll go easy on you,' I laughed, putting my hand on his shoulder. 'You know, I'm starting to see why you're so worried about the fifteen true gifts. They really are dangerous.'

'You have no idea, Ross. You have no idea.'

Romand shadowed me for the next three days, but whenever he wasn't around Cathy and I would spend time together. Most of the time we just talked about the movies and music we liked but some times we talked about our gifts. I told her how I discovered mine after my mother died and how I'd hidden it from everyone. Her story was very different; June knew Cathy had the gift of mind switching when she was only an infant, and had nurtured the gift throughout her childhood.

Cathy's life story was amazing. She'd grown up surrounded by people with true gifts. Both her parents had gifts and had mastered them and taught her the best and easiest ways to develop her own. That in itself was incredible, but she told me her parents' friends were all gifted and they often visited the farm. She'd seen so much. Precogs who could predict her every move. Electro-psychs who were able to draw visible electricity from the sky. Light tuners so powerful they could mimic a person's likeness from the light in a room. Sirens who could make you fall asleep by singing a certain note. I really was only taking my first steps into a bigger world.

As we learned more about one another our bond seemed to strengthen. We were real opposites, but that meant we had so much to learn from each other, which made us want to be together more and more. She was beautiful too. I would never tire of watching her. Never get bored with the sound of her voice. Never be indifferent to the touch of her hand. Never get complacent with her kisses. Never would I want to be without her.

My new home was a paradise, albeit with one dark cloud above it: Romand's training.

Each day there were new and increasingly difficult training exercises, but I mastered each technique. We did a lot of training, similar to the pebble duel, related to combat, but there were other, less exciting, tests I had to complete.

There were quite a few weight tests. I had to drag Romand's car along the dirt road surrounding the farm, I also had to lift a three-ton tractor around Mr Barnes' junkyard, there were also heavy rocks and I even had to lift Bebe and Pepe a couple of times. It was straightforward stuff but often left me worn out and irritable. They were nothing compared to the laborious training with multiple objects though.

Romand brought me to the forest where Cathy and I had done some combat training. He sat me at the base of a young tree then shook it as hard as he could and for as long as his arms had strength in them. I had to stop any falling leaves, and there were hundreds, from touching the ground. It took immense concentration and I usually had to rest after it.

The worst of the lot was the 'fistful of dirt' exercise. Romand scooped up a load of loose dirt with his hand then tossed it into the air. It was my task to bring the expanding cloud of dirt back together, into a ball, and to catch in one hand. It was mind-numbing and took me endless hours to get right, but Romand insisted it was necessary.

I'd been at the Atkinsons' house for over three weeks and I'd really gotten used to the way of life, but I could never get used to being woken at the crack of dawn by Romand, shouting that I had to get ready, and training all day. I told him over and over that I needed a few days off, but he wouldn't listen; he insisted that I had to be prepared for real combat, and that it could come at any time.

During my fourth week at the Atkinsons' house, Romand woke me one morning and told me the day had come to do some *proper* combat training. We spent a few hours practising Ala-Qush's defensive and offensive manoeuvres, and a few that Romand had invented himself then went back to the house for lunch and a short rest. When we finished our lunch, Romand asked Cathy and June to accompany us back outside. I thought we were headed for the barn, but he brought us to a section of the field that he'd mowed the previous evening.

'Since you are stronger than me,' Romand said, 'Cathy and June will be on my side of this fight.'

'That's not fair!'

'Yeah, Romand,' Cathy shouted. 'Give him a chance.'

'Life is not fair!' the tall Frenchman told us. 'Do you think it would be fair and evenly-balanced if he was to be attacked by Golding's assassins?'

'It's okay, Cathy,' I said. 'Romand is right.' I looked around at the square patch of short grass and there were no objects to use. 'So, how do we fight?'

'Using only our gifts. Cathy and June will periodically throw stones at you to break your concentration.'

Neither of the Atkinsons looked happy about the game, but both agreed to do what was asked of them. They gathered some small stones from the field and stood on the sidelines, waiting for the duel to begin.

'We will fight in rounds,' Romand said as he positioned

himself at the opposite end of the square to me. 'To win a round, one must knock the opponent to the ground. The first to win five rounds will be the winner. Prepare yourself.'

I psyched myself up and my mentor stood calmly with his feet close together.

'June, would you count to three,' he said.

'One… Two… Three!'

Romand spun on the spot and sent a powerful bolt of energy at me and I was sent into the air and crashed into the long grass outside the pitch. I sat up rubbing my chest and groaned loudly. 'Jesus, that hurt!'

'It was meant to. The first round goes to France!'

I took a moment to gather my thoughts before I took up my starting position again. June counted again and I sensed my opponent's next move. I jumped to the left as Romand fired a bolt at me. I summoned energy and used the spear technique to send a precise burst of energy across the pitch. Romand dodged it and laughed.

I fired another spear bolt but missed. I then had to leap away from a wave of energy that slid under my feet. A stone struck me on the forehead as I was preparing a counter attack and I stumbled and fell.

'England!' Cathy shouted and her mother gave her a high five.

'This isn't fair,' I muttered as I got to my feet. 'I'm fighting the united nations here!'

'Come on, Ross,' Cathy shouted.

'You cheer me on after you hit me in the mush with a bloody stone! I'll never understand what goes on inside a woman's head.'

'Enough!' Romand commanded. 'Round three!'

I took the initiative and levitated into the air. This seemed to take everyone by surprise and they didn't know quite what to do. Romand was dumbfounded for a moment and just stood there staring at me. I suddenly came back to the ground at great speed and fired a simple nudge at my opponent.

Romand ended up on his backside, rubbing his face.

'Ireland fights back!' I bragged. I winked at Cathy and she giggled. Her mother was not impressed with this and rolled up her sleeves and frowned at me.

The fourth round lasted quite a while; I was using my precognitive skills and was avoiding Romand's attacks and the stones being hurled at me from the sidelines. Eventually I ran at Romand and created a disk of energy that sent him off his feet and onto his back.

'Two a piece,' I said proudly.

During the next round Romand showed his experience and when he was under pressure he used body refraction to cloak himself. Nothing happened for a moment and I used my precog skills to sense where the attack would come from.

June threw a stone at me and broke my concentration for a second, before I knew it I was sent up into the air by soft burst of energy and came hurtling down heavily.

Romand appeared out of thin air and was smiling down at me. '*Vive la France!*'

I couldn't help but laugh as took up the starting position again. I would need something very special if I was to win the match; all the odds were stacked against me and Romand was a lot craftier than I expected.

The sixth round was an intense one. I manoeuvred around everything that was thrown at me and eventually caught Romand off guard with another spear of energy. The score was level once more.

'One ... Two ... Three!' June shouted and the game restarted.

The Atkinsons threw stone after stone at me, but I managed to deflect every one while still focusing my precog gift on what Romand was planning.

The Frenchman slowly circled me and sent constant little nudges to keep me off balance.

'Let's see what you're made of, old timer!' I shouted.

'Dodge this,' he replied as he twisted his wrist and created a white orb that grew from his tip of his index finger. Suddenly it was as big as a beach ball and was so bright that I had to shield my eyes.

June threw a small stone and it caught me right in the privates. I let out a long moan and fell to my knees. 'Oh, you ... how could you ... oh....'

'Oh, I'm so sorry, love!' she pleaded. 'Really I am. That was a lucky one … unlucky one should I say.'

'It's all right,' I said as Romand helped me to my feet.

'You okay to continue?' he asked. 'That looked painful.'

'It was.' I took a very deep breath and stood up straight. 'I'll struggle on.'

'You could say it was a low blow!' Romand chuckled. 'The score is my four rounds to your three,' he continued. 'If you lose the next round you lose the match.'

'I know, I know.'

'June, will you do the honours.'

'One… two… three!'

I opened my arms wide, created an outward wave and was immune to all attacks. I kept the wave flowing from my body until I sensed Cathy was about to throw a particularly heavy stone at me. When she fired it I cut off the wave, allowed the stone to reach me then used my power to deflect it and send it straight into Romand's privates.

June and Cathy snorted and laughed uncontrollably as he collapsed to the ground, roaring like a moose in heat.

'Sorry,' I shouted to my mentor. 'Low blow and all that.'

It took five minutes for Romand to compose himself and get ready for the last round of the match. He scowled at me and raised his fists, ready to strike out with all his power.

I stood very still, my face was blank and my fists were clenched. I was *not* going to lose this fight. I remembered the texts of Ala-Qush and decided to use the forced anger technique. I remembered the day my mother passed away, how angry I was and how confused I was when I first realised my power. Energy was drawn up from the ground around my feet and filled my body.

'One... two... three!'

I didn't wait for an attack; I forced negative energy into my right fist, raised it above my head then bent down and punched the ground. A tremendous wave of power blasted out in all directions and my three opponents were lifted off their feet and fell into the long grass.

I stood up and lifted my hands victoriously. 'I would say that is game, set and match to Ross Bentley.'

Romand sprang to his feet and went to the Atkinsons. 'Are you both unharmed?' he asked, helping June to her feet as he watched Cathy emerging from the long grass.

'I'm all right,' June said. 'But my hair's probably a mess.'

'Me too,' Cathy said.

'Good. Very good, Ross. You used anger to be victorious, but you managed to control it, and not harm us. The greatest danger is to lose control; innocent people can get hurt if that happens.'

'Enough of this for one day,' June said. 'The evening's upon us and I think we're all a bit tired and more than a little hungry.'

'Can we order a Chinese from town, Mum?' Cathy asked.

'Something wrong with my cooking?'

'No… but… maybe we can do something special to celebrate Ross' victory?'

'Chinese it is,' Romand interrupted. 'I'm buying.'

'Romand, you're the best!' Cathy cheered. 'Let's go have a look at the menu!'

Romand really splashed out on the dinner. There were dishes of Pork Chow Mein, Chicken Curry, Sweet and Sour Pork, Duck and Black Bean Sauce, lots of egg fried rice and BBQ spare ribs. We couldn't finish it off and a lot of leftovers went to Bebe and Pepe.

By nine, after a few glasses of wine, Romand was exhausted; the battle with me had left him no energy and his eyes were growing red. He was a bit tipsy and was starting to smile, which he didn't do very often.

'This wine has gone straight to my head,' he said with a goofy grin. 'I should probably go to bed. I will never tire of being able to simply go to bed and dream without fearing that some nasty little assassin will find me. You know, this is probably the safest place in the whole world. I am forever in your debt,' he said to June as he raised his glass.

He drained it, 'May your home always be a safe haven for you and future generations of the gifted.'

'Come on, Romand,' June said. 'You should get yourself to

bed, because if you fall asleep in that chair we'll never get you moving.'

'You're right,' he replied. He pushed his chair from the table and stood slowly. 'Good night all. Ross, I shall wake you at seven in the morning.'

'Good night, Romand.'

'I'm going up too,' June said. 'I'm dead on my feet.'

Soon Cathy and I were alone, even the kangals had padded out of the kitchen into the hallway where they slept off their meal. Cathy slipped off her seat and sat next to me. We held hands without even thinking about it then shared a long, passionate kiss.

'I've been dying to do that for days!' I whispered. I pressed my forehead against Cathy's and rubbed my nose on hers.

'Me too. Romand has been like a hawk though.'

'What's his problem?'

'When my father died he promised that he'd always look after me. He doesn't mean any harm by it, he's just a very loyal person and it makes him a bit over-protective. Think of him as a big brother.'

'I already do. I think he's hiding something really important from me, though. Do you know what I'm talking about?'

She leaned close and kissed me then wrapped her arms around my back. 'Let's not talk for now.'

'Suits me,' I said, hopping my eyebrows.

We spent almost an hour together before Bebe padded into

the kitchen and sat watching us very closely. We both knew June was controlling the dog so that she could keep an eye on us.

'I'd better head off to bed,' Cathy said. She turned and looked at Bebe. 'Seeing as we can't get any privacy here!'

The dog barked at her and she left the table and gave me a peck on the cheek. 'Good night, Ross.'

'Night.'

I waited for an hour in the kitchen for the house to grow silent. When I was sure everyone, including the dogs, was sleeping I crept to the sitting room and switched on the light. There was a telephone by the window and I sat next to it and lifted the receiver. I knew I was breaking their trust by making the call, but it was something I had to do. I couldn't leave Dad alone in Dullbrook worrying about me.

The conversation wasn't a pleasant one and there was lots of shouting coming down the line. Eventually I calmed him down and assured him I was safe, but couldn't return until the media attention died off. He seemed to believe me, even though I was lying through my teeth; I had no idea of when I could return to Dullbrook to see him. I wasn't sure if I'd *ever* return.

I told him I'd call again in a few weeks then ended the call. I was about to head off to my room when I thought about Gemma, my one true friend from home. She was probably worried about me and I thought it would be for the best if I made a quick call to her. Just to put her mind at ease.

The conversation started similarly to the previous call with lots of shouting, but she finally chilled out and told me she was just terrified that something might happen to me. I told her I was staying in England for a while and that I was with some really good people who were protecting me. She asked what I needed protection for, but I didn't tell her about all the things I'd learned about over the previous month. I cut off the call when I heard a thump from upstairs.

I switched off the lamp and quietly made my way to my room. I felt much more comfortable now that I'd made contact with Dad and Gemma and my night's sleep was a peaceful one.

Marianne Dolloway was sitting on the sill of the bedroom window of her London apartment, gazing out over the busy nightscape when a call came through on her mobile phone.

'Yes?' she answered coldly.

'Marianne,' a nervous voice replied, 'it's Golding.'

'I know who it is! You're the only one who has this number! What do you want?'

'I have some information that might interest you.'

'I'm listening.'

'Shaw, before his untimely demise, discovered that Bentley was close friends with Gemma Wright, a girl from his hometown. He instructed some of his intelligence teams to track her down and put a trace on her mobile phone. Obviously, without Shaw or Bentley working for me I no longer have any interest in her ... but ...'

'But?'

'But Ross Bentley just made a call to her.'

'Did you get his location?'

'Yes.'

CHAPTER TWENTY-THREE -

A Critical Mistake

Marianne woke early the next morning and stood naked in the bedroom gazing at her reflection in a full length mirror. Her preparations would begin before she even clothed herself. Her long silky white hair suddenly became alive, divided itself into long thick strands, then compressed and fused to form dreads. The dreads then wriggled around her head, medusa-like, and wrapped into an elaborate knot on the top her head.

When she was pleased with the way she looked Marianne opened a cabinet next to the mirror and applied white foundation to her face, then thick black make-up around her eyes and black gloss to her lips.

She paced to the wardrobe and spent a few moments rummaging then took everything she would need. First was a tight black body warmer over which she tied a leather corset. Then came a pair of leather trousers and boots with tall, sharp heels.

Then she took a small wooden box to her bed and opened it. Inside was a collection of rings and bracelets. She put a plain silver ring on each of her fingers and thumbs, then dragged at least twenty thin silver bracelets onto her wrists. There was a purpose to all the jewellery – she planned to melt the rings and bracelets into deadly projectiles and then fire them at lethal speeds. She needed no conventional weapons; her jewellery made her a walking machine gun.

Marianne returned to the mirror and gazed at herself again, now fully prepared for battle. She did a quick three-sixty and was pleased with what she was looking at. She was dressed to kill … literally.

By 11am she was on the street and her pursuit had begun. She felt like a predator; there was no fear in her and her confidence was flawless. She knew she could easily go to the location Golding had given her and collapse the entire house, killing everyone inside. That that would be too easy though and she would not get the answers she had sought for so long.

Killing Ross Bentley was just one part of her agenda. She also wanted to avenge Peter's murder by killing Romand, something she'd been desperate to do for many years. There was more to it than just murder though; this was also a priceless opportunity to obtain information from those who had been protecting Bentley and Romand.

For many years there had been a group of gifted individuals working against Golding's activities, but they were very good at covering their tracks. This was the lead she had been searching for so she could identify the shadowy group known only as 'the guild'.

Most important though was avenging Peter's murder. All the clues pointed to Romand. She'd had her doubts about the evidence at the time of Peter's death, but as the years went by she grew convinced of Romand's guilt.

Marianne was going to the house for revenge first, information second, but if her life was in danger she would cast aside her desire for answers and kill all in her way and dig for information after.

She paused on the pavement of a busy street and looked over a very flashy yellow sports car. It was perfect; just what she'd been looking for. She pressed a finger tip against the door lock and melted it, then turned the blob of aluminium clockwise until the door popped open. Once the alarm sounded she channelled both her psychokinesis and metallisir gifts into the engine bay and crushed the alarm siren. She then put her index finger to the ignition switch and twisted the barrel behind it and turned the engine on.

Seconds later she was rolling through the streets of London. The car growled loudly as she pressed her foot hard on the accelerator and she was pleasantly surprised, the car was faster than she'd expected. It wouldn't take too long at all to reach her destination.

Bentley and Romand would soon be dead and then she would squeeze answers from whoever was left in the house – and take pleasure in it – before they also were executed.

Romand and I took a break around noon and sat in the barn and talked about the true gifts, which was the weirdest, which was the strongest and which was the most dangerous.

I was stunned when Romand complimented me on how I'd improved over the weeks I'd spent with him. He even said I had the potential to be the most powerful psychokinetic that had ever lived.

'You really think so?'

'Yes. Perhaps one day you will be strong enough...'

'Strong enough for what?'

'Strong enough so that you and I can go searching for Marianne.'

'Why would we want to do that? She's seriously dangerous, *you* told me that!'

'Marianne is *too* dangerous. Too dangerous to be free... or alive for that matter ...'

'You want to hunt her down and kill her, don't you?'

'Yes,' Romand muttered, almost ashamed that he admitted it. 'Yes, I do.'

'You don't seem like the killer type, Romand.'

'You'd be surprised, Ross.'

'But why would you want to take such a risk?'

'I have a good reason.'

'Tell me.'

He turned to me and made me promise never to pass on what he was about to say.

'I can keep a secret, Romand. I swear I will never tell anyone.'

His mood was dark and he rubbed his forehead anxiously before he spoke.

'Romand?'

'You were asking about the sixteenth gift. I shall tell you so that you can make sense of my plans. The sixteenth gift was mentioned once, in an Egyptian manuscript dated to the time of Rameses the eleventh. One of the pharaoh's servants, a military leader, had four of the true gifts. It was said that during a battle with a rebel army he used the four gifts simultaneously and achieved the sixteenth power. It was thought to be a myth until 1989, when this mysterious gift reappeared.

'A young American man, James Barkley, had the gifts of psychokinesis, pyrokinesis, electro-psyching and precognition. A potent combination and he was courted by Golding Scientific who wanted him to work for them. He refused, no matter how much money they offered. This enraged Golding, who then hired a Mageleton to kill him while he was travelling in South-east Asia with some other young people, gifted people.

'The assassin tracked them down to the Indonesian island of Bali, murdered Barkley's friends, but failed to kill him. Barkley somehow used all four gifts together to defend himself and attained the highest power. The sixteenth gift.'

'What is this gift? This higher power?'

'It is the *Seductor Mortis*. This person has the power to bring death to the living and life to those who have passed.'

'You don't mean—'

'It's a monstrous gift. And it made a monster of a good man. Attaining this power shattered Barkley's mind and he grew demented within hours, which led to some appalling deeds on the island. His sixteenth gift meant he only had to brush off another living thing and they would die instantly. But more horrifying was the other side to this elusive power: he could raise the dead.'

'Like zombies?'

'I do not know exactly, the reports were not very detailed, but I do know that it is a power no human should command. He was given a name by the locals: "The Kematian". It's the Indonesian word for "death".'

'What happened to him?'

Romand's facial expression was troubled and he took quite a while to reply. 'No one really knows. Many have searched for the Kematian, but he has never been located. Ten years ago I accompanied other gifted individuals to Romania where there had been reports people rising from their graves. There was no sign of the Kematian though. A couple of years ago I heard a rumour that he had been captured and imprisoned.'

'By who?'

'Unknown.'

'What has all this got to do with Marianne?'

'When Golding's people first found her, as a child, they brought her into the science centre in California where I was living. She was a deeply troubled child and was often hysterical. Nobody could calm her down and I was asked to help. I was brought to the cell they kept her in and I tried to make her sleep by creating hundreds of tiny light orbs and spinning them around her room. To my surprise it seemed to make her drowsy and she gradually tired. I turned out the orbs as she fell asleep, but before I left the cell one orb reappeared. It was red in colour, was very faint and only lasted for an instant – but it was not of my making, I'm convinced of it.'

'She created it?'

'Subconsciously. Ross, she doesn't know she has a fourth gift. But if she were to find out … Marianne *has* read the story of the Kematian. She knows that four gifts used simultaneously releases the sixteenth gift. She cannot be allowed to achieve the *Seductor Mortis*, not someone as bitter and twisted as her. It would represent a threat to all humanity. I'm sorry to land all of this on you. It has been our greatest fear that she would realise her full power and this is a rare chance to remove her as a threat. We've never had someone as strong as you on our side, Ross, it is a golden opportunity to save the world from a disaster of immense proportions.'

I said nothing. I thought about taking the life of another

human being. Could I actually do that? I was no killer, but I guessed that if it was a choice between her and me that Romand would get his wish. I felt suddenly responsible for Marianne in some way, as if higher powers had created her, but could not manage her madness, and so I was given the power to destroy her. It was a crazy notion, but I couldn't get it out of my head.

'She has to be stopped, Ross.'

'I understand.'

'I have only been tough on you these last few weeks because I had to be. I needed to get you prepared for what you are going up against.'

'It's okay, Romand. I understand it all now. I understand why you're so serious all the time, you've had this heavy burden hanging around your neck for too long.'

'You will help me when the time comes?'

'Yes. Can I ask you a question though?'

'Go ahead.'

'Have you killed before?'

He said very little and began walking to the training barn nearby. When we got there he went to the briefcase containing his paper on the true gifts. He didn't open it, he carried to the house and led me to his room where he unlocked the case and took a single sheet and handed it to me.

I looked at the page, which bore an unusual logo, a wolf's head with sets of initials surrounding it.

'What does this logo mean?' I asked as I examined the page.

'It symbolises the fifteen true gifts and it often represents those who use them for the good of mankind.'

'It's a kick-ass logo.'

'It's your own choice whether you read this or not,' he said soberly. 'I will understand if you leave this place if you do choose to read it.'

CHAPTER TWENTY-FOUR –

An Uninvited Guest

I took the sheet of paper to my room and locked the door before sitting on the bed and placing it on my lap. I could clearly read the heading of the page and I really wasn't sure if I wanted to read on. I couldn't turn away now though. I braced myself and went to the first paragraph.

USING THE GIFTS TO TAKE LIFE
By Marcus Romand

It is with great regret that I admit to taking the lives of a number of people. My actions were never inspired by greed, hatred, passion or vengeance. It was always in self defence or at the behest of Paul Golding.

When I first came to work for Golding, as a young man, I felt liberated from a life of secrecy and shame.

The Golding Scientific centre was a bright new home for me. A place where I could openly display my gifts and meet others like me. I firmly believed my life was to be fulfilling and content.

As the years passed by, my gifts were exploited more and more by Golding and his minions. By the time I realised their true nature I was already in too deep and could not break free of the corporation. I became a reluctant assassin.

For many years I studied the works of military telekinetics / psychokinetics such as Ala-Qush, Roger McWilliams and Ali Homan, but also of warriors who used other gifts to take lives. I learned well from past masters. I was a reluctant, but efficient, assassin.

I owe my escape from Golding's clutches to the great electro-psych, Jonathan Atkinson. In my time with him, I learned of a way that is quicker and more effective than any other. Jonathan had incredible control over electricity and used it to send a small shock into the human heart, stopping it and killing instantaneously.

I have adapted this technique to psychokinesis. First I summon all my strength into my upper body then in one fluid movement I channel it through my arm and direct it out of my body through two pointed fingers (index and middle). A modest but very concentrated dart of energy is fired directly into the heart of the victim. The energy cripples the heart and death follows instantly.

It is the most efficient and humane way to kill. My only wish is that I never have to use it again. The true gifts should be used for the good of mankind but more often than not they are used by the corrupt and powerful of society to attain unnecessary wealth.

I will never be the good man that I once was. As soon as I killed my first victim my soul was to be a tortured one for all time. Using the gift to kill changes a person completely and they can never return to the life they once enjoyed.

I'd been very wrong when I said Romand wasn't the killing type. He *was* a killer after all, but he was wrong about a person being changed for all time. Romand wasn't a bad person, the fact that he regretted what he had obviously been forced into doing proved that to me. Would anyone have been able to do anything different if they had been in his shoes? I doubted it. I knew all too well how manipulative and influential Golding and his murderous puppet, Derek Shaw, were. Romand had actually saved me from a similar fate to his own by freeing me from Golding Scientific and all the evil people who were part of it.

Romand probably expected me to run a mile once I'd read

the page, but I was going nowhere. He'd saved me from an awful future and I intended to repay that debt. I was going to help him in his quest to save the world from the threat that Marianne posed.

I took the sheet and left the room to find Romand in his, sitting by the window smoking a cigar.

'Hey,' I said as I entered. 'You wanna put this back with the rest?'

He turned to see me holding the sheet of paper out towards him.

'You probably think I'm some sort of monster now.'

'No, Romand, I don't. I'll never think that and I'll follow you into hell when the time comes. I'm with you all the way.'

I could see he was smiling, but he refused to turn away from the window. I knew there were tears in his eyes. A man like him wasn't used to crying and I didn't want to embarrass him. I placed the sheet on his bed and told him I'd see him in the kitchen for dinner then left.

My mood changed once I reached the kitchen, where Cathy and June were chatting and giggling. They seemed so content in that moment, the way all families should be. Cathy looked at me when I entered and I knew she was the one for me. She had everything I could want in a girl: beauty, intelligence, creativity, humour – and of course one of the true gifts. I could fully understand Romand's attitude and why he was worried. There was so much to protect in that house and so much danger outside of it. I'd already lost my mother, and then been cut off from the home and family I had left. I wasn't going to let anyone take this new family from me.

I sat and watched and listened to them while dinner was prepared and tried to simply enjoy the moment. It was such a perfect evening. The patio doors that led to the back garden were wide open and a pleasant breeze blew inside to cool the kitchen after the stove had been on for the previous hour. Romand appeared as the sun was setting and darkness was creeping over the countryside.

He sat next to me and the atmosphere between us was calm, not like it had been before, when he was always so strict and secretive. I finally saw him in the way that Cathy did, as a big brother.

We shared no words as the dinner was placed on the table. Two bottles of wine were uncorked and a pot of hot tea was made. We were all set for yet another lovely evening together. I wished it would stay that way forever. The only thing that was wrong was Pepe who was sitting behind me panting and drooling. His breath was atrocious.

'Pepe, do you always have to breathe on me?'

He panted faster and barked loudly in my ear, which made the others laugh. I was half deafened though.

I was about to give out to the big, loveable mutt when he shuffled forward and licked my face, as he was very fond of doing. This made the others laugh even harder. Romand even managed a smile.

'Okay, okay, we can't have dinner with these two hanging around,' said June.

She left her chair and led both dogs out to the front yard and shut the door on them. Finally we could have our meal in peace.

When we were all seated and ready to eat Cathy decided to share one of her funny stories with us.

'I was in town this morning...' she laughed hard and covered her face.

'And?' June asked.

'I got even with Martin Brown!'

'Who's Martin Brown?' I asked.

'Oh, he is the world's crankiest man!' June replied, 'He makes everyone's life a misery in the town!'

'He owns a pet shop,' Cathy told me, 'I sat outside there today and switched my mind into one of his parrots and started talking to him.'

We all laughed, trying to imagine what the owner of the pet store was thinking and how white his face must have gone.

'Once I got inside the parrot's head,' she continued, 'I told him the sweater he was wearing smelt like ...'

Cathy paused and her mother slowly stood up and turned to the door to the hallway. There was an awful sound creeping through the house; the kangals were growling at something. Romand leapt to his feet, knocking over his wine glass as he stood. The dogs were baying loudly.

It got louder and louder until they were in a frenzy. We all knew something was terribly wrong. Some*thing* or some*one* unfriendly had arrived.

June instinctively turned to Romand for guidance, but he seemed stunned and for the first time I saw fear in his eyes.

Cathy, the only one still seated, dropped her chin and snapped her eyes shut. She'd switched her mind from her body. We all stared at her for a moment and the kitchen went dreadfully silent.

Suddenly she snapped out of it and crashed from her chair to the floor. She was utterly terrified by what she'd seen. Romand and I raced across the kitchen and lifted her up.

'What is it, Cathy?' Romand asked. 'What did you see?'

'She's here...' Cathy gasped. 'She's outside, Romand!'

'Who?'

'Marianne!'

June started crying and grabbed hold of Cathy. Panic was spreading in the kitchen and it got worse when we heard the terrible yelps from the front yard. I'd grown attached to Bebe and Pepe and it broke my heart to hear them being attacked. Cathy and June were growing hysterical; they loved those dogs as though they were family.

The cries of the kangals grew louder and more intense. It was hard to comprehend that any one person could fight, let alone hurt, such large dogs.

I felt frozen – one of the worst killers in history was right outside the house and I knew she'd come for me.

'What are we going to do, Romand?' June said, almost out of breath with worry. 'We have no way to get out!'

'To the attic, take Cathy and Ross with you.'

June pushed Cathy out of the room then turned and screamed at me to follow. I wasn't one for hiding though. I never backed down from a fight.

'I'm staying here with Romand!'

'No, Ross!' June shouted. 'Come! Now!'

'I'm staying right—' my words were cut short when Romand grabbed hold of my arm and flung me across the room like a rag doll.

'Protect Cathy and June,' he shouted. 'I'll try to draw her away from the house, when I do I want you to get out as fast as you can. Don't look back and don't stop for anything.'

'No!' I demanded as Cathy and June raced along the hallway and up the stairs. 'It's not going to end like this, Romand! It can't end like this!'

We heard a loud bang from outside the house and one of the dogs was silenced.

'Go, Ross!'

'You need my help. You know you can't do this alone.'

'Go!'

'Romand … I'm sorry … I called Dad and Gemma last night from the phone in the sitting room.' It had just dawned on me. It was I who had given our location away. 'I did this, didn't I?'

Romand stared at me and I knew he was fuming, but he simply nodded.

'You weren't to know. This conflict has been coming for a long time; I knew I couldn't hide forever. Do not allow guilt to overcome you, no matter what happens here tonight. Protect the others with your life, Ross. Go!'

I turned away and ran through the doorway then up the staircase and onto the landing. Cathy had already pulled down the wooden ladder to the attic and was climbing the rungs. I helped June up the ladder then followed and slammed the door shut. The attic was cramped and black. June was sobbing and Cathy kept whispering Romand's name over and over again.

There was no more noise from the dogs to be heard from outside the house. Bebe and Pepe had fought as best they could to defend their home and family, but it had been a fight they could not win.

I wanted to burst into tears, but I tried my best to stay composed and keep some measure of control. I had to do what Romand had told me. I had to for-sake him and to protect Cathy and June – if I could.

CHAPTER TWENTY-FIVE -

Duel

Marianne stepped over the broken and bloodied remains of the dogs then held out her hands. She sent a powerful shockwave towards the house and the front door smashed into a million splinters. She stepped through the open doorway and saw Romand standing, silhouetted by the light of the kitchen, waiting for her.

The fight with the kangals had been unexpected and the animals had been difficult to kill. Marianne had barely broken a sweat, though, and her inner power had simply been stirred by the tussle. As she stared down the short hallway at her nemesis, Marcus Romand, she felt her inner power begin to sizzle. That old anger was rising and it was rocket fuel for her gifts. She maintained self-control as she took a step forward. There would plenty of time to unleash her rage upon her old colleague.

'Good evening,' she said plainly. 'Hope I'm not imposing.'

'You'll regret coming here, Marianne.'

'Where is Bentley? I know you're hiding him ...' she craned

her neck and gazed up the staircase to her left. She sensed panic. It was coming from upstairs and it wasn't just Bentley. There were more people in the house. 'You are hiding more than just him.'

'This is between you and I.'

'Only for the moment. After I kill you I'll search the house and butcher the others one by one … after they've given me the information I seek, that is.'

'So everyone with a gift is now an enemy, Marianne? Did they *all* kill Peter?'

'You dare speak his name in front of me!' she hissed. 'After what you did to him?'

'Read my emotions, Marianne. Search my thoughts. My mind is open. You will see the truth.'

'There are only layers of lies in your mind, Romand.' Energy was coursing through her body as she grew more and more angry. She was ready for the fight.

'Let's see how good you really are.'

She stared at him, trying to read his emotions so she could guess his method of attack before he made his move. He had suddenly shut his mind though. Something Romand had always been able to do.

He didn't blink. He didn't move. He barely took a breath. Marianne would have to fight without the use of her emoto-magnet gift. This would be an old-fashioned duel: Romand's telekinesis and light-tuning skills versus her telekinesis and metallisiring abilities. She knew his gifts were not as pure and strong as her own – this was going to be fun.

She had fought the gifted before and knew the best method of attack was counter-offensive moves. That was why Romand was waiting for her to start the duel. She did, but not in the way he expected. She stepped forward then darted for the staircase, which forced Romand to act. He raised one hand and pointed his index finger at her.

A concentrated burst of energy came shooting out, cracked the banister in half and tore a hole in the wall. Marianne was unharmed and leaped from the stairs and into the hall.

She stared at him for a moment, as dust and debris fluttered around her. Marianne was naturally more powerful, but she knew Romand was very dangerous and was a skilful killer. They'd trained together many years before and she knew that only one would survive this battle. She had to be cautious until she landed a serious blow.

'I won't let you harm them,' Romand growled. 'Your days of killing the gifted end here.'

'Save your self-righteous bullshit for someone who believes in it. You and your guild are the ones who need to be stopped. I'm on the right side, Romand.'

'You are on your own side, Marianne. You care only for yourself. You've always been that way, even back when you were a child and we scooped you up off that street corner like a homeless kitten that no one wanted.'

She knew he was trying to make her lose control. She wouldn't give in to his taunts though. Her attacks had to be clinical yet powerful. It was time to put her old friend to the test.

She released a terrible blast of power that tore the plaster from the walls around her and blew Romand across the kitchen and up against the counter by the sink. It was only the first exchange, but it was clear that was a serious mismatch. Romand winced as he staggered to his feet. Marianne grinned at him from the hallway. She knew she'd broken a few of his ribs.

He quickly straightened himself and produced a strong defensive wave that swept the furniture in the kitchen towards the walls and pulsed into the hallway, keeping Marianne at bay for a few moments.

It didn't stop her for long. Marianne had a vast repertoire and quickly found a way of getting into the kitchen so that she could fight face to face with her old foe. It was a technique that only she knew, for she had invented it. She pulled energy into her body, up through her chest and cradled it in her arms. She caressed her hands in a circular motion and a sphere of psychokinetic energy was produced. When it was fully formed she flung it through the doorway and it bounced erratically around the kitchen, ripping a massive hole in the ceiling, smashing the tiled floor, cracking furniture and – most importantly – sending Romand darting for cover.

This was her opportunity and she seized it while her opponent was distracted. Marianne dashed through the hallway and slid across the kitchen floor behind the cover of the thick counter.

She didn't have any time to prepare her next move as Romand went on the offensive and started blasting precise bolts of energy at the counter. She couldn't risk staying where she was; if one blast broke through the counter she could be killed instantly.

She summoned her anger forward and released a powerful energy wave that shook the entire room and almost brought the ceiling down. She raised up and prepared a more concentrated attack, but Romand was waiting for her.

He fired a measured shot of energy at the kitchen counter and there was deafening blast. Glass, concrete and wood were blown to smithereens and sharp fragments of the debris doused Marianne. When the dust settled she casually plucked shards and splinters from her left arm as if she were flicking off dandruff. Marianne was powerful and she had a high pain threshold.

'I expected more from you,' she said grinning. 'After decades of training and all you can come up with are simple shockwaves and bolts you learned from reading old Mongolian manuscripts. How about I show you something more … *dynamic*!'

Marianne closed her eyes and sucked in breaths through

her nostrils then pointed at the ceiling and very slowly lowered her hand. She created a layer of energy that filled every millimetre of the room. It was so fierce that it was actually visible; the layer was affecting light and bright streams of white and red pulsed around the room. The layer of energy was falling lower and lower and would crush anything it touched. Romand's abilities could not defend against such a radical and dangerous technique. Marianne was finally getting the upper hand in the fight.

Suddenly there was a blinding light from across the kitchen that almost blinded her. A tiny blue light blossomed and grew rapidly into a large azure orb. Romand had created it and pushed it out across the room where it burst into a brilliant white explosion.

Marianne shut her eyes just in time. A second later and she would have been blinded by the light-tuning trick. It broke her concentration and the lethal crush-layer fizzled out.

She was losing patience with the battle, her old adversary just refused to die. Her anger rose and she opened her eyes. She intended to hit him hard ... really hard.

She spun her body and a bolt of psychokinetic energy struck Romand in the chest and sent him flying across the room where he crashed hard into the wall. His response was instant – an energy-slice came at Marianne. She tried to deflect it, but was clipped in the arm by the invisible disk. She looked at her bicep – there was a deep, clean cut and blood ran down across her wrist. She turned to Romand and her face tensed up as anger took control. Her rage drew in an incredible amount of power from her surroundings and every object in the room was blown to pieces.

Romand was thrown against the wall, his right arm smashed badly. It was almost finished; Marianne knew he could not fight her off for much longer with the use of only one arm.

The light bulbs in the kitchen had all been destroyed, the room became black, broken only by the glimmer of moonlight seeping in through the open patio doors. It was quiet too. She knew he was in pain, but his strength had not deserted him yet; there was not a wince, wheeze or even a heavy breath from the opposite side of the kitchen.

In the brief moments of calm after the explosion she began to sense his emotions; the pain from his wounds was opening his mind to her. She sensed his love for those he was protecting. They had been the only family he had ever known and he remained determined to guard them, even if it would cost him his life.

'A promise to an old friend to protect his wife and daughter. Eh, Romand?'

'It's not a weakness to have loyalty to those who care for you.'

'It *is* a weakness, and one I know all too well,' Marianne replied. 'I learned that lesson from my loss. Someone will probably learn it from the one you're about to suffer.'

'And the pain will be passed on. The conflict renewed. A never-ending cycle of hate.'

'You're about to die, but you're still philosophising. You are a strange one, Romand, but not too bright. You made a fatal mistake tonight.'

'Oh?'

'When the dogs attacked me you had a chance of winning this fight before it even started. I would not have been able to contend with the dogs, two psychokinetics and two mind switchers, yet you ordered them to hide in the attic.' There was a long moment of silence. 'Yes. I've read your thoughts. Bentley and two mind switchers are hidden above us. You failed them by not taking your opportunity, you fail them now by not shielding your emotions, and you will fail them yet again when I finish you off.'

'This is not over yet!'

Another large orb of blue light appeared in the centre of the room and became brighter and brighter. Marianne threw her arms across her face before it burned her eyes. She had dropped her guard just long enough for Romand to shoot a bolt of energy that sent her crashing against the metal stove. It was painful and her back stiffened, but Romand had grown weak and could no longer deliver a fatal blow.

She pushed all her residual energy across the room at him and he was struck head-on by an invisible tsunami that almost knocked him against the wall once more.

Marianne caught a glimpse of him scrambling out the back door. She followed, but he was invisible; he was using his old trick of body refraction to hide himself. The game was over; Marianne could hear his awkward footsteps and casually followed his trail of blood through the open patio doors and into the quaint little garden. She wouldn't be able to track him through the fields beyond the garden, though, and she decided it was time to bring a conclusion to the duel.

She revealed the ace she was holding up her sleeve: her gift of metallisiring. She raised her hands and used her abilities to pluck the eight silver rings from her fingers and bring them together in a line in front of her face. Without pause she used her metallisir gift to melt and shape the rings into razor-sharp arrowheads, then fired them across the garden.

Romand's light-tuning gift failed as the silver projectiles struck him. He slipped and staggered through the garden. There was no chance of escape for him; Marianne could see three of the arrowheads had ripped straight through his body and his wounds were too serious for him to go much further.

He fell to one knee and managed one last burst of power that merely disturbed Marianne's hair. She replied with a powerful thumping wave of negative energy that sent him tumbling twenty feet into the field beyond the little garden.

Still he refused to give in and tried to gain a few more yards from the house. Marianne took great pleasure in seeing her enemy's vulnerability. She would have liked to toy with him longer, but there was not time for such amusement. She pulled off one of her bracelets and allowed it to hover for a moment before metallisiring it into a sharp disk of silver. She took careful aim then shot it across the field. It sliced through Romand's leg and finally brought him crashing down into the grass. She took her time and walked slowly to him then looked down and smiled gloatingly.

'The mighty Romand,' she sighed. 'You should have killed me when I was a child.'

'I never wanted to kill you when we were in California, Marianne. I wanted to help you.'

'You? Help me?' Marianne laughed. 'You help no one but yourself, Romand!' She took the two remaining silver rings from her thumbs, formed them into arrowheads and prepared to fire them into Romand's heart.

'Why did you kill Peter?' she asked. A long-lost innocence had momentarily returned to her voice. '*Why?*'

'I didn't kill him. I never had a reason to.'

'Will you not speak the truth this one last time? I will make your death quick and painless if you do.'

'Your mind has been poisoned, Marianne. You cannot tell truth from lie. I pity you.'

'I don't need your pity, weakling!'

She fired one of the arrowheads into his right shoulder, just to prolong his agony and to make him pay for his lies.

She lowered her right hand and the second arrowhead slowly moved to Romand's chest.

'Who needs pity now?' she laughed. 'I just want to know this before I kill you: your friends will die a much slower and more excruciating death than the one I'm about to give you.'

The arrowhead began to burrow into his chest and Romand let out a loud, agonised roar. Marianne would not grant him the warrior's death that she'd given other gifted people. He didn't deserve it.

The arrowhead sunk through his flesh and worked its way to his heart. Marianne was standing directly over him. She wanted her eyes to be the last thing he'd see in life.

It was over ...

Suddenly Marianne was knocked off her feet and sent skidding violently across the field. She tried to stand up, but her head was spinning and she fell forward. Her body shuddered from the shock of the blow and blood spilled from her nose and a wound above her right eye.

How had Romand summoned such power? Even in his prime he was not gifted enough to deliver such an attack.

There was a moment of panic in her as she tried to stand; she could not allow him to hit her this hard again. The blow could have been fatal if it had been directed more precisely. She had to end this immediately.

Her vision was blurred and she stalked forward. She smeared

the blood from her face then rubbed her eyes then gasped as her sight finally cleared. Ross Bentley was stomping forward through the garden.

CHAPTER TWENTY-SIX

A Fight to the Death

I knelt next to Romand while Marianne was staggering and falling. He was in bad shape. His blood was splattered across the long grass, his face was purple and swollen and there were deep wounds all over his body.

'What are you doing?' he managed to ask.

'You saved me. Now I'm saving you.'

'*T'es vraiment stupide.*'

'I hope that means "thank you" in French.'

I spied Marianne getting to her feet and she looked mightily pissed off – the idea of facing up to her terrified me. I knew this would be a fight to the death. She would come at me with all her anger and rage, but I had powers of my own and would use everything I had to defend myself and those I cared about.

'Hold on, Romand,' I said as I stood up. 'I have to take care of this.'

'I knew you were stupid,' Marianne said as she approached me, 'but not quite this stupid. Didn't Romand warn you about me?'

'He did, but I don't take orders from him. You're going to pay for what you did to him *and* for that little stunt you pulled at the press conference.'

She laughed and shook her head. 'Ah, the press conference. You should have seen the look on your face, Bentley, when I snuffed out your gift. It was priceless.'

'You should have seen the look on yours when I sent you across the field just now.'

'Insolent little—'

I created an energy spear and she wasn't quick enough to dodge it. Again she was knocked into the long grass and when she stood up I saw blood trickling from her nose and mouth. She rubbed the back of her hand across her face and looked at the smudge of red. I could almost feel energy being sucked right out of the air and into her body.

My precog gift spiked and I darted to my left as Marianne fired a bolt of energy so powerful it flattened about twenty square metres of the long grass. I would have been torn to pieces if she had landed such a terrible blow.

'I'm toying you with, Bentley.'

'Let's stop playing around here, Marianne. Hit me with your best shot.'

'All in good time. I want you to suffer first, like Romand did.'

'I'm stronger than him. My gift is as pure as yours.'

'You're nothing more than a novice who uses his powers

to do skateboarding tricks. You have no idea how to use your gifts properly. Allow me to show you how it's done.'

She swung her arm and a deadly slice cut through the long grass. I was fast enough to dodge it and I hit back immediately with another spear. She easily avoided my attack and laughed mockingly at me.

'You need glasses. Romand should have brought you to an optician before he started teaching you cheap tricks!'

Another slice came fizzing through the grass and I jumped from its path. When I tried to get up I realised there was a deep gash on my leg. I hadn't been quite fast enough and I doubted myself for the first time. She was only getting started and I'd already used up most of the techniques I'd learned. I had to even up the scores, I *had* to put her on the back foot.

I jumped into the air and was going to replicate the ground thump I had beaten Romand with in our combat match, but Marianne was way too fast for me and channelled a fearsome bolt of energy that hit my chest and sent me far across the field.

I came down with an almighty thump and every inch of my body ached.

'Was that as good for you as it was for me?' she sneered. 'The earth moved for me, Ross.'

I couldn't even manage to say anything back and she continued to insult me as she waded through the long grass.

I was ready to collapse, but somehow tapped into some

deep, residual anger and used it to suck in negative energy from my surroundings. I stayed low, making it appear that I was too weak to stand. She thought she'd outdone me and approached while taking a bracelet from her wrist. I watched as she turned the simple ring of silver into a sharp disc the size of a DVD.

I raised my hand and released the energy from within, smashing the silver disc and forcing shards of it into her face. She hunched over and wailed in agony, but it wasn't enough to stop her; she was soon back on her feet and I could tell she was drawing in a lot of energy. I wasn't going to be able to avoid it and my body couldn't cope with another powerful blow. I did the only thing I could – I ran away. I needed somewhere to hide while I built up enough strength to continue the fight and there was only one place in sight: the training barn.

I ran as fast I could but was eventually downed by a small silver object that hit me in the back of the leg. It was burning hot and sizzled inside my hamstring. I reached down and yanked it out of my leg and my fingertips melted on its surface. How the *hell* could I contend with gifts like this? Romand was right about her, she was a weapon of mass destruction.

I scrambled off the ground and continued towards the barn. I don't even know how I managed to move one foot in front of the other; my entire body was aching and each step drained me. Marianne could have caught up with me if she really wanted to but she just strolled casually across the field.

She really *was* just toying with me.

I was swallowed by the shadows inside the barn, but I knew my way around inside and was able to traverse the hay bales until I reached the back wall. It would take a while to track me down and I used the time I had to suck the cool evening air into my lungs and try to build up my strength once more. I had some breathing space, but I knew I couldn't defeat Marianne; she was far beyond my skills. Romand had overestimated my abilities.

'Hiding, Bentley?' she called from somewhere in the barn. 'The poor young boy hiding in the dark, knowing that death is approaching. How afraid you must be. There is no need to prolong this. Give up those who you're protecting and I will allow you to live.'

'You're a liar,' I roared back. 'You're sick and twisted just like Golding.'

'I'm nothing like Golding.'

'Yes, you are! He made you into his mirror image. You're a murdering monster who only cares for money.'

'*I'm nothing like Golding!*' Her voice was filling with fury and hatred. 'You know *nothing*, you little fool!'

'I know he made you into his puppet. He had Shaw kill your boyfriend, Peter, and then blamed it on someone else. And you believed them! You're the foolish one, Marianne!'

'I know who killed Peter! It was Romand or one of his friends in the guild.'

I didn't know what she was talking about, but I knew Romand wasn't responsible. I also realised there was no way to reason with Marianne. She was hell-bent on revenge and wouldn't be convinced by anything I said.

There was a long eerie silence in the barn and my nerves were on edge. Where was she? What was she preparing? How the hell was I going to get out of the barn?

After almost two minutes, that felt more like two hours, there were *pings* overhead as the fluorescent lights came on. The interior of the barn was filled with light. I wouldn't be able to hide for much longer. She was getting ready to make her move.

I had expected it to take a while for her to find me, but I was outsmarted. The hay bales all floated into the air and hovered twenty feet above me. I was no longer hidden. I stood up and faced Marianne, who was standing near the front entrance. What would be her next move? I tried to sense what she was going to do, but my mind was blank; she was shutting me out somehow.

I contemplated an attack of my own, but decided against it when I heard clanking from above. I gazed upward to see the metal roof of the barn melting and shapes emerging from it. They looked like stalactites, they were growing fast and their ends were sharp as needles. They grew longer and longer, piercing the hay bales then stabbing the floor. One was coming right at my face! I had nowhere to run. I started to panic and was suddenly filled with energy. I felt as powerful as I had when I'd destroyed the pillar in Dullbrook.

I spun three-sixty and knocked a hole in the concrete wall, just about big enough for me to climb through. One of the spikes sliced my ankle as I pulled myself through the gap and I let out a yelp then fell onto the grass outside the barn.

I couldn't take much more of this. Marianne was not only powerful, she was really creative with her killing techniques! Where she could have learned that stuff was a mystery to me. Maybe she invented it herself. I didn't really care to know, I just wanted to get as far away from her as possible.

I needed somewhere to hide. Fleeing made me feel like a coward, but my life was in the balance. I had to do something to survive so I started hobbling towards Mr Barnes' old junk-yard.

When I reached the fence I leaned against a wooden post for a few seconds and tried to catch my breath. I stood there in disbelief as my enemy casually walked through the long grass as if the fighting had never even happened. How could anyone have so much power? Then I remembered that Romand said she was always angry, therefore she was always powerful and never got tired no matter how much she used her gifts. There would be no victory for me. She was unbeatable.

I limped through the junkyard in search of a hiding place, but then stopped and turned to face her. What was the point in hiding? She would eventually find me and I didn't want to die like a coward. I wanted to stand my ground and make a fight of it, just like Romand had done.

She stopped a few metres from me and put her hands on her hips and smiled. I expected her to say something dramatic, instead she let out a scream and flung her arms into the air. Before I knew it an engine block came at me as fast as a bullet. I spun and blasted it away just in time ... I barely had enough time to compose myself before another was shot at me; I deflected that too. I took control of a tractor wheel and fired it at Marianne, but she dismissed it with a wave of her hand.

I was all out of ideas and she knew it. Her eyes told me she was ready to finish it. She raised one hand and a stray car-door flew into the air, where she formed it into an immense metal disc that was spinning at an unbelievable rate. A smile grew on her face and I knew she intended to cut me in two. I transferred my strength into my precog gift and tried my best to predict her attack. I could read her better now, as if the excitement she was feeling was making it easier to predict her actions.

Her smile faded and she shot the disc at me. I tried to leap from its path when it came at me, but I was far too slow. It cut into my side and I crumpled to one knee. I saw blood pouring down from under my hoody and staining my jeans dark red; it was a bad cut, but I'd live, as long as I could prevent any further attacks.

'That'll leave a mark,' she said. 'It's time to end this, Bentley. I would have liked to say you were a worthy opponent, but I can't, you're pathetic.'

A small vehicle came flying at me. I used all my training to good effect, deflected it and sent it crashing across the yard. Almost immediately, it spun into the air and came back at me again. I dropped to my knees and it passed by my face by centimetres and rolled across the ground and clattered into a row of old vehicles.

Suddenly there were more vehicles whizzing around through the air. I used outward waves to deflect them but my power was sapped and I could not raise anger to strengthen my gifts.

The end was near and I could see it coming; an old tractor was rotating high above my head. I was too weak to deflect such an object. She'd beaten me and I had failed Romand.

Marianne raised her hands and prepared to send the tractor down to crush me like a bug. I closed my eyes and waited for the end to come.

Marianne prepared to bring the heavy vehicle down and squash Bentley into the dirt. She hesitated for a moment as she watched her enemy squirming in the shadow of the tractor. In that instant he looked so much like Peter, her one and only love. She wondered if that was how Peter had looked and acted before he was callously murdered.

Have I now taken the place of Peter's killer? she thought. *Have I become that which I sought to destroy?*

The moment of hesitation quickly passed. This was not Peter. This boy would soon grow to become a part of the group responsible for his death. Ross Bentley had to die.

CHAPTER TWENTY-SEVEN -

A True Gift

I don't know what came first: the sound of the gunshot or the sight of Marianne's shoulder exploding into a cloud of red. Either way, the bullet struck her in the shoulder-blade and hammered her to the ground. Her gift failed and the tractor came crashing down, but I was able to roll out of its way unharmed.

She was coughing blood and could barely keep her eyes open. The wound was horrific and looked fatal. Nobody, not even Marianne, could survive such an injury. I considered killing her while she was vulnerable, but I didn't want that on my conscience, she would surely die from the gunshot wound. She was still dangerous, but as the seconds passed I saw her lose consciousness. Her head hit the ground as her body went limp.

A group of armed police officers vaulted the fence and entered the junkyard then fanned out. One put his hand on my shoulder and told me to sit down and politely informed me that I'd lost a lot of blood. As if I didn't know that. After all, it was my blood that was all over the junkyard.

I fell onto my backside and watched the team of armed men surrounding Marianne and pointing their guns at her.

I was surprised they arrived so quickly. I'd called 999 earlier when I was sure Romand had led her out of the house. I'd given them the address of the Atkinson home and told them the person responsible for the massacre at the Laberinto was trying to kill us. Though the official story of the Laberinto explosion was a gas leak, I took the chance on the authorities being in on the cover-up and it had paid off.

I told Cathy and June to flee and that I'd follow them once I was sure Romand was safe.

I'd intended that the police would arrive in time to save the Atkinsons but they had arrived just in time to save me. Or had I been saved by those few moments of silence when Marianne held the tractor above my head? Why had she hesitated at the crucial moment?

The officers looked gobsmacked by the whole thing and kept throwing glances at the old and battered vehicles in the yard, as if they thought the cars and vans would suddenly come to life and start whizzing around once more. At any other time I would have worried about how to explain it, but now I was too exhausted too think about that.

When they were sure Marianne posed no serious threat they split up and searched the rest of the junkyard. Two of them helped me to my feet and led me back to the house, which was surrounded by more officers. Romand was still lying in the grass and a female officer was assessing his injuries. I wanted to see how he was, but they wouldn't let me anywhere near him. I was shown to the sitting room and told to sit there until a medical team arrived.

I figured that they would soon search through the entire house and anything they found would be taken in as evidence. That included the briefcase containing Romand's study of the fifteen true gifts. I couldn't allow them to find it. The paper would reveal all the secrets of the gifts and probably identify Romand's friends I kept hearing about.

When I was left alone I quietly made my way out of the room, crept up the staircase and entered Romand's room. I was in luck. He'd left the manuscript on his bedside locker the previous night and hadn't put it back into the bulky briefcase. I quickly stuffed the sheets of paper under my hoody then made my way back down the staircase.

'What are you up to?' one of the officers, who was coming through the open doorway, shouted. He pointed a handgun at me. 'What were you doing up there?'

'I was using the toilet,' I replied. I lifted my hands in the air and used my gift to keep the block of sheets from falling out from under my hoody.

'Right,' he said. 'Go back to the sitting room and don't move. There are some people coming who want to talk to you before you're brought to the hospital. I suggest you go sit down, you look like you've lost a lot of blood.'

I sat on the sofa and examined the cuts on my legs and the one on my side that was leaking a lot of blood; maybe I was in shock, because I wasn't in a lot of pain. How had it come to this? A simple decision to enter a talent contest had gotten me involved in a battle between two forces that most people wouldn't believe existed. My entire life had been turned upside down and now Romand was critically injured. Where would it all end?

'Ross Bentley.'

I turned to see two men wearing dark suits entering the room. I didn't know who they were, but the police officers nodded to them and although I feared they might be Golding's people, I suspected they were most likely Special Branch.

'The men in black?' I snorted.

'Not quite,' the older of the two said. He showed me an ID badge and my suspicions were confirmed; they *were* Special Branch. 'We know all about you and your friends though.'

'Friends?'

'Marcus Romand and Marianne Dolloway.'

'I wouldn't say Marianne is my friend.' I nodded to the blood on my clothes. 'Do friends do that to each other?'

The younger man stepped forward and grabbed hold of me. 'You're all the same, you lot are.' He dragged me off the chair and pushed me to the doorway. 'Get moving! You and the Frenchman are coming with us.'

He continued to shove me through the house until I was in the back garden again. There I was told to wait while they went to Romand. To my surprise they lifted him off the ground and started carrying him. The other officers told them he was at death's door and that an ambulance was on the way.

'He's coming with us!' the older man barked. 'Put in an official complaint if you have a problem with it.'

'He'll die if you don't get him to a hospital soon!' the female officer shouted.

'I don't care,' he replied. 'He's coming with us, and so is Bentley!'

'Who the hell are you people?' I shouted. 'You can't do this. He needs help.'

The younger man pushed me towards the little wooden gate that led to the country road that ran parallel to the house. I couldn't quite figure out what was happening, but I was beginning to suspect these men were on Golding's payroll afterall and that Romand and I were being led to our deaths. I wasn't going to let that happen. I hadn't battled with Marianne Dolloway just to be outsmarted like this.

They carried Romand along the dark road and to a silver car. I followed them from a short distance and as I drew closer to the car I saw there were two people sitting in the back. I couldn't see their faces, but they could have been Victor and Tsuyoshi for all I knew. I wanted to use the gift to escape but my strength was all but gone, I could barely walk. I tried to pull energy into my body as I watched them throw Romand into the back of the car. I thought it was a little strange that they'd put him on the laps of the two passengers and I paused in the road.

'Get into the driver's seat, Ross!' the younger man said as he closed the back door. 'There's no time to waste.'

'What?' I bawled. 'You want *me* to drive?'

'Yes! Hurry!'

'I've only had two lessons... Hang on! Why do you want me to drive? Why can't one of you do it?'

'Ross, get in the car and drive!' the older man shouted. 'I can't hold this much longer!'

'Hold what?'

'The mind-switch!'

Finally it dawned on me. I raced to the car and looked into the back. Cathy and June were both sitting there with their eyes closed and Romand was sprawled across their laps. They had transported their minds into the bodies of the dark-suited men and used them to get us free of the police.

'Hurry, Ross,' the older man said. 'My gift is failing.'

'I'm not a good driver.'

'Hurry!'

I sat in the driver's seat and slammed the door shut. I really was a terrible driver and I'd only ever had two lessons with my dad who swore he'd never get into a car with me again. There was no choice though; I had to get us the hell out of there.

I twisted the key in the ignition, pressed my foot on the accelerator and the car slowly rolled down the dark country road. I glanced in the rear view mirror to see the two special branch officers staggering around like a pair of drunks. One of them fell on his backside and the other went down on his knees and vomited on the road. Having their minds taken over obviously didn't agree with them.

I focused on the road ahead. I needed to get my friends away from the authorities and driving like a granny wasn't helping. I floored the accelerator and the car picked up speed. There were no streetlights and the route ahead was narrow with constant bends that slowed me down.

'Dear Lord!' June gasped when she'd fully released the mind switch and entered her own body once more. 'Romand, look at what she's done to you.'

'How is he?' I asked.

'Concentrate on your driving, Ross.'

'Tell me!'

'This doesn't look good. His injuries are very serious.'

'Will he live?' Cathy asked as she cushioned his head.

'I'm … not sure.'

'I'll drive to the nearest hospital,' I said. 'How long will it take to get there?'

'We can't go to a hospital,' June replied. 'That's the first place they'll look.'

'I don't care about being caught. We're talking about

Romand's *life*!'

'The nearest hospital is a two-hour drive from here.'

'He'll never hold out that long!' Cathy said. 'What are we going to do?'

'We can take him to Peter Williams; he'll know what to do. He's healed injuries like this before. His house is only an hour from here. Ross, take the next left turn.'

'Okay, but what if he's not at home?'

'Don't worry. Peter will already have sensed that we're on our way.'

'How is that possible?'

'Now's not the time, Ross. Drive!'

I pressed harder on the accelerator and the vehicle picked up speed. The bends came more frequent and I almost lost control of the car a few times. I didn't slow down though, I had to get Romand help.

I felt a strange sensation all of a sudden, like cold water was being poured into my mind and snapping me from my thoughts. It was my precog gift and it was telling me that danger was drawing near once more.

'We're being followed,' I told the others. 'Someone is coming up behind us.'

Cathy and June looked through the back window but there was only a wall of black.

'I see nothing,' Cathy said.

'She's right, Ross. There's nothing behind us.'

'I'm telling you there's someone following us. They're very close.'

'There is no one—'

Two headlights appeared behind us and they were gaining rapidly. After a moment there were sirens screaming and blue lights pulsed across the trees that lined the road.

'I thought our mind switch would have bought us more time,' Cathy said.

'We have to lose them!' I shouted. 'We can't be delayed.'

'Can you use your gift, Ross?'

'I'm running on empty, Cathy. I wouldn't be able to lift a feather right now. Can one of you switch your mind into the driver of the first car?'

'I can't,' June said. 'The last mind-switch took too much out of me.'

'I'll try,' Cathy said.

She sucked in a deep breath and lowered her head. Nothing happened for a moment but then the vehicle directly behind us swerved across the road, struck a tree and spun into the middle of the road.

'Did it work?' Cathy asked when she came to.

'Looks like it,' I said. I looked in the rear view mirror and the car was blocking the road. The cars had all come to a halt. 'That bought us a minute or two. It might be enough time to lose them.'

'I certainly hope so, I won't be able to do that again.'

I pressed harder on the pedal and increased speed. The road was winding, but my precog gift was helping me to manoeuvre the car while driving so fast – I could visualise what was ahead split-seconds before I got there and adjust my course to it. It was a skill I never knew I had, but I didn't get the chance to revel in this exciting discovery, not that I was in the mood for revelling, because the pulsing blue lights were in the distance again and were growing stronger. Three squad cars were moving up behind us and I was sensing *real* danger.

'I'm all out of ideas,' I said over my shoulder.

'Me too,' Cathy replied. 'Just keep driving as fast as you can.'

'They'll run us off the road soon enough,' I told her. 'I can sense it!'

I watched the lead car through the rear view mirror. It was coming at us fast and aggressively. They were going to strike us and send our car off the road or into a tree or a ditch. Our lives were all in grave danger now.

'There should be a cross roads up ahead,' June said. 'Go straight through.'

The police were right behind us now and I couldn't see any way out for us. I tried to find some energy to pull a tree down behind us but I had nothing left. I was totally exhausted and my injuries meant I was getting weaker each second.

'They're right on us!' Cathy shouted.

'He's gonna push us off the road,' I shouted. 'Put your safety belts on. This is gonna hurt.'

We braced for an impact, but suddenly the car behind us skidded to a halt. So too did the one behind it and the one behind that. I gazed into the mirror and saw the officers leaving their cars and gesticulating to one another. I didn't know what had happened but I was sure going to take advantage of it. I slipped the car into a higher gear and pushed the pedal to the floor.

'Why did they stop?' Cathy asked. 'They almost had us.'

'Maybe there's something up ahead,' I suggested. 'Perhaps a road block or something.'

'No, they wouldn't have had time to set that up'

'Why did they stop then?'

'Because they can no longer see us,' it was Romand, he'd woken up but his voice was terribly frail, nothing like it had been before. 'The gift of light-tuning has many uses.'

'No, Romand!' June said. 'You're too weak to do this!'

'Keep driving as fast as you can, Ross. I can't cloak the car much longer.'

'No, Romand!' Cathy screamed. 'Stop it! You'll die!'

'I'll die anyway ...'

'Romand,' I shouted, 'do as they say. Stop before it drains you too much.'

'I don't take orders from teenagers.'

I turned to look at him. His face was ghostly white and his eyes were glazed over like those of a mannequin. He tilted his head slightly and there was a hint of a smile in the corner of his mouth. He knew that cloaking the car would surely kill him, but he wouldn't listen to us.

'Keep them safe,' he said to me.

'Romand, don't do this!'

'Now you know the meaning of a true gift, Ross.'

'Romand!'

He didn't speak again. His head slumped against his shoulder and his eyes became totally lifeless. The cloak faded and the car was visible once more, but he'd given us enough time to escape. The police wouldn't be able to catch up with us before we reached the Williams home.

June shook Romand; there was no response. Cathy squeezed his hand and screamed his name, but he was gone and I knew it. My mentor, protector and friend was dead.

The Atkinsons cried for the entire journey and it was difficult to even get directions from June. It took a little over an hour to reach the tall metal gates of the Williams' place and it was the worst hour of my entire life. I felt so helpless. I couldn't do anything but drive that stupid car. I couldn't do anything for Romand. I couldn't even comfort my friends.

Peter Williams, a tall, elderly man, was unlocking the gates and pushed them open for us. He waved me on and I drove up the driveway and stopped outside the house where his wife was waiting.

I jumped out as soon as I killed the engine and helped the others to lift Romand from the back and lay him on the lawn. We crowded around him, looking for any sign of life, hoping for some sort of miracle.

'Let me take a look at him,' Peter Williams said. 'There may still be time.'

The old man crouched down and placed his hands on Romand's forehead and it looked as though he was trying to transfer energy from his own body into Romand's. I had a feeling it wasn't going to work and Mr Williams' face confirmed my suspicions.

He shook his head and wept, 'He is gone.'

CHAPTER TWENTY-EIGHT

Funeral for a Friend

They told me I collapsed soon after arriving at the Williams house and that I'd been out cold for over thirty hours. Someone dressed my wounds while I was unconscious and Cathy helped me into some fresh clothes when I felt strong enough to stand.

'Where's the manuscript?' I gasped. 'It was in my hoody.'

'Mr Williams took it.'

'He has no right to take that. It belonged to Romand!'

'Ross,' Cathy said calmly as she placed her hands on my shoulders. 'That manuscript is very important and Mr Williams can keep it safe. Just relax. The people here are all friends. Romand's paper on the true gifts needs to remain under their protection, not ours. Do you think Romand would have let you keep it anyway?'

'He might have...'

'Forget the manuscript for now. Come on, there's some people who would like to meet you.'

She led me downstairs and to the dining room where there

were over twenty people sitting around, drinking tea or coffee and looking sombre. They all seemed to know who I was, which wasn't really a surprise, but I hadn't a clue who they were.

Cathy introduced most of them and apparently they were all gifted and part of the network of friends that June had told me about. I didn't need to be told they had all known and loved Romand, the grief painted on their faces told me that much.

I sat by the double doors that led to the kitchen and listened to them sharing stories about my fallen mentor. It felt surreal that they were talking about Romand in the past tense. It still hadn't sunk in that he was dead. It showed how vulnerable we all were, when someone as strong as Romand could fall so easily.

I felt such intense hatred for Marianne as I watched June's frozen face. She was sitting on the opposite side of the room and gazing out the window at the front lawn. It seemed like something inside her had died with Romand. She didn't speak once or even acknowledge anyone's words. I felt so sad and fought the need to cry.

After three long and depressing hours I was told that Romand would be buried later that day, in the grounds of the Williams' estate. Apparently they were waiting on six more mourners to arrive before they could lay him to rest. I spent the rest of the afternoon wandering the estate with Cathy. We didn't speak much but there was very little to say. I simply held her hand and we both drew strength from being close to each other.

I eventually asked the question that had been playing on my mind since I woke. I felt somehow guilty and selfish for asking, but I needed to know the answer.

'What has become of Marianne?'

'I don't know, Ross,' Cathy said nervously, as if the mention of the name had made her blood run cold. 'Nobody does. Mr Williams knows some people who are close to the authorities, but apparently she was never brought to a hospital, a police station or a morgue. It was all covered up. What happened at our house wasn't even mentioned on the news.'

'Do you think she survived?'

'I don't know. Do you?'

'That bullet blew a hole in her the size of an orange. I doubt anyone could have survived that ... but I guess Marianne isn't just anyone ...'

'I don't want to think about her again, Ross.'

'I know.' I put my arms around her and held her tight. 'Neither do I.'

'I'm afraid of her, Ross. I don't want her to come back. Ever.'

'She won't.'

We held on to one another for what seemed like hours. We hardly spoke a word, for words were not what we needed; we needed only each other's presence. When Cathy finally spoke the sky was growing dim and the air was cooling rapidly. It was the first sign that the summer was drawing to a close.

'We should get back to the house now,' she said. 'I don't want to leave Mum alone for too long, she's hasn't taken Romand's death well.'

'Has anyone?'

'No, but Mum is acting very strangely. It's like she's lost part of her soul or something.'

'She still has you.'

'*Us.*' She grasped my collars and stared into my eyes. 'She still has *us*, Ross.'

We walked back to the house to find the six mourners had arrived. I'd expected them to be like the others at the house, older people who had gifts and had probably spent most of their lives hiding from the rest of the world, but I was wrong. The six looked more like soldiers who had returned from a tour of duty; they looked rugged and dangerous. They seemed powerful and well-used to using their gifts in combat, just like Romand had been.

Cathy introduced me to them before we returned to our seats. First were Angela and John Portman who nodded politely. Standing next to them was Linda Farrier who was in her mid-twenties and, disturbingly, reminded me a little of Marianne. Her eyes were intense and she showed that same sharpness of movement when she shook my hand.

Then there were three tall men wearing long, black coats.

They were the toughest-looking people I'd ever seen and their faces told of violent lives.

'Ross,' Cathy said, 'this is Jim Sterling, Dominic Ballentine and Mike Huntington.'

I shook their hands and nodded to each, but Huntington, a tall man in his thirties with a stern face, held my hand firmly for a moment longer than was necessary and his stare was hard to endure.

I said nothing to him and tore my hand away.

Everyone gathered at the rear of the house as the sun finally began to disappear and we walked to a tall oak with a patch of dirt in front of it. It seemed like a fitting headstone for such a great man. Romand had deserved something more than just a slab of stone that would weather over time and he got it, the tree looked robust enough to stand for all time. The same wolf's head logo I'd seen on some of Romand's papers was carved into the bark of the tree. It appeared out of place at first, but the more I thought about it the more it seemed fitting for Romand's grave.

We gathered round the grave. Most of us held old-fash-ioned torches that gave the scene a warm yet eerie atmosphere. Everyone but Ballentine, Sterling, Farrier and Huntington seemed grief-stricken. They remained serious, but very com-posed, as all around them sobbed.

Mr Williams said a few words then placed a rose on the grave.

'He was strong when the rest of us were weak. He preyed on evil while the rest of us fled from it. He will be greatly missed. Would anyone else like to say a few words?'

June took a step forward, but burst into tears and couldn't manage to say her piece. Cathy hugged her and they both wept hysterically. I thought about stepping forward to talk briefly about what Romand had meant to me in the short time we knew each other, but I was beaten to it by Huntington.

He stood next to the grave and raised his burning torch above his head as if it were an ancient ritual.

'I'm not one for speeches so I'll keep it short,' he announced in a thick Scottish accent. 'He wouldn't want me getting all emotional anyway. Romand and I faced many dangers over the years and he never took a backward step and never lost his nerve. We even searched the world for the Kematian, something few would even contemplate, and he never once spoke of caution or hesitation. He was always ready to put his life on the line for the safety of others.

'He was my friend. A man who had seen the worst evils of mankind, but kept his honesty and integrity and would always remain on the side of good. A man who knew the true value of life and never surrendered to greed. He was without doubt the bravest person I've ever known.

'When we had a meeting in this very house only a few short

weeks ago about …' Huntington glanced at me, '… Ross Bentley and how we could rescue him. We knew it was a task that could cost lives. Romand was the first the step forward to volunteer and I will always admire him for that. I regret now that I allowed him to do this alone. I regret that I was not there to save him.

'He was a good friend to all here, a brother to the Atkinsons, a rock for our community and a hero to all. A hero in life and in death. May he serve as an inspiration to all those who knew him. I will miss him greatly.'

Huntington nodded to the crowd, threw another glance at me, then strode away from the gathering and returned to the house. There was nothing more to be said.

I stayed by the grave long after all the others had gone. I felt so guilty. My stupidity had caused Romand's death. If I hadn't called Dad and Gemma that night none of this would have happened and I'd probably have been sitting down for dinner with Romand and the Atkinsons at this moment.

The guilt was unbearable, but I was also afraid. What would the others say if they knew I was responsible for Marianne finding our location? Would Cathy hate me? Would Huntington kill me? He seemed to have a beef with me anyway and he had the look of a killer.

I leaned against the tall oak and wept. My only comfort was that I had admitted what I'd done to Romand before he died, and that he had not judged me. For a moment I considered telling everyone at the house about the calls I'd made from the Atkinson farm, but I thought it best to keep the secret to myself, at least for a while. What good would it do if I told them? It would only cause more sorrow. Romand's death was something I would have to try to live with. Some day, when I came to terms with what happened, I would try to tell the others and then deal with the consequences.

I eventually returned to the house when my torch went out. I would truly miss Romand and I already felt lost without his guidance. I had no idea what was to come next. Where was I to go now? That question would be answered quicker than I thought.

The house was very quiet the next morning as I got up. I went downstairs to find only Cathy, Mr Williams and Mike Huntington in the kitchen by the table.

'What's going on?' I asked.

'We're discussing what should be done next,' Mr Williams answered.

'What *should* be done next?'

'It's too dangerous for you to remain here,' Mr Williams told me. 'My contacts in the police service say that this entire area is being scoured for you. And there are other undesirables lurking about.'

'Undesirables?'

'Most likely Golding's people.'

'I see. Where can we go?' I asked Cathy.

'I have to stay here with Mum, Ross. She's been getting worse since that night … her mind is—'

'She must stay here,' Mr Williams interrupted, '*I* can help her with the pain plaguing her mind. Cathy will be able to aid me, so she will also stay.'

'It won't be forever, Ross,' Cathy said, touching my hand.

'Okay,' I answered. 'I'll go back to my dad's place until it all blows over.'

'No,' Mr Williams said. 'You can't go back there. They will come for you if you return to your home, and they will almost certainly kill your father. You must remain under the protection of the guild.'

'The guild…?'

'What the old man is saying,' Huntington interrupted, 'is that you have to stay with one of the more … active members of our community.'

'Who might that be?'

'Take a wild guess.'

'When?'

'Now.'

I only had an hour before I had to leave the house. I wanted to contact Dad and Gemma, but they told me it was too much of a risk, and after what had happened at the Atkinsons' house I agreed. I'd write each of them a letter giving them some form of explanation once I reached my destination. I really felt bad about forsaking Dad, but it was for the best. I couldn't risk his safety. I was never going to put my loved ones in danger again.

I barely had time to say farewell to June and I had only a brief moment alone with Cathy while she gathered some spare clothes for me from one of the upstairs rooms.

'It's not going to be forever,' she said sorrowfully. 'I'll wait for you. We can be together again soon.'

'I hope so. I … er … I do like you a lot.'

'I'll say it even though you're afraid to. I love you, Ross Bentley.'

'I love you too.'

I kissed her and held her as tight as I could. I wanted to stay with her forever, but our time together was running out. Our paths were leading in different directions but I felt confident they would converge once more, in the near future.

'I know the address where you'll be staying,' Cathy told me. 'I'll write you letters every week.'

'Emails?'

'No, we can't communicate like that. We'll have to do it the old-fashioned way.'

'Cool. I've never gotten a love letter before.'

'You will soon enough.'

I gave her one last kiss before I left the room. I was about to take to the staircase when I heard voices from the hallway below.

Peter Williams was following Huntington down the long hallway. The old man had to jog to keep up with the younger man who strode purposely towards the front door.

'Hunter!' Mr Williams called. I figured this was Huntington's nickname, but that it might have a double meaning. 'Hunter, damn it, slow down!'

'What is it, Peter? I have a long drive ahead of me.'

'Go easy on that boy while you're in hiding.'

'Why should I?'

'There's something you're not aware of.'

'And that is?'

'I examined Romand's injuries and also listened to June Atkinson's account of that night before her mind closed up. It is my belief that Romand's physical injuries were not severe enough to kill him, which means the boy's intervention, in taking the fight to Marianne, would have saved your friend's life. Bentley is not the reckless kid you think he is.'

'How did Romand die if not from his injuries?'

'He extended himself too much during the escape from the authorities. He sacrificed himself for Bentley, but he was only returning the favour. The boy had *saved* Romand.'

Huntington didn't respond. He patted Mr Williams on the shoulder and paced out into the garden.

Huntington had ignored the old man's words, but they had an effect on me. They made me feel a little better about myself. Romand hadn't simply died from the injuries Marianne had inflicted. I had in a way saved him, given him a chance to survive the debacle that I had caused.

I *had* still caused it though …

I plodded down the staircase into the hall and headed for the garden. Mr Williams was standing just outside and stopped me as I passed.

'Huntington isn't all bad when you get to know him,' Mr Williams said. 'He was Romand's best friend. He's just upset.'

'He blames me for it … and maybe he should.'

The old man put his hand on my shoulder and stared at me intensely. 'Listen, young Bentley, whatever happened that night, or will happen in the future, I know when it really mattered you didn't hide. You came out fighting and put your life on the line for Romand and the others.'

I had the feeling that somehow he knew that I had led Marianne to the farmhouse. Tears welled up in my eyes and my mouth went dry.

'Listen, Mr Williams, it was because of me—'

'What happened is not because of you or anyone on our side. It was because of Paul Golding's greed. Nothing else. Put any guilt you have aside. You need to be strong and you need to stay safe. Romand gave you another chance at life, I suggest you don't waste it by drowning yourself in guilt.' He smiled and nodded at the house. 'There's a remarkable young woman in there who cares a lot about you, and needs you to overcome this and return here as the same young man she fell in love with, not a young man who has been crushed by remorse.'

'Thank you, Mr Williams. Thank you for everything.'

There were no more words between us. He simply shook my hand and returned to his house.

I felt a little better, but it didn't last more than a second. I turned to see Huntington leaning out the driver's side window of his beat up 4X4 and scowling at me.

'I don't have all day,' he grunted.

CHAPTER TWENTY-NINE -

The Silent Wilderness

I climbed into Huntington's beat up 4x4 and he floored the accelerator before I could even close the door. I could tell by his mood he didn't want to talk to me so I didn't attempt a conversation.

We left the Williams estate before noon and drove hard and without a break until late in the night. He seemed determined that neither the journey nor his concentration be interrupted until we reached his home. I didn't feel like talking anyway; my injuries were hurting me greatly and it was a constant battle to hold back tears. I felt I had missed out on a lifetime of discovery with Romand. The sense of loss was horrendous.

The digital clock on the dashboard read 2.45am as we drove along a winding country highway. I thought the journey would never end, but then Huntington took to a dirt road that led to his home, a small white cottage surrounded by tall pine trees, with the Scottish highlands climbing into the night sky beyond.

The 4x4 slid to a halt on the path outside the cottage and

Huntington left the vehicle without so much as a word. In fact, he hadn't said a single word to me for the entire journey. My time with him would not be pleasant. This would not be anything like the weeks I'd spent on the Atkinson farm.

He unlocked the front door and stooped under the low doorway. He left it ajar which was the only invitation I was going to get. I noticed a carving on one of the wooden porch posts as I went to the door. It was the symbol that had been etched into the tree where Romand was buried. Huntington and Romand must have both been part of some secret society. I was sure of it.

When I got inside I found it cold, not just in temperature, but in atmosphere. There were no personal items; there was furniture and the usual fixtures, but nothing that betrayed his personality or his life.

'Down the hallway,' Huntington grunted as he sat on a wooden chair in the sitting room. 'Room at the end's yours.'

'It speaks,' I said, my instinctive sense of humour appearing from nowhere.

'We're not here to hold hands and be friends,' he raised his voice. 'We're here so you can stay out of trouble. I do have other, more important, things that I could be doing so you might want to watch that smart mouth of yours. Otherwise you'll be out on your ear and the wolves can have you.'

'You get wolves in Scotland?'

'I was speaking metaphorically, dumbass.' He reached

down and untied one of his boots. 'I'm getting tired of all this talkin'. Don't make any noise at night. I'm a light sleeper.'

All this talking? We'd spoken for two minutes that entire day and he was tired of talking? I really hoped my exile wouldn't last too long.

My bedroom was cramped and smelled stale, like an old garden shed. The narrow single bed wasn't all that bad though, I was grateful for that. Within moments I crawled under the covers and stretched out my aching limbs. My whole body seemed to be cramping up and the wound on my side stung like hell. The deep cut above my cheekbone wasn't much better and Mr Williams had told me I'd have a nasty scar for the rest of my days. I didn't care though. Such things seemed trivial now.

Before I slept I thought back to Romand's final words and tried to figure what they meant. 'Now you know the meaning of a true gift,' he had said just before he died. I couldn't quite figure out if he was talking about the true gifts or was he talking about the gift of sacrifice? Did he mean a true gift, a *real* gift, to someone was to put your life on the line to save them, or that having a true gift meant it was your duty to put your life on the line for others?

I would probably never understand, but either way it made sense to me. If I wanted to be a good person I would have to use my abilities for the protection of those who needed it. Romand had been a good person, and a very wise one. I now realised that. It made his loss even greater.

There was a loud bang and I jumped out of the bed with my fists raised. Huntington was standing there with his arms folded, looking even grumpier than usual.

'What is it?' I screamed. 'What's wrong?

'It's time for breakfast.'

I looked at the clock on the wall then turned to him and shouted, 'It's six in the morning! I've only had three hour's sleep!'

'We have to have an early breakfast.'

'Why?'

'Because your training will begin at seven each morning.'

'What the hell do I need training for?'

'You'll need proper training if you're to take Romand's place in the Guild of the True.'

'What the hell is the Guild of the True?'

'Warriors with true gifts who protect our kind against any evil that threatens us. Do you want in or not?'

I seemed destined to live a strange life. I had thought things were about to calm down in my world, but now I was stuck in a cottage in the middle of nowhere with some weird gifted warrior who wanted me to join a brotherhood with a stupid name. Could it get any worse?

'You want me to join your guild?' I asked as a startled smile grew on my face.

'Well?' Huntington asked as he pointed at me. I noticed the slightest hint of a smile in the corner of his mouth, so fleeting that I'd have missed if I'd blinked. 'You want in?'

'Hell, yeah!'

The next 'Ross Bentley' adventure ...

coming soon

Turn the page for a taste of what's to come!

After the terrifying events at the Atkinsons' house and the horror of Romand's death it might seem like Ross Bentley would be glad of some peace and quiet. But when that peace and quiet involve being holed up in a remote Scottish farmhouse with Hunter, the Guild-member tasked with protecting him, Ross finds he's never felt so alone.

With his mentor Romand dead, Ross is cut off from family and friends, separated from the girl he loves, in hiding, miles from civilisation – and he's really miserable. Hunter's no replacement for Romand; Ross just can't seem to connect with him. Even the hope of joining the Guild of the gifted, learning to use his gifts to protect others and perhaps one day having the chance to take revenge on those who killed Romand now seems an impossible dream. All Hunter will say about it is, 'All in good time, Bentley,' as he makes Ross train, study and practise his powers relentlessly.

But suddenly the monotony is broken – Hunter is summoned by the guild. A gifted child has been kidnapped. Hunter needs to track her down, and he has no choice but to take Ross with him.

The search for the missing child, and the dangers it uncovers, take Ross to the darkest place he's ever been. He must face danger and great grief and learn to harness his powers to face down his greatest nemesis yet ...

F SOM